# NECROMUNDA

# BLOOD ROYAL

## IN THE HEART OF A ROGUE
## BEATS ROYAL BLOOD

MEET KAL JERICO: rogue, bounty hunter, swashbuckler and self-proclaimed 'suavest bounty hunter' in the towering urban hell of Necromunda. The illegitimate offspring of the planet's ruler, Kal shunned his royal roots to take up the career of hired gun.

Following a botched job with former rival turned bounty hunter, Yolanda Cattalus, Kal is 'invited' to an impromptu family reunion with his father and is made an offer that he would be very foolish to refuse. To get through this one, Kal has to hope that blood really is thicker than water.

# NECROMUNDA

# BLOOD ROYAL

## WILL MCDERMOTT
## & GORDON RENNIE

*To my mom and dad, who never once complained about
their little boy who spent too much time alone in his room
reading. For Harriet, my mom, who drove me to the
bookstore every time I needed a new Larry Niven novel. And
for Jerry, my dad, who bought me my first role-playing game.
Without them, this book wouldn't be possible.*

*– Will McDermott*

**A BLACK LIBRARY PUBLICATION**

First published in Great Britain in 2005 by
BL Publishing,
Games Workshop Ltd.,
Willow Road, Nottingham,
NG7 2WS, UK.

10 9 8 7 6 5 4 3 2 1

Cover illustration by Clint Langley.

A CIP record for this book is available from the British Library.

ISBN 13: 978 1 84416 190 4
ISBN 10: 1 84416 190 0

Distributed in the US by Simon & Schuster
1230 Avenue of the Americas, New York, NY 10020, US.

Printed and bound in Great Britain by
Bookmarque, Surrey, UK.

See the Black Library on the Internet at
# www.blacklibrary.com

Find out more about Games Workshop
# www.games-workshop.com

In order to even begin to understand the blasted world of Necromunda you must first understand the hive cities. These man–made mountains of plasteel, ceramite and rockrete have accreted over centuries to protect their inhabitants from a hostile environment, so very much like the termite mounds they resemble. The Necromundan hive cities have populations in the billions and are intensely industrialised, each one commanding the manufacturing potential of an entire planet or colony system compacted into a few hundred square kilometres.

The internal stratification of the hive cities is also illuminating to observe. The entire hive structure replicates the social status of its inhabitants in a vertical plane. At the top are the nobility, below them are the workers, and below the workers are the dregs of society, the outcasts. Hive Primus, seat of the planetary governor Lord Helmawr of Necromunda, illustrates this in the starkest terms. The nobles — Houses Helmawr, Cattalus, Ty, Ulanti, Greim, Ran Lo and Ko'Iron — live in the 'Spire', and seldom set foot below the 'Wall' that exists between themselves and the great forges and hab zones of the hive city proper.

Below the hive city is the 'Underhive', foundation layers of habitation domes, industrial zones and tunnels which have been abandoned in prior generations, only to be re-occupied by those with nowhere else to go.

But... humans are not insects. They do not hive together well. Necessity may force it, but the hive cities of Necromunda remain internally divided to the point of brutalisation and outright violence being an everyday fact of life. The Underhive, meanwhile, is a thoroughly lawless place, beset by gangs and renegades, where only the strongest or the most cunning survive. The Goliaths, who believe firmly that might is right; the matriarchal, man–hating Escher; the industrial Orlocks; the technologically–minded Van Saar; the Delaque whose very existence depends on their espionage network; the firey zealots of the Cawdor. All striving for the advantage that will elevate them, no matter how briefly, above the other houses and gangs of the Underhive.

Most fascinating of all is when individuals attempt to cross the monumental physical and social divides of the hive to start new lives. Given social conditions, ascension through the hive is nigh on impossible, but descent is an altogether easier, albeit altogether less appealing, possibility.

excerpted from Xonariarius the Younger's
*Nobilite Pax Imperator – the Triumph
of Aristocracy over Democracy.*

# PROLOGUE: SOMETHING WICKED

ARIN BESTER SLIPPED out the door of Hagen's Hole and leaned against the wall outside. His once-green body armour, faded and stained from years of use, disappeared into the shadows of the Glory Hole twilight. The light coming from the barred windows and narrow doorway behind him provided the only illumination for blocks around. The Underhive settlement had barely enough power to heat and light central dwellings during the hours of 'day', let alone outlying streets and alleys at night.

The old bounty hunter took one last long draught of his purloined Wildsnake before tossing the empty bottle into the alley. The dark liquid burned his throat, and he could feel the dead snake from the bottom of the bottle slide past his tonsils. I must be drunk, he thought, that last swig tasted *good*. As he scratched at the coarse, black hair on his neck, Bester absentmindedly checked his weapons – chainsword on hip, shotgun tied to his back. The rest he could check later.

He closed his eyes to concentrate on standing. The dull-grey wall behind him once hummed with power, but that was in a time before remembering, back when Hive Primus wasn't even a mile high. The dome that was now home to Hagen's and the surrounding Glory

Hole settlement had been a crown jewel of the young Hive, its inhabitants slaving away at their machines to make the nobles rich. But time and the pressing weight of the ten-mile-tall Hive had pushed this once glorious dome, cracked and crumbling, into the depths of the Underhive.

Few amongst the Hive City Houses deigned to enter Glory Hole these days, let alone those prissy nobles high up in the Spire. Not, that is, unless they had fallen from grace or had been forced to flee their enemies, or their family, often one and the same. That was, in a round-about way, how Bester had come to the Hole. He'd been a little too boisterous for the serious leaders of House Van Saar, and after one long and costly drinking binge, his loving family had finally cut him loose.

He'd clawed his way out of the gutter the only way he could – by beating all comers in the pit fights. His fame spread through the Underhive after that, and eventually he made his way to Hagen's. As far as Bester knew, the joint had always been called Hagen's Hole, even though the original Hagen had been dead for centuries. Each new owner tried to make a name for themselves, but the patrons – mercenaries all – insisted on calling every bar-keep Hagen, and so the name persisted.

The Hole had been a merc bar almost as long as it had been named Hagen's. That was probably the reason the rundown place had lasted so long. It wasn't much to look at. In fact, it was nothing more than an abandoned power substation on the outskirts of the dome. Blown-out conduits and cracked pipes ran across the ceiling and down the walls inside, making the small rooms feel even more cramped. Iron gratings covered a maze of rusted pipes underfoot, while hundreds of years of debris, congealed into a brown sludge by spilled drinks and spilled blood, filled the voids between the pipes.

Hagen – the latest Hagen, if Hagen was his name at all – didn't so much sweep the floor at night as scrape the ooze through the grating.

For all its decay, the presence of mercenaries brought a constant stream of gangers downhive into the settlement and into the bar and business at Hagen's remained steady. They came seeking extra muscle for upcoming battles or guides for treasure-seeking trips beyond the White Wastes. Sometimes they came to town to make a name for themselves by taking down a famous merc. More often than not, the only name they made was chiselled into a headstone.

Merc bars were sacred spaces to those who didn't give a ratskin's snout for the affairs of house or gang, unless they were being paid of course. To the mercs, Hagen's Hole was a place of business and a source of drink and other bodily pleasures. The Hole was where you sold your services and where you spent, or lost, the rewards. It was a home away from home. No ganger or gang had ever won a battle inside Hagen's Hole. No ganger had ever *survived* a battle fought inside the Hole. The mercs protected their own. They took care of Hagen and his Hole.

Bester reached into a pocket in his skin-tight battle-suit and pulled out a crumpled pack of tox-sticks. Only one left. Damn. He flipped the stick up into his mouth and tossed the crumpled pack toward the discarded bottle. As he lit the stick hanging from his lips, Bester thought he saw movement in the buildings across the street. He switched his augmetic eye to nightvision and scanned the area.

The ruins of an ancient machine shop stood across from the Hole. A huge gash had been blasted in the front wall long ago by archeotech scavengers, and the shop had been picked clean well before Bester's time.

It made for a good flop house now when he'd had one too many Wildsnakes. Another flicker of movement drew his attention to the hole in the wall. He adjusted the brightness on his eye and peered into the shop, but saw nothing. He checked the roof. Again nothing. Just a few rats scampering across the conduits that ran from Hagen's Hole to all the other buildings in the area.

The merc knew from personal experience that these pipes no longer carried power. He'd crawled through them often enough to escape the attention of the Watch or to bypass the Glory Hole gates through a hidden escape tunnel beneath Hagen's. All the wiring in these pipes had also been scavenged long ago. Along with machinery parts and abandoned weapons, copper wiring was just about the most valuable archeotech a hiver could find in a sunken dome.

The stink of sweat, sludge and Wildsnake wafted from the doorway into the slightly less toxic night air of Glory Hole, snapping Bester from his reverie. The stench nearly made him puke, and he forgot about the suspicious movement in his flop house as he swallowed the bile. The Hole smelled like a mixture of salty vinegar, fuel vapour, and mouldy hivewasp honey. The odour stuck to your nose hairs and stayed with you long after you left the bar.

Leaving the stench behind, Bester ambled across the street toward the abandoned shop to check on the unwanted guest. It was time to make himself scarce anyway, lest his card-playing buddies come looking for their money. He'd told his companions that he needed to step outside to get a breath of 'fresh' air. But, in reality, he was up three hundred credits and knew that Skreed, Beddy and Dungo wouldn't let him out of the game until they'd won their money back, but he needed these credits to pay off Jerico. Bester had no intention of heading back into the Hole tonight.

No, it was time to sleep it off, and now it appeared he would have to kick out a squatter before he could bed down. He sidled up to the hole in the wall and peered inside. The bare workshop shone in shades of green to his augmetic eye while shadows loomed and danced in the periphery of his normal eye, giving the room an eerie, otherworldly appearance, but Bester was used to the odd duality and found that the shadows often gave up more information than the stark, black-and-green world of his nightvision eye.

As he scanned the room, the shadows transformed from amorphous blobs into a series of sharply focused images. Twisted scraps of metal that once held machinery in place dotted the shop floor. The far wall was scorched by fire and laser blasts. A crack ran diagonally from corner to corner. To the side, a crumbling stone stairway led upstairs.

A shadow on the stairs moved abruptly as Bester glanced toward it. He twisted his head to catch the intruder in his nightvision eye, but once again he saw nothing.

'Damn fast,' muttered the bounty hunter. Bester reached over his shoulder and grabbed his shotgun before creeping into the room. He pumped a shell into the chamber and called out. 'I ain't got nothing against you, but this is my place. Get out now and I won't have to shoot you.'

He listened intently, but heard only echoes. Whatever was upstairs moved fast and silent, and seemed to like to keep to the shadows. Maybe it was just a rat. A big rat. Ratskins were known to come into town. Bester had even met a couple of Ratskin mercs acting as guides to the Underhive. They seemed alright to him, but this was his place.

He snuck to the base of the stairs and peered into the darkness above. A man-sized shape flew past the opening, leaving just a streak of black across the green nightvision field. Bester fired. The blast turned the green world blinding white for a moment. From his normal eye, he thought he saw a billowing black shape like wings or a cape.

Bester pumped the shotgun again and moved up the stairs. He blinked away the afterimage of the shotgun blast and then, switching back to normal vision, flicked on the torch attached to the barrel of his weapon.

'Let's see how you like the light, Mr Shadow!' he yelled. As Bester neared the top of the stairs, he unloaded two more cartridges into the room before running in after the shots. He did a quick pirouette, shining the torch around the room. Again, there was no trace of anyone in the place. Not even movement in the shadows.

He raised the shotgun to pump another cartridge into the chamber, and then he saw it. A black shape loomed above him. It grabbed the barrel of the gun and pulled Bester from his feet, up into the air. He pulled the trigger, but there was no cartridge in the chamber.

The creature slammed Bester into the ceiling. He let go of his weapon and dropped to the floor. Rolling to the side to escape an immediate assault, he heard a clatter behind him and the lights went out. The bounty hunter scrambled to his feet, switched back to nightvision, and unsheathed his chainsword. With a flick of his wrist, the chain began screaming along the length of the blade.

His shotgun lay in the middle of the room. The barrel had been crimped and bent in half. The attached torch lay shattered nearby. He searched the room, but saw nothing but a ragged hole in the ceiling that led to the roof.

Bester looked again at the crumpled shotgun and then at the hole he'd have to crawl through to follow the beast he'd seen. The next decision came easy to the battle-hardened mercenary. 'Okay!' he called out. 'You keep the place. I can sleep mine off somewhere else.'

Chainsword still screaming in his hand, Bester walked over to pick up his ruined shotgun, muttering, 'Whatever you're on will take more than a night's sleep to clear up.' As he bent over to get his gun, the bounty hunter felt a shift in the shadows. He raised his chainsword toward the hole, but it was too late.

The figure swooped through the hole in the ceiling, grabbed Bester by the neck and sword arm, and vaulted back through the hole. Bester finally looked into the face of his assailant just before the hand holding him under the chin twisted, snapping his neck with a loud crack. The chainsword, still screaming, slipped from the dead merc's grasp and fell through the hole, landing next to the shotgun in the room below.

# 1: FAMILY BUSINESS

Sun streamed past thick, velour drapes – a luxury not known nor needed in the sunless depths of Hive City – and glinted off gold-flecked cords hanging in loops across the bank of windows. The glittering light fell on the back of Gerontius Helmawr, Lord of Hive Primus, and thus ruler of all Necromunda. Helmawr, who normally towered over every room, his political and economic power giving him the stature of a demigod, now sat head in hands and nearly curled into a ball on one of the soft, leather couches arrayed beneath the windows.

From his vantage point atop the spire, the Lord of Hive Primus was used to the sun beating on his back and the rich appointments of the Imperial quarters. In fact, they were a birthright. House Helmawr had ruled Necromunda in the Emperor's name since time immemorial. Helmawr himself had ruled for hundreds of years, longevity was just another commodity his immense wealth and power easily afforded him.

But as brightly as the sun shone on this glorious day, it was a dark mood Lord Helmawr found himself sinking into as he looked at the macabre scene before him. It was hard enough to hold onto his sanity at the best of times, but the stress of today threatened to tip him over the edge. Helmawr was not used to the sight of blood and dead bodies – at least not in his home. Assassination was one thing, many a noble had succumbed to the assassin's blade or a vial of poison emptied into a bowl of soup, but those deaths were clean, artful even, and were accepted practice within the Noble Houses of the Spire. Brutal murder, though, that belonged in the world beyond the Spiral Gates. Violence was a fact of life in Hive City and a way of life in the Underhive. Violence of this nature did not belong in the Imperial palace.

And yet, here it was again.

Helmawr heard himself giggle at the absurdity of the scene before him, and then tried to get a hold of himself. Murder was no cause for laughter.

A palace guard lay dead on the velvet rug at Helmawr's feet. The pool of blood surrounding the body blotted out most of the house crest woven into the fabric. 'That will have to be replaced,' said the lord, pointing at the rug. Four attendants, who always hovered around him like moths fluttering around a flame, jotted down the order on four separate notepads. 'And I suppose we'll need to order some more guards.' Another small giggle escaped his lips.

The body of a second guard lay half on and half off the mahogany four-poster bed that lay opposite him, across the chamber. He'd been cut in half, perhaps while rushing toward his attacker. Blood still dripped off the edge of the silk sheets onto the floor where the rest of the guard's torso and legs had fallen. The blood had probably soaked through the silk sheets all the way to the down mattress, Helmawr realized. The entire bed would have to be destroyed. 'What a waste,' he muttered.

Details. That's what the doctors told him. Concentrate on the little details. He must re-train his mind to be able to maintain focus. 'Have that bed destroyed,' he said to the attendants. 'Or better yet, clean it up and send it to Lord Ty as a birthday present.' The attendants scribbled furiously. It didn't matter whether it was Ty's birthday or not. None of Helmawr's attendants would ever contradict him.

Helmawr was getting bored with this gruesome detail. He felt that there must be some important meeting or another he should be attending. That fact was that he rarely remembered where he should be at any point during the day or, for that matter, what had happened at the last meeting. The attendants kept him apprised of the details he often forgot, but it fell to the royal chamberlain to keep track of his daily itinerary and ensure that Helmawr didn't miss any important meetings.

But that was not possible this day, which made this affair all the more intolerable. The third and final body in the room had belonged to Stiv Harper, Gerontius Helmawr's royal chamberlain and most loyal servant. The battle for the chamberlain's life must have been gruesome. He had been literally hacked to death. The man's severed arms and legs lay at odd angles to his body, forming a crude 'W' on the floor. Helmawr didn't know if it meant anything, but had the attendants make a note of it anyway.

It was the chamberlain's head that most upset Helmawr, though. The top had been sawed off and most of the contents spilled across the polished hardwood. Unlike the two guards, though, there was very little blood around the dismembered chamberlain. Of course, the man had been more machine than flesh. Stiv had been with Helmawr since the beginning, and no expense was spared to keep such a trusted advisor alive. But this time, there would be no saving Stiv. His wayward son had seen to that. The damage was too severe for even Lord Helmawr's physicians and augmetists to fix.

As Helmawr broke from his pondering, he noticed that the guards who had been searching the room had finished their investigation. They stepped hesitantly up to their lord and awaited further orders.

'What?' Helmawr asked, looking up from the couch.

The guards glanced at each other and hesitated. Finally the sergeant spoke up. 'We didn't find it, my lord,' he said.

'Find *what*?' asked Helmawr.

The sergeant looked confused and pointed at the chamberlain. 'The royal chamberlain's… um… his… er…'

'Oh yes, *that*!' said Helmawr, as one of the attendant's leaned down and whispered into his ear. 'No I didn't expect you would find it. Details, though. Mustn't lose sight of the details. I'm sure the little bastard took it with him.'

He rose and strode across his son's former quarters, kicking Stiv's legs out of the way as he came to the door. 'Clean up this mess!' he called back. 'I'm sure I have important matters to attend to.'

Yes, brutal death had once again come to Lord Helmawr's palace. And once again, it seemed that his homicidal son, Armand, had fled, leaving a tangle of bodies in his wake. But this time the troublesome boy had really gone too far. His son had stolen from his father, and *that* Helmawr could not forgive. He strode down the hall. The attendants ran to keep pace, feverishly writing down names of advisors, who were to be brought before his lordship immediately.

'KAL! DON'T SHOOT him!' yelled Scabbs.

Jerico glanced over the edge of the catwalk to see his buddy scrambling up the service ladder. The numerous scabs on the little half-breed's face cast odd shadows that made it look like he was wearing war paint. 'Why not?' he called back. 'Look what he did to my shirt!' Kal grabbed his sleeve to show Scabbs the rip, tearing the fabric even further in the process. He never should have taken his leather coat off, but it was getting in the way when he climbed the ladder.

'That was my best shirt,' Jerico sneered. The thin, balding man pinned beneath his knee squirmed and tried to speak, perhaps trying to apologize, but all he could do was squeak. 'Hell. It's my only shirt!' added the bounty hunter. He shifted his weight to bear down on the captive's chest.

'So now I think I'll just put a hole in your only head.' Jerico flipped his two blond braids up out of his eyes and pressed the barrel of his lasgun against the forehead of the mousy little man. He released the safety catch and started to put pressure on the trigger.

Scabbs barrelled into Jerico and the laspistol fired, searing a hole through the metallic ledge and taking a piece of the captive's ear with it. Scabbs and Jerico tumbled toward the edge of the catwalk, both screaming and clawing at the other.

'Don't shoot!'

'What the hell are you doing?'

'We need him!'

'Get off me!'

Jerico felt the edge of the catwalk bite into the small of his back and knew he couldn't stop in time. 'Crap!' he yelled as they tumbled over the ledge. He dropped his weapon and grasped at the ledge with his free hand. 'Hold on!'

Kal's fingers scrambled for purchase as the two men fell in tandem. His hand slapped against a pipe beneath the catwalk and he closed his palm around it as the lasgun clattered and clanged through pipes and cables down to the dome floor twenty metres below.

Jerico's shoulder popped as his torso whipped around beneath the catwalk. Scabbs, arms clenched tightly around Jerico's chest, slipped down to his waist, leaving several streaks of dead skin, as the duo came to a sudden stop. He hooked his fingers into Kal's belt. Above them, Kal could hear his former captive scrambling down the ladder.

'You let him get away!' yelled Kal. He tried desperately to get his free hand onto the pipe.

'I let him get away?' asked Scabbs. 'You were going to shoot him.'

'I was just trying to scare him.' Kal swung back and forth and grasped at the pipe.

'You fired your gun.'

'Only because you tackled me.' Jerico's trousers slipped past his waist and Scabbs began to claw at his partner for purchase. 'Watch it!' yelled Kal. He grabbed Scabbs around the wrist just as his trousers fell to his knees.

'Perhaps you two would like to finish your argument up here?' asked a familiar female voice from the catwalk. 'Perhaps with your clothes on?'

Jerico looked up into Yolanda's brown eyes, which were framed by the Wildcat gang tattoos that ran across her forehead and down both cheeks. 'This is his fault,' he muttered. A moment later, Scabbs was pulling himself up a rope, using Kal's body to push his feet against as he climbed. Jerico followed shortly after. He rolled onto the catwalk and pulled his wayward trousers up as he spun.

When he got to his feet, he saw the squirrelly captive trussed up and lying on the grating. Blood oozed from the man's shredded ear. A nasty bruise blossoming at his temple was just barely covered by thin wisps of hair. Jerico smiled at Yolanda. 'Good work.'

'Next time you might want to tie up your informant before you two decide to discuss interrogation tactics,' said Yolanda.

Jerico's smile faded. Before Yolanda could react, Kal snatched the laspistol from her holster, and then smiled again. 'Mind if I borrow this?' he asked. He knelt down next to the captive and flicked the safety off. 'Now, you may have heard me say that I wasn't going to kill you,' said Kal. He waved the gun in the face of the quivering informant. 'But that doesn't mean I won't shoot you.'

Jerico grabbed the bound man by the wrists and pointed the pistol at his fingers. 'You might want to unclench your fists and spread your fingers... unless you want me to shoot all of them at once.'

'GIVE MY TROOPS a day, sir, and we'll have that murderous son of a bitch standing before you locked in irons,' said Captain Katerin. His round, red face flushed as he spoke. The sweat that had been beading on his bald head dripped into bushy, black eyebrows.

'And would I be the bitch in this scenario, captain?' asked Gerontius Helmawr. The Lord of the Spire lounged in a high-backed leather chair behind an enormous oak desk. There were no windows in this room, and the only light came from an array of lamps on Helmawr's desk, arranged to keep him in shadow while shining brightly on his staff. The private office was tucked away in the centre of the royal palace, completely shielded on all sides from eavesdropping devices. Long forgotten sound dampening technology made it impossible to hear what was said unless you stood within ten feet of the speaker.

An emergency meeting of Helmawr's top advisors had been called to deal with the Armand situation. Six men stood in a semi-circle facing Helmawr in his private office: Katerin, the captain of the royal guard; Vin Colouri, the guardian of the coffers; Morten Croag, Helmawr's top aide in matters of law; Malchi Prong, the chancellor of the Spire; Hermod Kauderer, master of security and intrigue; and the ranking political officer, a somewhat junior official named Obidiah Clein.

The meeting had not been going well. Helmawr's attendants, who stood behind him taking notes, constantly had to remind the lord who the advisors were and why they were meeting. The royal chamberlain would normally run these meetings, but he was no longer able to perform those duties. The resulting chaos had obviously left Helmawr even more confused than normal.

'We're talking about my son... what did you say your name was?'

The military man glanced at the other advisors before answering. 'Katerin, my lord, Captain Katerin.'

'Armand is still my son, Katerin,' said Helmawr. 'He may be a little rambunctious at times, but you would do well to regard him with some degree of civility.'

'Sorry, my lord,' Katerin said, bowing slightly. 'My enthusiasm gets the better of me.' The captain of the royal guard dabbed at his forehead with the handkerchief he kept constantly at hand for this very purpose. The sweat began to flow a bit more freely under Helmawr's stare and even the tangle of beard covering Katerin's face glistened with perspiration. He straightened his uniform before continuing. 'All I meant to say, sir, was that my men are ready to tear apart the Lower Hive searching for your... wayward son.'

'I think, perhaps, a more subtle approach would be in order,' stated Hermod Kauderer. 'Kauderer, my lord. Your master of intrigue,' he added. Kauderer was easily a head taller than everyone in the room and towered over the other advisors, but it wasn't his abnormal height that put people off. His narrow face, piercing eyes and sharp features gave one the impression of staring into the face of a hawk who was about to swoop down and rip out your eyes. 'I have agents in place throughout Hive City and enquiries are well underway. I'm sure we can bring this matter to a quick and quiet conclusion, within the hour.'

'Hah!' scoffed Katerin. 'Your agents could never handle that pit b– Um, powerful son of our lord. They wouldn't last a minute against him in battle.'

'You assume he would still be standing when my agents got to him,' said Kauderer. He tilted his head slightly and arched his eyebrows as he stared at Katerin. 'If your men storm through the Hive, it will result in a blood bath that will make Armand's indiscretions look like afternoon tea. Discretion is the wise move here.'

'Those were my men he killed up there, Kauderer!' stormed the captain. 'I owe it to them to find their murderer and bring him to justice.' He turned to Lord Helmawr, and continued. 'I could lead a small number of men into the Underhive, sire. A simple search and retrieve mission. Very little collateral damage'

'I can guarantee no collateral damage,' stated Kauderer. 'And no witnesses.' His lips tightened into a thin smile, or perhaps more of a sneer. Kauderer always looked like he was sneering.

The other advisors smiled as well. Colouri even nodded his head at the last statement. Captain Katerin felt his influence in the matter waning. He looked around for allies. Colouri, Croag, and Prong all dropped their eyes to the floor to check on some speck of dust on their shoes. They rarely took sides openly in battles between Katerin and Kauderer. Both men had considerable power and influence throughout the Spire, and that influence grew stronger as Helmawr's faculties waned, as they most certainly did now, with his mind scattered by recent events and his most trusted advisor cut into pieces. The captain's gaze fell upon Obidiah Clein, the junior political officer. 'You agree with me, don't you, Clein?'

Clein was only present in the meeting because his superior was the recently dismembered Stiv Harper. He was a small, unassuming man with short-cropped hair and a soft, doughy face topped by wire-rimmed glasses. He was about half the girth of Katerin and half the height of Kauderer. This was Clein's first time in the spotlight of the big office, but if Katerin thought the little man would be easily cowed without the chamberlain around to back him up, he had obviously misjudged Obidiah Clein.

'From a strictly political standpoint,' said Clein, pushing the glasses up his nose and looking back and forth at Katerin and Kauderer, 'I believe both plans are deficient in one important regard. The other Houses... '

The two strong-willed advisors interrupted and tore into the newcomer before turning on each other again.

'We must show strength in this matter!'

'My agents will never be seen.'

'The other Houses must see our resolve.'

'Agents of the other Houses can be dealt with.'

'Your agents will never get close to him.'

'Your men let him escape in the first place.'

'Your agents couldn't find their rears with a stick and a mirror.'

'What will your men do, bleed on him?'

A sudden crash from the desk ended the argument. The advisors all turned toward their lord. The shattered remains of a crystal decanter lay scattered amidst a puddle of liquid on the desk. Helmawr stood, his face impassive, yet with an almost comical smirk spreading across his lips. He still clutched the broken glass handle in his hand. Nobody spoke. Nobody moved. After a moment, Helmawr dropped the handle onto the desk and sat down in his chair. 'Gentlemen,' he said. 'I believe – that man there – had a point to make, and I would like to hear it.'

All eyes turned toward Obidiah Clein, who took a moment to clean his glasses before proceeding. 'Obidiah Clein, my lord,' he began. 'I am the ranking political officer after the untimely... accidental death of the royal chamberlain.'

'What did you want to say, Mr Clein?'

'The real problem is not apprehending your wayward son,' replied Clein. 'It is more important to retrieve the item he – um – liberated from my predecessor. We need to get the item your son stole, wouldn't you agree, sir?'

Clein looked at Helmawr expectantly, almost demanding an answer before continuing. Katerin found the tactic brilliant and wished he had thought of it. The addle-brained Helmawr was easily led, if you knew how to guide him.

Helmawr's response was immediate. 'Yes. We must recover what my son stole from me, no matter the cost,' he said. 'Take care of it, will you, Clein? I feel I must take a nap now.' With that, Helmawr leaned back in his leather chair and closed his eyes. A moment later, his soft snoring could be heard wafting across the desk.

Katerin dabbed at his forehead as he looked back and forth at Clein and Kauderer. 'You heard our lord,' he said. 'We must retrieve the item, whatever the cost may be.'

Clein strode over to the captain and stood directly in front of him. 'The problem with a frontal assault is not the casualties you will inflict on the hivers,' he said, 'although I'm sure Mr Colouri would not enjoy paying for your little escapades downhive. The problem is that as soon as you pass through the Spiral Gates, every other Noble House will track your every move. It's too visible, and this matter must be handled delicately.'

'Exactly,' said Kauderer. 'My agents are the epitome of tact. No one will even know they were there.'

Clein turned and sauntered over to the intrigue master. Kauderer glared at the top of the little man's head. Clein hopped up onto Helmawr's desk to look at Hermod eye to eye. Katerin was starting to realise that the diminutive man before him was much more than a novice bureaucrat, and that might be dangerous.

Clein glared back at Kauderer. 'As soon as one of your agents ask a single question about Armand,' he said, 'spies from every other Noble House will report back to their superiors and the race will be on to see who can reach him first. Are you willing to bet your life on your spies against the rest of them down there?'

Kauderer was silent.

'I thought not,' said Clein. He jumped off the desk before straightening his glasses which almost fell off his face as he descended. 'That is what we are fighting for here, gentlemen. The information Helmawr's son has access to could ruin this House – that is, it could ruin us all.'

Katerin knew that he had lost this battle. It was time for a united front. 'If we can't send my guards or Kauderer's agents, then what do you suggest?' he asked.

'A third party,' said Clein. 'Someone not officially tied to House Helmawr, who won't raise suspicions amongst the other Houses.' He adjusted his glasses again and smiled. 'We're looking for a criminal hiding out in the lowest reaches of the Hive. I suggest we employ an expert for the task. I suggest we hire a bounty hunter.'

'Ridiculous,' said Kauderer, obviously unable to side with Katerin on anything, no matter how sensible it might seem. 'You can't trust scum like that. They're little better than gangers or muties. They'll turn tail and run at the first hint of trouble, or worse, take our money and then sell us out to the other Houses anyway. We'll be no better off at all – *worse*, in fact. My agents will be a step behind whichever House buys the information.'

Clein just grinned. He had long been ready with the answer to such concerns and, like a true politician, had simply led his counterparts into debating the matter for no reason other than to make himself appear all the more impressive when the time came to impart his own wisdom. 'You see,' he began, 'if my information is correct, I think there is a bounty hunter we can trust.' He was smiling the wide smile of a child who holds the answer to a question that all of the adults have been asking. 'This bounty hunter and Lord Helmawr have a somewhat *special* relationship,' Clein concluded with a grin.

'Now, ISN'T THIS more comfortable than climbing around in the ductwork?' asked Kal.

Jerico, Scabbs, Yolanda and Derindi, the wretched little informant who had nearly cost Kal his trousers, were all sitting at a large, round table in the middle of the Sump Hole, Kal's favourite Underhive dive. It had all the charm of a rat-infested slave pit decorated with trash, only the rats were much larger and carried weapons.

The ropes around Derindi's hands and feet had been removed and the bounty hunters were all smiles. To prying eyes, the scene appeared to be nothing more than a group of friends enjoying a drink.

'I'm a dead man,' moaned Derindi. He stared at the bottle of Wildsnake – a foul, brown liquid in a dirty, brown bottle. Still, it was more expensive than Second Best, so things could be worse. No. They probably couldn't. Even the snake in the bottom of the bottle was staring at him. Perspiration matted what little hair Derindi had left above his ears and his palms were so slick that, when he finally picked up the bottle, it nearly slipped from his grasp.

'Don't be like that,' said Yolanda. She giggled and tossed back the blonde locks of hair that had fallen over her cheeks. But Derindi could tell it was all for show; Yolanda didn't giggle. Not unless she wanted something from you.

The show was for the audience that had been forming at the bar and nearby tables. He noticed the icy edge to her words. 'I stopped Kal from shooting your fingers off, didn't I? We're all friends here.' Yolanda's voice grew suddenly loud on the last line, obviously for the benefit of the surrounding gangers and mercenaries.

'You should have let him kill me,' grumbled Derindi. He dried his hands on the rough cloth of his clothes before trying to pick up the bottle again. Perhaps the foul liquid would kill him. 'Bleeding to death through a bloody stump would be like dying in bed compared to what'll happen to me if I talk.'

Derindi thought about running. He looked at the door some metres past the bar and wondered about bolting for it, heading further downhive where neither Jerico nor Svend and his gangers could find him. Jerico wouldn't dare shoot him in the back if he ran, would he? They needed him, and even in the Underhive murder is – well it's at least frowned upon, especially in front of this many witnesses. Derindi looked at the bounty hunter, his teeth clenched into a tight-lipped smile as he picked at the hole in his shirt. Jerico was obviously still pissed off about the rip. And then there was the matter of the trousers. Kal was clearly a man fond of his clothing, and Derindi had thus far made an impressive fist of ruining damn near all of it. Derindi decided not to chance running.

'Oh, it won't matter whether you talk or not,' said Jerico with another forced smile. 'Everyone will think you squealed either way.' He reached into his pocket and Derindi flinched, spraying sweat from his chin onto his shoulder. But when Jerico's hand came back out, it was full of tokens and bonds. He picked one bond from his palm and held it up to look at it.

Derindi saw the gangers at the bar ogle at the ceramite piece as Jerico pretended to check its authenticity. Then, with a flourish, the bounty hunter slapped the bond onto the table and spoke in an overly loud voice. 'That's just the down payment, Derindi. You'll get the rest when we get our bounty for Svend. Thanks!'

Kal flicked the ceramite bond across the table at Derindi, who caught it out of reflex before it slammed into his stomach. Scabbs reached out and shook Derindi's hands, his wide smile causing a cascade of loose skin to fall from his cheeks. 'Yeah, thanks, Derindi. You did the smart thing here,' he said out loud. Far louder than was necessary, in fact.

Then, in a softer voice, Scabbs added, 'You're right, Derindi. Don't tell us anything. Besides, all we need to do now is sit back and wait for Svend to kill you, and then capture him while he's digging that bond out of your pocket.' Derindi pulled away from the scabby bounty hunter, and immediately noticed that the ceramite piece was no longer in his hand. Scabbs's smile looked more sincere now.

Yolanda leaned in toward Derindi. 'Or you can tell us where to find Svend right now, and maybe we'll get to him before he gets to you.'

'Maybe,' said Jerico. He picked at the hole in his shirt again. 'Maybe.'

CAPTAIN KATERIN TOOK a break from the mound of paperwork on his desk and rubbed two podgy digits into his tired eyes. He hated this part of the job. Weapon requisition forms, guard rotation schedules, disciplinary reports, promotion applications, leave requests – it all came across his desk. Most of it simply needed a signature, but he had to read every piece of paper to make sure his subordinates were doing their jobs correctly and, more importantly, that they weren't trying to deceive him in some way. The last three Captains of the Royal Guard had lost their positions due to 'gross incompetence', which was just a fancy way of saying their subordinates had screwed up. That was not going to happen to Almar Katerin.

The blurry office came back into focus after he pulled the fingers from his eyes, and Katerin practically fell off his chair. 'How the hell did you get in here?' he roared, staring up into the hawkish features of Hermod Kauderer. He jumped to his feet, snatched a laspistol from his hip, and pointed it at the head spy. 'Explain yourself, Kauderer. How did you sneak into my private office?'

Kauderer remained calm in the face of the captain's rage. He flicked at some invisible piece of fluff on his black robes and raised an eyebrow. 'Your door was not locked, Captain,' he said. 'And I never sneak. I do not, however, make any sound when I walk, unlike you soldiers, who announce their presence from down the block.'

Katerin decided not to rise to the bait. Instead, he dropped the laspistol on top of the pile of requisition forms and slumped back into his chair. 'What do you want, Kauderer?' he asked. 'I have a great deal of work to do, so let's just skip the normal banter portion of our conversation.'

'Gladly,' said Kauderer. There were chairs facing Katerin's desk, but the master of intrigue did not sit in the presence of others. He enjoyed looking down at people and never gave up the high ground, literally or figuratively. Before continuing, however, he pulled a small device from the pocket of his tunic, flipped a switch, and set the item on Katerin's desk. 'To protect us from prying ears,' he said. 'Now, down to business as you requested. Armand Helmawr must die, and I don't think either of us believes that bastard bounty hunter is the man for the job.'

Katerin pushed the pile of papers aside and leaned forward, suddenly interested in what his rival was saying. 'What do you propose?' he asked. 'That weasel Clein was probably right about using house resources. Our men will attract too much attention.'

'That doesn't mean we can't direct others to do the job that you and I both know must be done.'

'And done right this time,' added Katerin. He spun the laspistol on his desk as he imagined Armand meeting with various, gruesome deaths. 'Done completely and finally.'

'You know what I'm talking about, don't you?' asked the Kauderer.

Katerin nodded, a smirk growing on his face. 'Spyrers.'

'For a start, yes.'

* * *

DUNGO BAIN STRODE into Hagen's Hole, his metal-tipped boots clanging against the mesh floor, and slapped a token onto the bar. 'Hagen!' he called. 'Snake me.'

The current Hagen, a round man with a long beard and longer, stringy hair, sidled over to the end of the bar. After wiping his podgy hands on a brownish apron that might once have been white, he grabbed a bottle of Wildsnake from the shelf behind the bar and opened it with his last remaining teeth. He slammed the bottle down in front of the bounty hunter, making the credit token jump and sending a plume of the bitter drink sloshing onto the bar.

Hagen wore no shirt beneath the apron, and his flabby chest and protruding gut peaked out around the edges whenever he moved. The patrons never asked nor checked to see if he wore pants. Hagen leaned over the bar to collect the token, dragging his hair and beard through the puddle in the process.

Dungo pulled the helmet off his head and ran a hand through his thick hair as he checked himself in the mirror behind the bar. He still had helmet head, and the scar that ran from ear to ear across his chin seemed redder than usual. He scratched at the stubble around the scar as he gulped the foul liquid in the bottle, and then looked around the bar. A game was already under way in the back room, but there were few other patrons in the Hole at this time of morning. 'Seen Bester?' he asked.

'Not since last night,' said Hagen. 'I thought he left with you.'

'Nah, he stiffed us,' Dungo replied. 'Ran out for a smoke with three hundred credits in his pocket and never returned.' He drained the bottle and spat the snake onto the floor. It flopped onto the grate, but didn't quite make it through to the pipes. Hagen had another open bottle in front of the bounty hunter before his token even hit the bar.

'That's right,' said Hagen. He owes me for a Snake, too.' Hagen flipped his hair back over his shoulder, and it hit the mirror with a wet slap. 'When I see that rat… '

He never got to finish the statement, for at that moment Jak Skreed entered Hagen's Hole carrying a body over his shoulder. Jak was a bull of a man, easily topping two metres tall and nearly twice as wide at the shoulders as he was at the waist. Sweat seemed to constantly glisten on his bulging, black biceps. 'We have a problem,' said Skreed.

'Ya sure do, Jak,' said Hagen. 'Ya know better than to bring your bounties in here. It's not sanitary.'

'Not my bounty,' said Jak as dropped the dead body on the floor. The corpse made an odd sound as it hit the metal grate, like a burlap sack full of sticks. The mouth on the body was wide open and the eyes bulged, as if the poor soul had been screaming at the moment of his death. The skin on the arms and face was cracked and leathery, and had shrunk so much you could see the contour of the bones underneath. He looked like he'd been dead and buried for months. But Dungo noticed the faded green battle suit and knew immediately that couldn't be the case.

Jak confirmed his suspicion. 'It's Bester,' he said. 'Or it was yesterday.' To drive his point home, Skreed dropped the mangled remains of Arin Bester's shotgun on top of the body. Dungo could see the hash marks etched into the barrel.

'Thirty-six,' he said counting quickly. 'Seven tallies of five and one extra – that's Bester's gun alright. He just bagged number thirty-six last week. Bought us all a round of Snake. What in the Spire happened to him?'

'Can't say,' muttered Skreed as he stepped over the body. He walked up to Dungo, and pulled a huge handful of credit tokens mixed with a few ceramite bonds out of his pocket and dropped them on the bar. 'His winnings were still in his pocket, and all of his weapons were sheathed except the shotgun and his chainsword, which we found still running in his flop spot across the street. The body we found... elsewhere.'

'It weren't no robbery then, huh?' asked Dungo. Skreed shook his head.

'What could have done that to him?' asked Hagen, pointing at the desiccated corpse of their former friend. 'He looks, I dunno, deader than most bodies I seen.'

Jak plucked a token from the pile and flipped it to Hagen, who got him a bottle of Wildsnake. Skreed took a long pull at the bottle before answering. 'Beddy thinks it's a vampire,' he said after a long burp. 'I think she's read too many of those pulps, but near as we can tell, all of the blood's been drained from his body and there are a couple of small wounds on his neck – puncture-like, you know.'

He tilted his bottle up above his face, letting the liquor flow into his open mouth. He caught the snake between his teeth when it flopped out of the bottle, bit it in half and swallowed. 'Beddy's out hunting vampires right now.' He pulled half a snake from his lips and flicked it onto the floor. 'Says it's better to do it in the daylight. I told her it don't matter when you can't even see the sun, but you know Beddy.'

Dungo didn't want to ask the next question, so he took a swig from his second bottle to steel his nerves. He swallowed hard as he realized too late that the snake had slid down his throat. He hated the damn snake. 'Where d'you find the body?' he asked after a coughing fit that failed to expel the slithering beast.

'That's the damndest thing,' said Skreed. 'It was stuffed into the power pipes – not the ones running from the Hole over to the machine shop – the main lines hung from the ceiling of the dome.'

Hagen's jaw dropped. 'You mean the pipes nobody's ever scavenged because they're too high up?'

Skreed nodded. 'That's right. We never would have found the body, except there was a pile of copper wiring on the roof. Beddy looked up and saw the feet sticking out. I shot a line into his boot and pulled him out.'

'Lucky he was wearing his body suit, or his body would have got crushed when he fell,' said Hagen.

'Yeah, lucky,' said Dungo. He grabbed a token from Bester's winnings and tossed it to the barkeep. 'Do you think that suit would fit me?'

NEMO SAT IN the darkened chamber and contemplated the day ahead. The Underhive's most notorious crimelord (as Nemo liked to think of himself) enjoyed the dark, and often dimmed the various vid screens that surrounded him. He'd lived in the dark most of his life in the twilight world beneath Hive City. That city was dimly lit compared to the golden splendour of the Spire, but it had power enough for luxuries like light and heat. In the Underhive, there was precious little power for anything.

For the crimelord, the choice had been simple. Life was uncertain enough downhive without relying on tools that could fail, get lost or be stolen without a moment's notice. Instead, he had learned to see, to live, to thrive in the dark. Nemo lived on pure instinct, sensing danger before it arrived, 'seeing' contours in the shape of the darkness around him, and relying on reflexes honed by the strap of experience to the unnatural sharpness of a power sword.

A faint hiss from above alerted the crimelord to an incoming message. One of the most recent technological luxuries Nemo had installed in his subterranean base of operations was a message tube. Powering the tube had been easy; he simply tapped into the tube's power source. The logistics of keeping the tube a secret had been monumental, however. The Hive City end of his tube rotated to a different nexus after passing each message into his network. There were simply too many tube stations in the Hive for the authorities to check, so it was nearly impossible for them to track the tubes back to his base.

Once he had connected to the tube network, a well-trained, highly intelligent rat had been fed into the system that searched for the special capsules Nemo's associates had to use, and routed these capsules to his tube network. Nemo had considered using the rat to hunt down messages to or from important figures in the Hive, but had ultimately decided the security risk was too high. If someone ever suspected their messages were being hijacked, or found rat droppings in one of the capsules, the game would be up.

Very few people had access to Nemo's special capsules, and those that did still needed a special code to send a message to Nemo. He periodically changed those codes to ensure that only his business associates could use the system. But the tube had been a profitable expenditure. His most lucrative jobs always arrived via the tube, generally straight from the spire.

This particular message, like dozens before it, dropped from the tube into the inky blackness of the crimelord's chambers, and Nemo grabbed the capsule before it hit his desk. His fingertips tapped another code – one only he knew – into the end of the capsule. This extra layer of security deactivated an acid trap that would destroy the message before it could be read. In addition to conditioning his senses to life in the dark during his long years in the Underhive, Nemo had also cultivated a healthy sense of paranoia.

The capsule clicked open in his hands and a roll of paper dropped onto the table. Nemo flicked on a lamp to read the message – not because he needed the light, but because the lamp was part of the message system itself. The page practically glowed in the eerie, black luminescence, illuminating words that would have been invisible under any other light.

Nemo read the message twice, not quite believing it the first time. He turned off the lamp after committing the details of the message to memory and then tossed the paper into a different tube that led directly into an Underhive sewage pipe with effluent so corrosive it would destroy the paper quicker than an incinerator. He sat in the dark for a few moments longer, letting his eyes readjust until the shadows came into focus again, then began to write a series of carefully worded notes to be sent to select members of his organisation. This job would require strict discipline and a certain finesse that only his top operatives possessed. Nemo thought he might actually have to get involved in this job personally, but it would be worth the risk. Well worth it, in fact.

# 2: PLAN 'W'

KAL JERICO STOOD astride an air duct high above Glory Hole. His long, leather coat billowed around his legs, blown by a steady stream of air from a crack in the duct at his feet. He leaned out to see the settlement below with a pair of infrared goggles held up to his eyes in one hand. His other hand rested on the butt of the laspistol at his waist.

Jerico had chosen this spot for the ambush carefully, sitting as it did above a crossroads that Svend Gunderson, rogue ganger from House Orlock, would have no choice but to pass. Assuming, of course, that Derindi's information could be trusted. Plus, the cracked airduct allowed Kal to look heroic while he waited.

'How long are you going to stand like that?' asked Yolanda from one side.

Kal looked over. The daughter of Lord Catallus turned Escher gang leader turned bounty hunter was flipping her sword from hand to hand. The look on her face told Kal she was ready to use the weapon, on him if necessary.

'Until I see Svend coming down the street,' he replied, putting the goggles back up to his eyes.

'Or until we push him off,' added Scabbs. 'It's not a fashion show, Kal. You don't have to strike a pose.'

Kal turned to his old partner, who was picking at one of the perpetual sores that dotted his ugly face. 'A lot you would know about fashion shows,' he sneered. 'Look, one thing you two need to learn about bounty hunting is that it's as much about style and looks as it is about strength and courage.'

'With you, Kal, it's mostly about luck, dumb luck,' said Yolanda. She sheathed her sword and grabbed the goggles from Kal. 'Let me look for a while.' She pushed the swarthy bounty hunter out of her way and took up position above the crossroads.

Kal and Scabbs watched in dumbfounded silence as Yolanda's breech cloth flapped in the breeze coming from the cracked pipe, showing tantalizing glimpses of her inner thigh. She must have felt the warm air rising between her legs, because a moment later, Yolanda gave up on her heroic pose to move away from the crack.

Kal drew a deep breath, shook the images from his head and regrouped. 'Did you ever think, Yolanda, that maybe my style and grace bring me good luck?' he asked, as he sat on the ductwork to take a break. 'It's hard work being this good looking. I should get something out of it, don't you think?'

'Besides all the women, you mean?' asked Scabbs.

Kal nodded. 'Yes. Besides all the women.' He slapped Scabbs across the top of the head and was immediately sorry he had, as he looked for somewhere to wipe his hand. Eventually he gave up and wiped it on Scabbs's legs, leaving a slightly less disgusting smear on his palm.

'Alright,' said Kal. 'With Yolanda watching for Svend, this is a good time to go over the plan one last time. According to Derindi, our Orlock bandit has been hiding out in an old hole out in the White Wastes. But he's

supposed to come into the settlement today to get sup-
plies from Derindi.'

'What if Derindi was lying just to get us to let him go?'
asked Yolanda. She had crouched at the edge of the air
duct, well away from the crack to watch the road.

'I thought of that,' said Kal. 'But I don't think Derindi
was smart enough to lie to us. And, if he did, well he
wasn't that hard to find the first time.' Jerico pulled out
his lasgun and used the barrel to draw a map in the
dust. 'Now, Svend will have to pass this crossroads right
beneath us on his way to meet Derindi. When he walks
into the intersection, I drop down in front of him, while
Yolanda drops down behind him… '

'Where do I go?' asked Scabbs. He leaned down to get
a better look at the map, and his stench hit Kal like a
hot blast of wind from the air duct.

'Helmawr's rump,' said Jerico. 'Get downwind. How
can you track anything when you smell that bad?' he
shooed the half-breed ratskin back a pace with his pistol before continuing. 'As I was about to say, you,
Scabbs, will drop down on this side of Svend. With us
blocking three of his exits, Svend will be forced to run
down this street, which we have already blocked up, so
he'll be trapped. With any luck, he'll come peacefully
and we can get the full bounty.'

'Here he comes!' said Yolanda. She dropped the goggles and drew her sword.

'Remember,' said Kal, 'the bounty on Svend is tripled
alive, so if he tries to fight his way out of the trap, shoot
to wound.' He pushed himself back to his feet. 'Okay,
Scabbs, Yolanda – get into position.'

'Um, Kal?' said Scabbs.

Kal dusted himself down, before looking up. 'What is
it, Scabbs?'

'Don't shoot me, but Yolanda's already gone.'

Kal looked at the empty spot where the buxom but deadly ex-ganger had crouched moments ago, just as he heard the distinctive 'skrak' of a laspistol shot from below.

'Crap,' said Kal. He pulled out his second pistol and jumped off the ductwork. 'I guess we go with plan W as usual.'

AT THE OPPOSITE end of Glory Hole, Beddy Bor'Wick ran along a rooftop in a slight crouch, her pulse rifle cradled in her arms. She was following a trail of fresh blood. Intermittent spatters steamed on the cold, concrete roof. The vampire couldn't have gone far. She scanned the adjoining buildings, the barrel of the rifle following her eyes. But she saw no movement nor any sign of recent visitors beyond the regular vermin.

Beddy glanced up as she ran, worried the vampire might swoop down on her, but there was nothing but cables, ducts and conduits running along the dome above her. Her black boot felt the edge of a hole, and Beddy instinctively jumped. She'd nearly fallen through an old blast hole in the roof. As it was, the small, wiry but fairly buxom bounty hunter lost her footing when a chunk of concrete fell away as she landed.

Her momentum pitched Beddy forward as she fell through the roof. Her knees scraped against the edge of the hole before her pelvis slammed into the roof, knocking the wind out of her and sending her rifle flying from her hands. She began to slip backward into the hole, scrabbling with her legs and arms against the dusty concrete for purchase.

Beddy winced in pain as she got a knee up against the ragged side of the hole. She knew there was more fresh blood waiting for her when she finally climbed out of this hole. Both knees burned and she could feel a warm trickle of liquid running down her legs into her boots. She gritted her teeth through the pain and climbed out of the hole, rolling over on her back to keep her knees elevated for the moment.

As she lay there, taking deep breaths and working through the pain shooting down her legs, Beddy noticed for the first time that all of the cables, ducts and conduits running along the top of the dome in this section of Glory Hole seemed to converge on a nearly vertical shaft above her. Forgetting her aching knees for a moment, Beddy pulled herself over toward her rifle, keeping an eye on the shaft as she moved.

With rifle in hand once again, Beddy took a moment to check her knees. The shredded skin looked like something a butcher had run through a grinder. Blood and pus oozed from the six-centimetre wounds. She pulled a canister of spray adhesive from a pouch on her belt and administered a bounty hunter's field patch. It would have to do until she could get to a surgeon, because now she had a vampire to kill.

She stood and looked around. The trail of blood definitely ended on the far side of the blast hole. The vampire could have dropped into the building through the hole but, remembering how she and Skreed had found Bester, Beddy was betting on the shaft. As far as she knew, there was no bounty on a vampire, but it had already killed and drained Bester, and probably at least one more victim, so somebody would pay for this waste-spawned monster's death.

Beddy unhooked a grapnel shooter from her belt and took aim at the side of the shaft up as far as she could see. When she fired, the magnetic grapnel rocketed toward the shaft, trailing a thin strand of monofilament from a spool attached to her belt. The wire cable was as light as string, but as strong as steel.

The grapnel was good for getting into hard-to-reach places, and the cable could also be used as a garrotte. Its versatility made the grapnel Beddy's favourite piece of equipment.

As soon as the grapnel attached, a winch within the spool began to reel it back in, pulling Beddy up into the shaft. When she got to the end of the line, the bounty hunter wedged her feet in between several pipes to hold her body in place, and looked up into the shaft. It was pitch black beyond the meagre light that streamed in from the noonday streetlamps in the dome below. Beddy took a moment to don a nightvision visor, pulling it down past her tightly-curled, wiry, black hair. The shaft continued on into the darkness, well past the limits of her visor.

'Nothing for it but to keep going,' muttered Beddy as she lined up another shot with the grapnel. The line whizzed out past the edge of her sight before the grapnel clanged into metal and held. The winch began pulling her up farther into the shaft.

When she released her feet from their holds, Beddy felt like she was falling, but only for a moment before she began to rise up into the shaft. She held her rifle in one hand and used the other to steady herself during the ascent. She had to concentrate on the walls to keep from banging into the pipes and conduits that snaked their way up through the shaft.

As she reached what should be the end of the line, Beddy glanced up, but instead of seeing the grapnel attached to a wall, it was held out over the shaft by some dark form lurking in a side tunnel. She raised her rifle to shoot, but the figure jerked the line, and whipped a loop around Beddy's neck. The loop snapped tight, slicing through leather, skin and bone like scissors through paper.

In the distance, the rats heard the clang, clang, clang, thud of a falling object, and scurried over the concrete roof to see what treasure they might find.

By the time Jerico hit the street, Yolanda was chasing Svend the wrong way, away from the dead end. Even worse, they were both heading toward him, and Yolanda was shooting wildly. The Orlock's leather vest flapped open as he ran, showing a bolero decked out with frag grenades hanging over his dirty white shirt. Kal pointed his own lasgun at Svend, but had to dive to the side as a stream of Yolanda's lasblasts sizzled the air, right where his head had been.

Kal rolled to the ground and tried to kick Svend in the knees as he ran past. The ganger's metal-clad boots slammed into Kal's leather-protected shins with a crack, spinning the bounty hunter around and leaving him face-down at the edge of a sewer grate. 'Crap! That stinks worse than Scabbs,' he groaned.

A moment later, Yolanda charged through, her hair whipping across her face and her chest heaving and straining at her cotton shirt. The buxom bounty hunter nearly kicked Jerico in the ribs as she vaulted over him. She let loose with several more blasts at the retreating Svend as he weaved back and forth across the street. Her last shot singed the ganger's ponytail. She was shooting at his head!

'Alive!' yelled Kal. 'Yolanda, alive! Don't you listen to me?'

'What?' screamed Yolanda. She turned to look back at the prone Kal. At that moment, the fleeing Svend tossed a grenade over his shoulder.

'Oh crap!' muttered Jerico. He rolled away from the bouncing grenade as he screamed. 'Never mind! Run! Grenade!'

Jerico heard the grenade clinking as it bounced ever closer. He knew there was no way he could roll out of the blast radius. He also knew that by the time he stood up, it would be too late anyway. So he rolled and hoped his luck and good looks would save him once again. A pair of boots and a distinctive odour flashed past Jerico. A moment later he heard a dull thunk, followed by a deafening explosion.

The shockwave turned Jerico's roll into an out-of-control tumble. Shrapnel rained down around him, some of it biting through his leather coat into his flesh. But the explosion had sounded too far away and the fragments seemed sparse and weak. What in the Spire had Scabbs done?

Kal tumbled to a stop and pushed himself up to his hands and knees. Scabbs lay sprawled on the ground down the street, one leg sticking straight up in the air. His already tattered clothes had been shredded by flying fragments, and Kal could see blood soaking through his shirt in numerous spots.

The building next to Scabbs had a new entrance on the third floor. A charred hole between two windows bore witness to the power of pyrotechnics. A pile of new rubble littered the street beneath the hole. Somehow the grenade had exploded against the side of the building, three storeys up. Kal stood and glanced back and forth between the blast hole and the bleeding Scabbs.

'You son of a ratskin!' he exclaimed as he ran over to his partner's side. 'You kicked the grenade. Of all the scav-minded, dumb things to do. You could have blown your foot off.'

Scabbs groaned as he finally lowered his leg. He tried to sit up and groaned again. 'A little help, Kal?' he asked in a pitiful, small voice.

'Quit yer whining,' said Kal as he kicked Scabbs in the rump. 'I'm not done yelling at you for being stupid.'

'I was saving your life,' protested Scabbs. Kal couldn't help but notice that the half-breed's voice was stronger and clearer all of a sudden.

'That was your first mistake.' Jerico leaned down and offered a hand to his friend, surreptitiously checking the little man's injuries as he helped him to his feet. Amazingly, all the cuts seemed superficial. The blood-stains had grown no larger while they talked. 'I take that back,' said Kal, with a smirk. 'Your first mistake was being born.'

'Uh, boys?' asked Yolanda, appearing from behind a doorway across the street. She was completely unharmed, and seemed to have had time to comb her wayward hair before returning.

'Or perhaps teaming up with someone even more reckless than me.'

'Boys?' asked Yolanda again.

'What?' they both yelled together.

Yolanda sauntered over, a smug look on her face. One eyebrow arched, giving the tattoo on her forehead several more lines. 'While you've been gabbing, did either of you think to look for our quarry?'

'Helmawr's rump,' said Scabbs. 'He must have gotten away in the confusion of the explosion.'

'Unless the blast got him, or one of Yolanda's shots put a hole through his head,' said Kal as he scanned the street. 'Yolanda, don't you realise that "dead or alive" means we can bring some of them in alive? They're worth even more that way.'

'Yeah, but they're more trouble that way, too,' said Yolanda. She put her hands on her hips and stared hard at Kal. 'Frag 'em all and sort out the heads later. That's what I always say.'

'But we had a plan,' said Kal with a pout. 'I drew a map and everything.'

'It's called "Plan W",' added Scabbs.

'No, that's something dif–' Kal stopped. He looked at the debris from the bombed building. There was something sticking out from beneath the concrete rubble. It looked like a steel-wrapped boot. Jerico smacked Scabbs on the back of the head and pointed out the buried remains of their bounty to his partners. 'Damn, Scabbs. You killed him. There goes two-thirds of our bounty.'

He walked over to the pile and began pulling chunks of concrete off of the body. 'Don't just stand there,' he called back to Yolanda and Scabbs. 'Your share is under here, too.'

Later as Scabbs rolled a block out of the way, he asked, 'Kal? What is "Plan W"?'

Kal sighed, thinking about all the bounty that had disappeared with a bang. 'The W stands for wing it, Scabbs.'

'Then why do we use it so often?'

Kal looked at the crushed remains of Svend Gunderson. 'Because nothing else works quite so well.'

IN JUST A few hours, Nemo the Faceless, self-appointed Spymaster of Hive Primus, had collected a dizzying amount of information concerning the current affairs of one Kal Jerico. He knew that his old nemesis had met with a snitch named Derindi in the Sump Hole. He knew that Jerico and his crew had travelled to Glory Hole tracking a rogue Orlock ganger named Svend Gunderson. In fact, Nemo was currently enjoying the antics of the swarthy bounty hunter and his filthy comrades via a remote camera as they dug through rubble to unearth Gunderson's body. Most importantly, Nemo knew the identity of Jerico's next assignment *and* employer, even though the bounty hunter had no idea what fun his immediate future held.

Nemo looked up from his control console and noticed that the balding little snitch was still standing in his office. How long had he been there? Nemo didn't actually care. At least he's been quiet, like a mouse or, yes, a weasel. In fact, Nemo had to admit that Derindi really did look like a rodent as he stood in the dark, wringing his hands. Is a weasel a rodent? Nemo pondered. Ah well, probably some ratskin blood in him. They do make the best informants, though. Be a shame to lose Derindi.

The Kal Jerico show went on the road on the small screen to Nemo's left. It was time to get back to work, so time for Derindi to be elsewhere. Nemo touched a control on one of the many panels arrayed around him. A moment later a door slid open quite noiselessly behind Derindi. Meagre light entered the chamber along with two of Nemo's henchmen – Orlock twins named Brynn and Riyl wearing matching but colour-coded clothing. One always dressed in indigo while the other always wore crimson. The only problem was that nobody could ever remember which one wore which colour.

'Sir,' said Brynn and Riyl in unison as they came to attention behind Derindi. The snitch jumped a foot into the air.

The twins – and only Nemo could call them that as they despised being considered a pair, even though they were never apart – liked to call themselves Seek and Destroy. They looked tough enough with their black leather vests over red and blue sleeveless shirts, bandanna-covered shaved heads and dark sunglasses, which they wore even in Nemo's shadowy office. In reality, though, Brynn and Riyl were little more than errand boys that Nemo used for small tasks, like taking care of rats.

'Hello, boys,' he said. The twins winced, but remained silent. They had learned not to correct the boss. Nemo smiled behind his mirrored, black mask. He enjoyed their constant displeasure at his use of collective pronouns. 'My business with Mr Derindi is completed. Show him out, and make sure he gets what he is owed for his services.'

Panic streaked across Derindi's face as the twins grabbed him under both arms and hoisted him up off the ground. 'I swear I didn't know Svend was in your employ, Mr Nemo, sir. I woulda let Jerico kill me before giving him up if I'd known I was crossing you.'

The little weasel was shaking so hard, Nemo thought he might slip right out of the twins' grasp. 'Not to worry, Derindi,' he said. 'Your particular services are far more valuable to me than even a hundred Svends.'

Derindi's shaking transformed into vibrations as his head began bobbing up and down like a jackhammer. 'That's true, Mr Nemo, sir. We both deal in information. We're information brokers, you might say.'

'Well, I am a broker, Derindi,' said Nemo. 'Actually, *the* broker. And you are nothing more than a small-time gossip collector. But I see your point.' As he talked, Nemo triggered several more controls on a few different panels, but he didn't like what he saw. Kal Jerico's face, larger than life, filled one of Nemo's screens. The view kept tilting and twisting, and he could see fingertips at the edge of the screen. The damn bounty hunter had spotted the tail Nemo had placed on him earlier that day!

'Mr Nemo, sir?' Derindi's whining voice floated across the chamber. Nemo snapped his fingers and the snitch stayed quiet.

When Nemo looked back at the screen, the view had shifted. He could now see a Delaque agent – his agent – held off the ground with Yolanda's hands around his neck. A moment later, Nemo saw the ground rush up at the camera and then the screen went black. Nemo sat and seethed. He needed to stay close to Jerico, but the bounty hunter was too suspicious, especially of the Delaque.

A soft whimper from the twice-forgotten Derindi made Nemo twist his faceless head around toward the weasel. It was well past time for the snitch to die. Even through all the platitudes, Nemo had always intended to kill the snitch. He just enjoyed torturing them with hope first. But now, as he looked at the offensively inoffensive little man, a thought occurred to the spymaster.

'Yes boys,' he said to the twins. 'Pay Mr Derindi for his trouble and give him some gear. Derindi, I have an assignment for you.'

'WHAT IN THE Spire was that thing?' asked Scabbs. He kneeled down next to Kal and looked at the broken remains of Nemo's spy camera strewn on the ground. Before Kal smashed the device, it had looked like a weapon of some sort, except with a glass lens stuck in the end of the barrel. Scabbs had thought it might be a new type of laspistol.

Scabbs picked through pieces on the ground. The casing had cracked open, revealing circuit boards, miniaturized motors and gears, and two curved pieces of glass that apparently once moved up and down the barrel. On the back end, above the handle, was what looked like the smashed remnants of a tiny pict screen.

'Spy camera,' said Kal. He ground his boot into the circuit boards, catching one of Scabbs's fingers under his heel. 'See that metal rod at the top?' Scabbs nodded as he sucked on his finger. 'An antenna. Somebody was watching us. Spying on us!'

'Any idea who?' asked Yolanda. She looked at the dead ganger lying crumpled at her feet, his head twisted almost completely around.

'Too many ideas,' said Kal. 'He's a Delaque. I'd guess from the colours he's wearing that he belongs… used to belong to the Silent Vipers. House Delaque doesn't like me much. Perhaps another bounty hunter hired him to follow us to Svend. Or, maybe he's just one of my hundreds of adoring fans, and all he wanted was an autograph.'

'More likely he was one of your hundreds of enemies looking to cash in the bounty on your head,' said Yolanda.

'I paid that months ago.'

'Maybe he didn't get the message,' said Yolanda, pointing at the dead ganger. She bent down and began searching his pockets. 'No. No bounty posters,' she announced. 'Some loose credits and weapon reloads, though.' She pocketed the found treasures. 'Killers keepers, I always say.'

'Nemo,' said Scabbs a moment later. He was still poking through the shattered spy camera.

'Yeah. Could be Nemo,' said Kal. 'He's got a thing for messing with my life.'

'No, I mean this is Nemo's gadget,' said Scabbs. 'I recognise the imprint pattern on these circuit boards. Only Nemo uses anything this sophisticated downhive.

'He could have been outfitted by one of the Noble Houses,' said Yolanda as she stuck the ganger's weapon in an extra holster. 'Most of his other gear is pretty standard Hive City issue.'

'Nemo,' said Jerico. He dropped his head and ran a hand through the locks of braided blond hair that constantly flipped into his eyes. 'Helmawr's rump. It's Nemo alright. I can feel it. Something nasty has been crawling up and down my spine all morning. Our lives are about to get a lot more interesting.'

'What do you mean *our* lives?' asked Yolanda, a note of hysteria entering her voice. 'The last time Nemo got his claws into you, *I* almost died. You can handle this round on your own.' She kicked the dead Delaque agent in the ribs and stalked off down the street, her loin-cloth slapping her legs in a syncopated rhythm with the steady beat of her boots.

'Yolanda!' called Scabbs. He stood and started running after her.

Kal grabbed his scab-covered sidekick by the shoulder as he ran past, almost pulling him over backwards. 'Let her go, Scabbs,' said Jerico. 'She'll be back. Besides, if Nemo is after us, we have more than enough problems of our own. We don't have time to deal with women issues.'

'But she might get into trouble without us to back her up,' whined Scabbs.

Kal looked into the scabby face and saw real concern in his friend's beady eyes. Possibly for the first time, Kal realized that the little half-breed really cared for the Amazon-sized bounty hunter. Scabbs constantly complained about the time he had spent as Yolanda's partner. She was reckless, he said, even more reckless than Jerico, and had almost gotten him killed on more than one occasion. But he obviously enjoyed the danger. Why else would he stick around with both Kal and Yolanda, as they took him to death's door every other day? And then forced *him* to knock on it.

Jerico softened a bit toward his sidekick and put an arm around Scabbs's shoulder, instantly regretting the contact as he was sure he could feel some small critter crawl up his arm. He cringed and kept the arm where it was. 'Yolanda can handle herself just fine,' he said. 'She's tougher than a Goliath and trickier than a Delaque.'

'Yeah,' sniffled Scabbs, 'and crazier than a scavvy.'

'That's our Yolanda,' agreed Kal with a chuckle. 'What in the Underhive could possibly threaten her?'

'I WANT THE head of Yolanda Catallus!' screamed Vicksen Colteen as she stormed into the Wildcats' hideout. Spiky blue hair waved around above the Escher gang leader's eyes like an enraged sea anemone. The sides of her head had been shaved clean to allow the Wildcats tattoo on her forehead to wrap around her ears, but behind the shock of blue spikes, auburn locks flowed straight over Vicksen's head into a long ponytail that reached the small of her back.

She wore a spiked collar on her long, muscular neck, to which were attached the straps of a skin-tight half-vest that ended well above her pierced and tattooed navel. This was no frilly, feminine vest like those a Spire noblewoman would wear over a silk blouse. This leather vest was pulled taut around the ganger's ample bosom, and was studded with brass rings that held live grenades or empty pins from used munitions.

Below the half-vest, the Escher wore a double bandolier as a belt. The bandolier, which swayed up and down atop Vicksen's hips as she strode through the doorway, was filled with shotgun shells and also held the sheath for her chainsword. A pair of tight, tan breeches that looked almost painted on hung low on her hips and hugged her long legs all the way down to her knees where they met black, spike-heeled boots that shone in the candlelight.

'What's she done now?' asked Themis, Vicksen's second-in-command. Themis Van'Upp had grown up inside House van Saar, but struck out on her own at eleven, fed up with her role as a housemaid in the male-dominated van Saar world. She'd been a Wildcat ever since Vicksen had found her, half-naked and screaming at the top of her lungs, in the middle of a street brawl over a loaf of bread. Themis had run off into an alley with the loaf, while the boys she had beaten limped away, bent over and groaning.

Themis wore a vest similar to Vicksen's, but topped by a leather overcoat with long chains that hung down from the shoulder to bang against her waist. Her long, blonde hair fell in sheets around her round face, outlining the Wildcat tattoo that circled her eyes and ran down her cheeks to her jaw-line. She was sitting at a makeshift table crafted from a petrified piece of wood that might once have been a door lying across cinderblocks. Themis's heavy stubber sat in several pieces on the table in front of her. She finished wiping down the firing pin and laid it on the table as Vicksen dropped onto a cinderblock across from her.

'It's not anything that witch has done,' she began. 'It's her scavving legacy!' She snapped her fingers twice and a moment later a scrawny man wearing dirty, cotton shirt and breeches scurried into the room through a rusted iron door near the back of the room. Vicksen and Themis sat in the burned-out remains of what must have once been a bar or bistro back when this dome had been a thriving hub of commerce. The front walls were all but gone, just a few blocks to either side of the entrance giving little more than the suggestion of walls, and the furnishings had long since been stolen or rotted away. But in the back, the Wildcats had found a complete kitchen with working stoves and ovens, once power had been redirected to the dome.

The bistro was the nerve centre of the Wildcat camp, which encompassed all the buildings on the square. Most were nothing more than burned-out shells, but the gang members found more than enough prime sleeping quarters in the houses, shops, and inns situated on the square, and Vicksen herself lived above the kitchen, which was both warm from the ovens, and close enough to the kitchen for the mavants, who were little more than male slaves, to hear her frequent summons.

The soiled servant shuffled up to the gang leader, hanging his head low to avoid eye contact. 'Yes, mistress,' he said. 'What do you wish?'

'Soup,' she demanded, 'and a bottle of Wildsnake.' She kicked the male slave in the rear as he turned to trundle back toward the kitchen. 'Make sure the soup is hot and the 'Snake cold this time!'

'If only I could get that kind of fear and respect from the other gang leaders,' sighed Vicksen as she turned back to the table. Themis was busy rebuilding her weapon, and the gang leader watched with awe as her second-in-command snapped pieces together with almost unnatural speed and precision. After a few seconds, the heavy stubber sat gleaming on the table. Themis picked up the large weapon and spun it twice in her hands before slinging it through the chain hanging at her side.

'What's the problem?' asked Themis. 'We need to show the Manic Miners, the Circuit Breakers and all the other local gangs who rule this section of the Underhive again?' Her eyebrows furrowed and a frightening glare flared in her eyes as she spoke.

'Perhaps,' said Vicksen. 'Since Yolanda left, the Circuit Breakers have encroached on several territories and taken archeotech that is rightfully ours, while Trogan, the Orlock gang leader, has nearly convinced the merchant guilds that the Wildcats are a leaderless, outlaw gang so they won't deal with us.'

'But you're the leader!' snapped Themis. She grabbed the butt of her heavy stubber and swung the weapon forward. 'Let me show them some fear and respect.'

'The real problem is Yolanda,' huffed Vicksen. 'A Wildcat leader doesn't just leave. A Wildcat leader dies defending the tribe or at the hands of the new leader in a challenge battle. Until Yolanda is dead, the Wildcats have no leader.'

'What can we do?' asked Themis.

'We must find and kill Yolanda Catallus. *I* must kill Yolanda to claim my rightful place as leader!'

'Then find her we will,' said Themis, still holding her heavy stubber. 'No matter who or what gets in our way.'

'Gather the cats,' said Vicksen. 'We're going hunting.'

YOLANDA STORMED THROUGH the mostly deserted streets of Glory Hole like a hivequake rumbling through layer after layer of domes. At this time of day, most residents of the Underhive settlement were out prospecting for archeotech or still sleeping off the previous night's 'Snake. Those settlers who were on the street took one look at the dark cloud surrounding Yolanda's face and the swift gait of her long, muscular legs, and quickly decided not to be there any longer.

The constant slamming of doors and scurrying of feet in front of her didn't improve Yolanda's mood either. 'Rotten, moth-eaten, slug of a scav-worm,' she grumbled as she walked. 'Acts like the whole Hive revolves around him, like he's the emperor of the scavving universe. Didn't even try to stop me from leaving. Too much trouble to be around. What in the Hive is their problem anyway?'

She yelled at a retreating figure carrying several bags overflowing with bread and meats, some shopkeeper heading to the market, or perhaps a thief retreating from the market, who had paused to glance at the stalking bounty hunter. 'What are you looking at?' she demanded. Then, when the plump, little man scurried off, she added 'That's it! Run away from me. I'm a scavving nuisance to your pitiful life!' Yolanda drew her pistol in a flash and shot at the now running man, barely missing his head and chipping off a chunk of concrete from the partially-collapsed wall behind him.

Yolanda's feet had taken her nearly to the far side of Glory Hole, but she hardly even noticed where she was going or where she'd been since stomping away from Kal and Scabbs. 'At least Scabbs had called after me,' she grumbled, continuing her running rant against Kal Jerico. 'But no! Don't let my former partner show any loyalty to me, Mister High-and-Mighty-Bounty-Hunter. You don't own the whole, scavving Hive, Jerico!'

This last line was screamed at the crumbling buildings of Glory Hole with an intensity and rage rarely witnessed in the Underhive. At least, rarely witnessed by anyone who survived to tell the tale. The entire street went quiet in the wake of Yolanda's primal scream. The only sound was the rhythmic stomp of the bounty hunter's boots.

In the almost unnatural silence, a shadow passed over Yolanda's head. Pistol immediately in hand, her eyes darted toward the rooftops. A flash of movement drew her gaze to the conduits emerging from the top of the building next to her. She fired.

'WHERE WE GOING, Kal?' asked Scabbs as they wandered the streets of Glory Hole. Jerico's meanderings since Yolanda left had led the scabby half-breed to believe that they were searching for their wayward partner. They'd been going up one street and down another all afternoon, often going in circles or retracing their steps from hours earlier.

They had currently stopped in front of a burned-out factory that Scabbs was sure he'd seen at least twice already. The rear of the building no longer existed. A hivequake had long ago brought an entire section of dome down on the stone and steel building. All of the useful equipment inside the factory had been demolished or buried under tonnes of stone, never to be recovered, at least not until the next quake shifted it all into a deeper cavern. The quake had opened a handy escape passage that Scabbs knew about, which led from Glory Hole out to an abandoned strike in the wastes.

As Scabbs looked at the landmark they had passed twice in as many hours, he knew one thing was certain; if Kal Jerico was actually trying to get somewhere, they should have been there long ago.

Jerico ran his fingers though the dyed gold locks dangling in front of his face and gave Scabbs a sheepish grin. 'I'm looking for Hagen's Hole, but I think it must have moved.'

'You mean you're lost, don't you?' admonished Scabbs.

'Not lost exactly,' said Kal, now smirking like a mischievous cat. 'I'd say more like momentarily between landmarks.'

Scabbs sighed. 'What you need,' he said while pointing one podgy finger at the nose of his smirking partner, 'is someone skilled at finding their way through the back alleys of the Underhive, perhaps a tracker who knows shortcuts, secret paths or just the most direct route from one side of the scavving dome to the other.'

Kal slapped Scabbs on the back. 'Excellent idea. A guide. We can hire one at Hagen's.'

'If you can ever find it,' muttered Scabbs. He took a deep breath. He could tell that Kal was never going to ask for help, let alone admit he was lost. But the little man was determined to give it one more try. 'I do have some skills as a tracker, you know.'

'Picked that up from me, have you?' asked Kal, his grin broadening across his chiselled face.

'Helmawr's rump!' exclaimed Scabbs. 'The Hole is just around the corner.'

Kal walked to the intersection and looked down the street. 'So it is. I've found it!' he said.

'Go in there and find yourself a new tracker, you ungrateful…' Scabbs fell silent as Jerico strode out of sight and then, after only a moment's reflection, ran to catch up to his partner.

HAGEN'S HOLE WAS abuzz when Kal stepped through the door. Oddly, though, the noise all came from the front room, which was filled past capacity with bounty hunters from all over the Underhive. At least two dozen mercenaries packed the room. Kal could see Dungo and Skreed, regulars in Hagen's for many years, along with Gorgh, Hern, and Lebow from Dead End Pass, and The King (nobody knew his real name), who rarely came up from Down Town unless chasing some mutie that was trying to escape uphive. Big names all, and Kal couldn't remember a time when he'd seen them all in the same watering hole.

The gaming tables in Hagen's back rooms, which normally would be the focus of attention for most of the patrons this time of night, sat vacant except for those poor souls on the perimeter of the throng who couldn't push their way through to the centre of all of the attention.

That wasn't a problem for Kal Jerico, though. He pulled out his trusty lasgun and fired at the ceiling. The sharp report of the blast and the sudden hiss of air escaping the neat hole he'd just put into the grey conduit above him brought all eyes in the room to Kal Jerico.

The moment would have been perfect if not for the untimely arrival of Scabbs, who rushed through the doorway and slammed into Jerico's back, sending them both to the floor in a heap. The room erupted into laughter as Jerico tried to roll over and kick the scabby half-ratskin tracker off of him and onto the floor. For his part, Scabbs must have realised what would happen to him once Jerico got to his feet, and simply scuttled over and over Kal as the much larger bounty hunter rolled around on the crowded floor.

The laughter had reached a fever pitch when Jerico stuck his lasgun into Scabbs's gut and shouted, 'Get off of me you little runt or, so help me Helmawr, I will turn you into a pile of ratskin droppings!' This had the effect of redoubling the laughter in the room, but also scared Scabbs enough to make him jump off and dash into one of the back rooms.

A hand reached down and grabbed Kal by the arm, hoisting him easily to his feet. Kal looked down into the smiling and still chortling face of Hern. Tears rolled down his plump, red cheeks and fell the short distance from his stubbly chin to his huge, rounded shoulders. Hern was a short man, but had arms the size of most men's thighs. What scared the renegades that Hern hunted the most was that the muscular bounty hunter wore no visible weapons. Most of his friends called him the headhunter, but never to his face.

'Thanks for the laugh, Kal,' said Hern as he released his grip on Kal's arm. Jerico was sure the five red imprints on his forearm would still be there in the morning. 'We can always count on you for a moment of levity at our darkest hours.'

Kal and Hern easily pushed their way back through the crowd to the bar where a bottle of Wildsnake awaited Jerico. 'Darkest hours?' he asked. 'What's happened? Why's everyone here tonight? Did old Helmawr finally die?'

'Now why would that upset any of us?' asked Dungo. 'No, we're all here about the Underhive vampire. Hadn't you heard?'

'Underhive vampire?' asked Kal as he took a swig of 'Snake. Hagen's best was just as bad as he remembered, but he forced it down and enjoyed the warmth that spread through his body a moment later.

Hagen spoke up. He seemed to be the local authority on the subject. 'It's killed two people in Glory Hole so far,' he said while mopping the bar with a drab cloth as well as part of his long beard, which had gotten stuck to particularly nasty stain in the cloth. 'Killed 'em and drained all their blood.'

'Anybody we know?'

All the heads in the bar bobbed up and down as one.

'Bester,' said Dungo.

'Arin Bester?' said Kal, almost spitting out the 'Snake. He swallowed hard. 'Nah. It'd take an army to kill that old pit champion. He's stronger than Hern.'

'He's dead all right,' said Skreed. I brought him in myself. Vampire snapped his neck like kindling and bent the barrel of his shotgun.' He dropped the ruined weapon on the bar as an exclamation point.

'Damn. Not Bester?' Jerico slammed his bottle onto the bar. 'Damn. He owed me two hundred credits!'

'Beddy also found the body of Pete Parcher earlier today,' said Hagen. 'He runs a guild shop over on the south side of the dome…'

'Or used to before his body was drained and left on the roof of his shop,' added Dungo.

'I take it the guild has put out a bounty?' said Kal hopefully. Maybe he could get the money Bester owed him, with interest.

'Two thousand credits!' said Skreed. 'Beddy's out there right now trying to cash in.'

Credit symbols danced in Kal's eyes. The debauchery he could wreak in watering holes throughout the Underhive with that kind of money made the bounty hunter's heart thump as fast as a repeating rifle. But another more immediate yearning, one that had quickly developed below his beltline, forced Kal to retreat from the throng, which had now broken into several groups who all seemed to be planning their attacks on the vampire.

In the alley beside Hagen's Hole, Kal relieved his watery burden against the wall while pondering the best way to track and defeat the vampire. It was obviously some mutant beast from the deepest depths of the Underhive. How else could The King have heard about it? It was strong and apparently attacked without warning.

But Jerico knew that none of that mattered. Sure the beast had taken out Bester, but the man was getting on in years and anybody can be taken by surprise. Jerico, though, had three things that even the best in the business, all of whom were in the Hole tonight, did not have. He had Plan W, which was a tried and true method to defeat any kind of surprise. He had two partners to draw the beast's attention while he lined up a shot. And he had the fabled Kal Jerico luck.

Kal heard a noise behind him and turned too late. Helmawr's rump. That's just my luck, thought Jerico to himself.

# 3: HEADS OR TAILS

YOLANDA'S LASPISTOL BLAST echoed in the empty streets. A shape dropped from the conduit above her. When it hit the street in front of her, something rolled off into the ever-present rubble. The object at her feet was about a metre long, brown, furry, and headless. Bare patches of skin dotted the body, showing old sores from battles and diseases that had never quite healed over.

It was a rat. She'd been startled by a lousy Hive rat. Good thing Kal and Scabbs weren't around to see her so jittery. Her paranoia circuits must be working overtime. Stupid Jerico. This was all his fault, she remembered. With Nemo on them again, even a rat could be dangerous. Yolanda kicked the headless rat into the rubble.

That's when she saw it. The head. But it wasn't the rat's head. She'd blasted that clean away. This was a human head, covered by tightly-curled, black hair. Yolanda had a sick feeling in her stomach as she walked over to get a better look. Not from the shock of seeing a human head. She'd carried enough of those into the guilder's offices as proof of her bounties. No, she was fairly sure she recognised this particular head, even though she could only see the back of it.

She picked up the head to get a better look. Much of the skin and underlying muscles on the face had been gnawed away by rats, leaving a gruesome, bloody patch-work. But the thick, black curls with roughly the texture of steel wool, along with the gold teeth clearly visible within the lipless mouth confirmed Yolanda's fears. It was Beddy Bor'Wick.

Yolanda examined the head to see if she could figure out what had happened to her fellow bounty hunter. The skull seemed to be intact, and what was left of the skin had no burn holes or scorch marks. Beddy could have been shot in the torso and her head severed after-ward.

She examined the cut marks. Luckily, the rats hadn't eaten their way down to the neck yet. The cut was clean, but it hadn't been cauterised. So, not a laspistol, power sword or laser scalpel. The cut was too clean for a chainsword, though. And who, or what, would have the strength to make such a clean cut with only the strength of their bare hands behind the blow?

Yolanda opened her pack and pulled out a blood-stained cloth bag. She stuffed Beddy's head into the bag and dropped it into a special compartment in her pack. She looked at the pile of rubble. It sloped gently up toward the roof where she had shot the rat. Probably the local thugs and thieves had shaped it for an easy escape. She would use it for a different purpose. It was time to hit the rooftops and find Beddy's killer. Or at least the rest of Beddy.

Rats scurried off across the conduit pipes as Yolanda reached the top of the pile. She reached up and pulled herself onto the rooftop. Standing with her hands on her hips, she surveyed this section of the dome from her elevated vantage point. It looked exactly the same as every other part of Glory Hole. The once glorious dome now held little more than partially-destroyed buildings and rats. Lots and lots of rats.

Yolanda decided to follow the rats. If there was a body anywhere up here, the vermin would find it first. She looked at the bundle of pipes that stretched to the building across the street. The rat she had killed had been scampering across with Beddy's head when she'd taken its own head. The conduit looked sturdy enough, and the bounty hunter could see footprints in the dust from recent vermin traffic of the human variety, so she decided to chance it.

She loped easily across the pipes and dropped onto the roof on the other side. Judging from the huge exhaust tubes rising up from the building all the way to the dome, she was atop an old factory of some sort. The rats had all vanished before she arrived but a trail of blood led away from the pipe, probably from the rat dragging Beddy's head. She followed this across the roof and another set of conduit pipes to a large, flat roof with a blast hole in the middle.

Two trails of blood led away from the hole: a fresh one coming toward her that she was now sure had come from the severed head in her pack; and another, leading off from the other side of the hole. There was no body in sight, though, and an eerie silence had descended around her.

Yolanda slipped her sword from the sheath banging against her bare thigh. Her other hand found its way to the butt of her laspistol as she scanned the rooftops. Nothing. Not even the rats scurried about anymore. As she crept toward the hole, she began to hear a strange scrabbling sound. There was more blood at the edge of the hole, but it didn't seem to have any connection to either trail. She could also see that the other blood trail had already dried.

The scrabbling sound was louder, and she could hear what she recognised as the chirping sound of rats again.

She looked down into the hole. There, twenty feet below, just barely visible in the deepening gloom of the Glory Hole twilight, was a body. Yolanda flicked on a torch and shined it into the hole, revealing a headless body covered in a swarm of huge rats. She shot a blast into the pack beside the body and the swarm dispersed. It was Beddy alright. Her rifle was still sheathed on her back, and a spool of grapnel wire laid coiled atop her body. Oddly, there was no blood visible, not even oozing from the numerous rat bites.

'What in the Hive?' asked Yolanda.

KAL JERICO AWOKE to a bright light shining in his eyes. His side ached. He couldn't move his arms or legs, and he had a headache that started at the base of his skull and wrapped around his head to dig into his eyeballs. 'I won't tell you anything!' he cried out automatically. 'I don't care how much you beat me, how much you torture me, I…' He paused as he looked around at his surroundings, '…am yours to command.'

The bright light streamed in from a bank of windows over the massive bed where Kal lay. He was pinned to the mattress by a slim brunette in a shear bodysuit snuggled up against one shoulder, a buxom blonde in a black corset and stockings lying on the other shoulder, and a voluptuous redhead in a long satin nightgown sprawled across his legs. Kal's leather coat and trousers had, at some time during the night, been replaced by red silk pyjamas.

The Spire. Even without the golden rays of sunshine beating down on him and the bevy of gorgeous ladies who smelled of lilacs instead of sludge, he would have known where he was. The walls of the room were white. Not even the grungy, brownish white of Hive City, but pure, alabaster white; whiter even than the pale skin of the redhead at his feet.

And the air. It didn't hang there in your mouth and nose like a haze of grease in a fry kitchen. It simply passed through to your lungs with just the barest whisper of pine dew. Of course, the air was thinner. He was, after all, about ten miles higher within the Hive than when he went to sleep.

Sleep. No. Drugged. Or stunned. Or both. The night before started to come back to him. He'd stepped outside Hagen's to shake out the snake. Then he'd turned to find Spire guards surrounding him and a needle gun jammed into his ribs. That explained the pain in his side. The headache must have come from whatever the needle had injected, which also put him out for the rest of the night.

He looked at the girls and the silk pyjamas again. 'If this is a jail, then I'm signing up for a life sentence.' He extracted one arm and started stroking the bare shoulder of the blonde on his right. Her tanned skin was smooth, supple, and freshly bathed. A far cry from the grungy and sometimes scaly women he normally had on his arms downhive.

'A man could get used to this,' said Kal. All three women were still deep in sleep. He watched their bosoms rise and fall as they breathed, mesmerised by the rhythmic dance of soft flesh. His headache persisted, but what bothered Jerico even more was that he couldn't remember anything after losing consciousness. Here he was with perhaps the three most beautiful women he'd ever slept with, and he was pretty sure all he had done was sleep. Well, that would change soon, he said to himself as his hand strayed from the blonde's shoulder toward her neck.

But his suspicious mind, attuned to life in the Underhive, wouldn't relax and let go of the fact that he had been kidnapped and drugged by someone as yet unknown. Plus, the oversized paranoid region of his brain told Kal that it couldn't be a coincidence that the kidnapping had occurred only hours after he'd found Nemo's man spying on him.

He should get up, he knew that. He should get out of bed, find his clothes and weapons, figure out where he was and deal with whoever had brought him here. The brunette on his left moaned and shifted in her sleep, brushing her entire stocking-clad body up against Kal's side. 'Or I could stay here and interrogate the girls,' he said. 'Repeatedly. It could take hours, but I'm sure it will be fruitful.'

Maybe it was a prison after all. A prison specially built to hold Kal Jerico.

DERINDI CROUCHED BEHIND the large conduit pipe and watched the entrance to Hagen's Hole below. Beads of sweat dotted his bare head from just above his eyes all the way down to his neck. He wiped one temple, running his hand through the thin wisps of hair above his ears, only succeeding in plastering the little hair he had against his head. He wiped the other side, forgetting again about the bandage over what was left of his ear.

Clenching his teeth to hold in the scream, Derindi groaned and grumbled, 'Damn Jerico. He'll pay for this!'

'Concentrate,' purred a voice in his good ear. 'Where is Jerico?' asked Nemo through the radio his men had so graciously implanted in the snitch's eardrum.

A subvocal transmitter attached to his vocal cords was obviously broadcasting everything he said back to the spymaster. It had been a shock when he realised it earlier at Pinky's Parlour in Down Town. He had since resigned himself to the fact that he was now an owned man. 'My sources say he and the half-breed went into

Hagen's several hours ago. Nobody's seen them leave, so I assume they're still in there.'

'You assume!' roared the voice. Derindi's inner ear felt like it was going to explode. He definitely didn't want to make Nemo angry anymore. 'Go in and find out, you fool!'

The protest came out before he could think to hold his tongue. 'But the place is crawling with bounty hunters,' he blurted. 'They've come from all over the Underhive to catch some mutant vampire.'

There was a pause that was almost more frightening than the impending scream. 'Interesting,' came the sub-dued response. 'I had not heard about a gathering of hired guns in Glory Hole or of this mutant vampire.'

'Yeah, it killed Bester last night,' said Derindi under his breath, happy to have something of value for his new master. 'Supposed to be huge. Some say it's invisible.'

'Hmmm. Doubtful, but possible.' Another pause. Derindi knew better than to interrupt Nemo's thought processes. 'Get into that bar,' he said after a moment. 'Find out everything you can about this so-called vampire – and find Kal Jerico!'

The ringing in his ears subsided after a moment, but the headache that followed would linger for quite some time. Derindi knew there was one way he could get into Hagen's undetected, but it would mean crossing the conduit to the roof where the first vampire attack had supposedly taken place. This was not something he wanted to do. But the alternative was to fail Nemo, which was just as deadly, and probably more painful.

He looked across the street at the dark roof where Bester had fought the vampire. The shadows loomed and seemed to move. Fear gripped the little man and he wished, not for the first time, that he'd picked a different line of work. Of course, in the Underhive, you didn't so much choose your life as it chose you, often for dinner.

'Okay,' he said to himself and Nemo, if only to give that final push he needed to get up, 'here I go.' There was silence from the other end of the radio. Derindi climbed out from his hiding place and crept across the conduit.

Halfway across, he remembered that the twins, Seek and Destroy, had given him some new gear as well as the implants. Derindi wrapped his legs around the pipe and opened the pack. Inside was a pict camera with an attached antenna, a grapnel, a needle gun and a pair of goggles. He slipped the goggles on and flipped them to nightvision.

He scanned the roof and the dome overhead, but saw nothing moving against the greenish background of conduits, cables, and broken concrete. Feeling only slightly better (they said Bester never saw the monster coming), Derindi crawled the rest of the way across.

'Now, where's that access panel?' he asked himself. He felt along the end of the conduit until his fingers found the hidden clasp. *Depress for two seconds, wait three seconds, depress twice for one second each.* A hatch slid open and Derindi crawled inside the pipe. The panel slid shut behind him.

The trip back to the roof of Hagen's was far easier on his nerves. The vampire was said to be three metres tall and as broad as a Goliath. It would never fit inside the pipe. Halfway back, something banged on the end of the pipe behind him. Derindi fell flat inside the pipe and didn't move. Another clang came shortly after the first, and this one was closer.

Bang. Bang. Bang. Something big was running down the pipe. Derindi scrambled to get onto his hands and feet and ran like a crab the entire length of the pipe. He dove into the shaft at the end, plummeting into the darkness toward the basement of Hagen's Hole.

'So, DO YOU mean to tell me that you girls don't know where we are either?' asked Kal.

The blonde, whose name was Candi, currently sat behind the bounty hunter, giving him a back rub while he in turn stroked the back of Sandi, the redhead. Brandi, the brunette, was taking a break in an over-stuffed chair next to the door. All three girls worked at the infamous Kitty Club, renowned the whole Hive over for their beautiful and accommodating employees.

Brandi sucked on a grape before answering. 'We were hired for a private party by some guy,' she said. 'That's all we know.'

Candi nibbled on Kal's ear as her hands rubbed his bare shoulders. 'We were blindfolded and brought here,' she whispered. 'I still have the blindfold if you like that kind of thing.'

Kal took a deep breath and shook his head. He had to stay focused and Candi was making that difficult. The interrogation had been enjoyable, but not terribly fruitful. Whoever had imprisoned him certainly wanted Kal to enjoy himself, but the door was locked and outside the window was a ten mile drop to the base of the Hive. Worst of all, his clothes and weapons were nowhere to be found within the small apart-ment.

'What did he look like,' he asked, 'this guy who hired you?' In his mind Kal was taking a cold shower, desper-ately trying to maintain some control as Candi licked at his earlobe. Sandi turned around in front of him and began kissing Jerico's chest. The water in Kal's imaginary shower began to steam.

'I don't know,' said Brandi. 'He was a guy. All I saw was the top of his head.'

'Yeah,' added Sandi, 'They never look you in the eye.'

All three girls laughed at the private joke. Kal had to admit he would have a hard time looking them in the eyes. As beautiful as their faces were, there were just more interesting aspects to these girls than their eyes.

'He had short hair and professor glasses,' said Brandi. 'You know the little round ones with the wire frames? The kind that all the bookish types always wear.'

Kal exhaled in several short gasps as the girls' ministrations threatened to break his concentration. 'What was he wearing?' he asked after a few minutes.

'Why all the questions, lover?' asked Brandi. 'Enjoy the party. If you're good, I'll show you something fun I can do with these grapes.' Brandi grabbed a handful of grapes and sauntered over toward the bed.

Before she could show Kal her grape trick, the door opened and a short man with a buzz cut and wire-rimmed professor glasses walked in, flanked by two House Helmawr guards.

'Good morning, Mr Jerico,' he said. A smile crept across his face as he looked at the shirtless bounty hunter and the semi-clad ladies. 'My name is Obidiah Clein. I hope you have been enjoying Lord Helmawr's accommodations. But I'm afraid this party is now over.'

DERINDI SAW THE bottom of the shaft rushing toward him in the green glow of the nightvision goggles. He slammed his hands and feet against the sides of the chute in a desperate attempt to slow down. At the last second, he ducked his head and used his hands to absorb some of the impact. He rolled out of the shaft and spun across the room, crashing into a stack of kegs before he could stop. He could hear the Wildsnake

slosh around inside and scuttled away before any of the
kegs fell over on top of him.

'Ow, ow, ow, ow, ow!' he cried. Luckily, it seemed
Nemo was attending to other matters, for there was no
response from his ear drum receiver. Derindi took stock.
He had no protruding bones, no gushing blood, and
the rocking keg hadn't fallen. Pain shot up his forearms,
though, and it felt like somebody was pounding a beat
on both of his elbows. Plus a drip, drip, drip on his
cheek told the snitch that his wounded ear had bled
through the bandage.

But he was alive and inside Hagen's Hole. At least
that part of the plan had worked out. He listened at the
shaft, but heard no more banging. Whatever had been
following him had gone, or was simply waiting for him
to climb back out. From here, he could climb up into
Hagen's, spy on the patrons from a special panel that
he was sure none of the bounty hunters even knew
about, or move one of the kegs and gain access to an
escape hatch that would get him out of Glory Hole for
good.

Derindi sighed and crept under the stairway into a
crawl space. This area was filled with old pipes and conduits from the time that Hagen's had been a power
station. It was a maze that extended throughout most of
the basement. The floor was sticky from centuries of
ooze and muck mixed with layer upon layer of dust. It
was like walking through paste.

After several twists and turns, the snitch stopped and
looked up at the low ceiling. This was the worst part.
The spy panel was a simple sliding door, but he knew
from experience what lay on the other side. The panel
opened up beneath the grate floor in the middle of
Hagen's front room; the grate that constantly filled with
the effluvia from the bar above.

There was normally a table set over the panel. Derindi and a few others who knew about the panel would always 'help' each new Hagen find the best layout for the place, taking care to preserve their own special spyhole. But Derindi knew the table only protected the panel so much and Hagen's would likely be busy at this time of day. He slid it back as quickly as he could, pulling his aching arm down and away with a jerk.

It didn't matter. No matter how quickly Derindi moved, the mixture of Wildsnake, spit, blood and too many other liquids too awful to imagine always sluiced through the opening and coated his forearm. He waited another minute to let the last drop of ooze drip onto the floor, and then climbed onto the pipes to stick his head through the opening.

A small section of floor above the panel had been cleared of most pipes, giving Derindi a clear view of the bar through the grate floor. A commotion must have erupted at the front of the bar just moments earlier because everyone in the bar was rushing toward the door. All he could see was feet and legs running past him, and he could hear nothing but shouting.

A moment later a single voice rang out and quieted the mob. 'Shut up, you band of scum,' yelled Yolanda, 'and let me through.' The Hole went completely quiet, and the next thing that Derindi heard made his heart skip a beat. It was the clang, clang, clang of boots against the grate, just like he'd heard on the pipe. As the crowd parted, he saw the normally graceful, long-legged Yolanda stomping toward him under the weight of a body slung over her shoulder.

As Yolanda came closer he lost sight of her face and the body as they were blocked by the table. With a thump, the body was slung practically on top of

Derindi, making him jump. He almost screamed when he saw that the body was missing its head.

'It's Beddy all right,' he heard Yolanda say. He pulled his eyes away from the headless corpse and looked at the legs surrounding the table. There were Yolanda's bare thighs, Hern's camo pants and thick boots, Gorgh's knee-high snakeskin boots with the hidden boot knife, and Lebow's suede boots sticking out from his tight, red pants. Across the table from this group stood someone wearing white leather strides and matching shoes: The King! Derindi knew he didn't want to be seen in this bar today.

'She's been completely drained of blood,' said Yolanda. 'Damndest thing I ever saw.'

'She's not the first,' said another voice. It was Hagen. Derindi recognised his shabby grey dungarees with the stains on the thighs where he wiped his hands. 'The beast got Bester two nights ago and a shopkeeper yesterday.'

'Beddy thought it was a vampire,' said another voice that he knew to be Skreed. 'She went out to search for it to get the bounty.'

'I'd say she found it,' said Yolanda.

'Where'd you find her?' asked Hern

'That depends,' said Yolanda.

'On what?'

'On how big the bounty is on this beast.'

'Two thousand credits,' said a voice Derindi recognized as Scabbs. 'Hi Yolanda. Am I glad to see you!'

'In that case, Hern, that is information for me and my partners only.'

'Make that partner,' said Scabbs.

There was a pause and Derindi gulped as he guessed what was coming next.

'Why? Where's Jerico?'

'I don't know,' said Scabbs. 'He's been gone for hours. I kinda hoped he was with you.'

Oh crap, thought Derindi. He dropped down to the floor and closed the panel. He needed to make a report to Nemo. The spymaster wasn't going to be happy about this.

OBIDIAH CLEIN AND an entourage of royal guards escorted Kal, fully clothed once again, through the lush quarters of Gerontius Helmawr's estate. The affluence of the palace gave the bounty hunter some pause. The walls were a mosaic of individually carved and highly polished stones arranged to depict scenes from the history of House Helmawr. The floors were carpeted in a plush, white fabric that made it feel like he was walking on piles of fur. At one point, the guards marched him past a series of real wooden doors, carved in bas relief with the busts of House rulers from ages past.

Then there was the light. The light never ceased to amaze Jerico. Sure, he'd experienced it before. He'd grown up a Spire brat, and had even spent some time recently above the Spiral Gates. But this was his first good look at the palace, and the sunshine shone with a brilliance here that was unsurpassed anywhere else in the Hive. The light streamed in from banks of windows. Every room, every hallway, every corridor was bathed in the golden rays of the sun.

It was almost enough to make Kal think of giving up his life in the gloom of the Underhive, but as he looked at the faces of the guards who, even without their uniforms, all looked alike, Kal knew he was not built for this life. Too many rules. Too much boredom. March here. March there. Do what you're told. Don't talk back. Kal Jerico had never been very good at obeying orders.

But now here he was, marching to the beat of Lord Helmawr. The whole thing left a bad taste in his mouth, like a half-bitten snake. Of course, the Spire did have its perks, like sunshine, liquor that wasn't strained through Hagen's old socks, food you could actually taste and clean women who could do interesting tricks with grapes. Hell, just eating fresh fruit was a trick in the Underhive.

So, he'd listen to his lordship's proposal, for why else go to all the trouble of dragging him up to the very top of the Hive except to make him do something he didn't want to do? Kal didn't do anything without payment, and Helmawr would have to come up with some amazing bounty to make Kal Jerico sit up and salute, and perhaps that same payment might just make it worthwhile.

As he ruminated on what his price might be, the group came to a sudden stop outside a plain-looking door. Kal noticed he was no longer bathed in sunlight. In fact, he now realised that the last few rooms had gotten gradually darker. The door opened. It was thick, like the door to a vault, and moved slowly inward. The room beyond was pitch black, except for a bank of lights shining in the distance.

The guard behind Kal pushed him into the room. Kal instinctively swivelled and kicked the man in the groin. The other guards drew weapons and pointed them at the bounty hunter. 'Sorry,' said Kal with a slight smirk on his face. 'He touched me, I touched him.' He looked down at the guard curled into a ball. 'Better get some ice on that.' Kal turned and strode across the black room toward the light. Clein followed, but the guards remained at the door.

The scene at the other end of the room was almost surreal. A lone desk sat in the dark with lights blaring into the faces of five men, two of whom obviously dominated the others. One freakishly tall with sharp features who glared at everyone and another who reminded Kal of a battle tank, a massive battle tank ready to run over anything in its path. There were also shapes in the shadows behind the desk, but with the light in his eyes, Kal couldn't see anything much beyond the top of the desk.

'Who is this?' asked a voice from the shadows.

Clein answered. 'Kal Jerico, your lordship. As you requested.'

'I requested?' asked the voice. 'Why would I request to see someone I don't even know?'

Kal heard the collective sigh from the other men in the room. All, that is, except Clein, who leaned in to Kal and whispered, 'He has good days and bad days.'

'I can guess which this is,' replied Kal. He pushed his way past the hawk and the tank and jumped up on the desk. 'It's me, Father,' he said into the darkness. He kicked at Clein who began pulling on his ankle. 'Kal Jerico, bounty hunter.'

'My son?' asked the voice. 'I don't have any sons.' Kal could hear another noise in the darkness, like rats scrabbling on the ground. He squinted to see in the gloom. There were four young men in white tunics and breeches, busily writing on parchment they held in their hands.

'Yes, you do, sire,' Clein said. He'd given up on pulling Kal off the desk, and was obviously trying to move the meeting along. 'Many, in fact.'

'I doubt you remember Mother,' said Kal. He sat down on the dark side of the desk and looked at his father. Helmawr looked like a man of fifty, with a thick shock of silver hair and chiselled features that reminded Kal of his own face. Of course, Jerico knew that the Lord of the Spire must be well over two hundred years old. The body had held up well. Too bad about his mind, though. 'I'm your son, all right,' he said. 'Not that you ever gave me any birthday presents.'

'Never?' asked the still confused Helmawr. The scribes busily wrote down everything said in the room. 'Clein, give my son something fitting,' he said. 'I know. Give him the spear I received on my last birthday.' He leaned in toward Kal. 'I think you will like that one, and I don't have much use for spears these days.'

Kal easily resisted the urge to give the old man a hug. A slight cough from Clein behind him made the bounty hunter realise he should move this along. 'Well, I've taken up enough of your time,' he said as he stood. 'I'm going to go talk with these men about that job you wanted me to handle.'

The light of recognition still failed to flare in the old man's face, but the canny Clein was more than ready to handle the situation. 'Yes, sire,' Clein interrupted, 'young Kal is the man who I earlier recommended might be of use to use in the… present situation.'

'Ah yes,' groaned Helmawr. 'The Armand problem. My other son. Well, one of my other sons. Very bad one at that. Stole from me. Go find him, Kal. Find him and bring back–'

'Yes sir!' cut in Clein. 'Mr Jerico's right. We won't take up any more of your time. I can brief Kal on the *particulars* while we retrieve that birthday present.'

Without another word from Clein, Jerico found himself surrounded by guards again, who hustled him out of the room. The one he'd kicked kept his distance and glared at the bounty hunter as they left the gloom and made their way back toward the light.

'HE'S NOT COMING back, is he?' Yolanda asked. Hagen's hole had finally calmed down. Most of the mercenaries had left to search for the vampire. Yolanda was fairly certain it wouldn't come out of hiding for a while after its large Beddy meal, so she wasn't worried. Besides, she was the only one who knew where to start looking.

'No, I don't really think so,' replied Scabbs. 'He didn't even say goodbye. He must have been pretty mad at me.'

'Wasn't you he was mad at,' said Yolanda, staring into the nearly empty bottle of Wildsnake. She'd been nursing the bottle for an hour or so, waiting for Kal to return. She hated the vile stuff, but you couldn't be one of the boys unless you drank the 'Snake. The whole 'Snake. So there she sat, staring at the little guy wriggling in the bottom of the bottle. It would be so much easier if she could just shoot it, but no, the code said you had to swallow the snake or bite it in half. Neither was all that much fun, really, but if there was one thing Yolanda was known for, it was for taking the whole snake, usually in one go. 'I guess I shouldn't have walked out like that, but he didn't even try to stop me, so good riddance I say.'

Scabbs nodded, which caused a cascade of dried skin to flake off his face. 'It's not like this is the first time he's done this disappearing act,' he said. 'And we do just fine together without him.'

'You saying you want to team up again?' asked Yolanda. The snake was still wriggling.

Scabbs nodded again. 'Yeah. We had fun together.'

Yolanda smiled. 'Like that time with the plague zombies? Now that was a hoot.' Scabbs had stopped nodding, but Yolanda barely noticed. She was getting caught up in the moment. She picked up the bottle, swallowed the last swig along with the snake, then slammed the bottle down and jumped up from the table and grabbed Scabbs around the shoulders as he peered around the bar, as if looking for a means of escape.

'Besides, Scabbs, old pal,' she said as she pulled him hard against her leather-encased bosom, 'when our partner left us, he took the bounty with him.'

'You mean?'

Yolanda nodded again. 'Yep. We're broke.' She pulled him towards the door. 'Now, let's go find us a vampire. I've got a great plan. We'll wait until it's hungry again, and then give it something really scabby to eat.'

DERINDI SAW YOLANDA and Scabbs leave Hagen's Hole from his hiding place on the roof of the bar. He was still a little spooked from his last trip across the conduits, but now realised that the heavy footsteps had belonged to the amazonian Yolanda weighed down by a dead body. He slipped out from behind the pipes and scrambled across the top of the conduit to cross the street behind the retreating duo.

With Jerico missing, Nemo had told Derindi to follow Scabbs and Yolanda. They would almost certainly lead him back to the wayward bounty hunter. As he landed on the roof where the first vampire attack took place, Derindi felt the hair on the back of his neck tingle. The place spooked him, and he didn't want to become a vampire meal, but it was still preferable to the unbearable and unending torture he would face if he failed.

He ran across the roof, keeping his eyes up in the air to spot incoming vampires. Unfortunately, he didn't see the hole in the roof. As he fell into the darkness, Derindi yelled, 'Oh crap!' and then instantly regretted it as his inner ear exploded with the response from Nemo.

KAL STRAPPED ON his weapon belt and checked the many daggers placed strategically about his body to make sure he hadn't missed any. They had returned to the quarters where he had spent a sleepy night and fun-filled morning with the girls. Sadly, their contract had obviously run out, because they were no longer in the suite.

'So, basically, you just want me to find this Armand Helmawr,' said Kal, 'who, if I understand you right, is bat crap insane and sporadically homicidal, and then relieve him of some item. But you won't tell me what the item is, you have no idea where he's gone, and I can't tell anyone else what I'm doing or who I'm looking for. Does that about sum it up?'

'Yes,' said Obidiah Clein.

'Not a problem,' said Kal. 'And my fee for this bounty hunt is?'

'I have been authorised by Lord Helmawr to grant you full diplomatic privileges as an heir to the throne of House Helmawr, rightful and just rulers of Hive Primus.'

'Would I get an allowance with that?' Kal asked as he searched his pack and bags.

'Each of Lord Helmawr's legitimate heirs gets an annual stipend in the amount of 100,000 credits.'

'Annually? Huh! That's a decent bounty.' Kal straightened up. 'Say, you didn't see a head in my stuff when you guys stripped me, did you?'

Clein cringed. 'Yes. It was disgusting. We had it incinerated.'

'Then you can add fifteen hundred credits to that stipend,' Kal said. 'That's what that head was worth.' He slung the much lighter pack over his shoulder. 'Oh, and before I go, where's my birthday present?'

'I sent Valtin Schemko to get it,' admitted Clein. 'He will meet us at one of the secret entrances to the Helmawr estate and escort you back to Hive City.'

'Whoa,' said Kal. He stopped and stared down at the short administrator. To Clein's credit, he didn't flinch a bit. 'I thought I was to work alone. You know, not tell anyone about who I'm going after? I don't need some pernickety bureaucrat hanging around while I'm working. I have a certain style, and that tends to get crimped by little toadies getting themselves killed around me.'

'This is non-negotiable,' said Clein. 'Valtin will accompany you and return with you and the item if you are successful. You need not fear for his safety. He is one of my personal guards.'

Kal looked around at Clein's entourage. One of the guards was missing. He got a bad feeling in the pit of his stomach as he searched their faces. Yes. He was right. The missing guard was the very same one he had kicked in the groin. This was going to be so much fun.

Clein smiled. 'Please take good care of my guard. Without him, you'll have a very difficult time getting back into the Spire once the job is done. Remember, 100,000 credits per year, plus access to girls like Candi, Brandi, and Sandi any time you like.'

'And grapes, right?' asked Kal. 'Lots and lots of grapes.'

'WHAT THE HELL was that?' asked Captain Katerin. He had paced back and forth in his office for almost an hour after the Jerico meeting waiting for Kauderer. Sweat streamed down his bare head in every direction. His handkerchief practically dripped in his hand. 'We've lost all control. And that bounty hunter – I've never seen such insolence.'

'Patience, captain,' said Kauderer. He pulled out a tox stick and placed it between his lips. 'We must endure some trials if we are to triumph.'

'Trials?' asked Katerin, his voice almost on the edge of hysteria. 'That was agony. Keeping my mouth shut in that ludicrous meeting was absolute torture. If that man is ever added to the line of succession, it will be my last day in this house.'

'You may very well be looking for a job sooner than that, my dear captain,' purred Kauderer. He paused to light his tox stick and take a long drag. Katerin was practically vibrating by the time the intrigue master continued. 'House Helmawr is at a critical juncture. Our lord's mind is failing. That much is obvious. I do not know how much longer we can hold his leadership together. And when he falls, he may well take the entire house down with him.'

Katerin sat on the edge of his desk and mopped his brow with the wet cloth. 'This much I know,' he said. 'There are simply too many heirs. After two hundred years, the old man is still siring possible successors. The power struggle will make the last House war look like a gang brawl. But what can we do about it?'

'I believe we must find the "rightful" heir and make sure he takes the throne when the time comes.' Kauderer puffed on his tox stick and smiled.

Katerin's eyebrows furrowed as he tried to fathom the meaning of the oft obtuse spymaster. 'But who is the rightful heir?' he asked. 'I doubt even the old man remembers, even on his good days.'

'The rightful heir is whomever we can control once we place him on the throne.' Kauderer's smile widened even further, which on his face was an even scarier sight than the hawkish scowl he usually wore.

'But what of the others?' asked Katerin. The military man was not used to all of this cloak and dagger work. He preferred a simple, stand-up fight. 'There will still be opposition voiced from all sides when the old man passes.'

'We will have to eliminate all the opposition before it can be voiced, starting with that murderous Armand and that smug, self-important bounty hunter. Our

Spyrers will make sure of that, and bring the item back to us for a little insurance when the time comes.'

NEMO WAS WAITING for a call. It was long overdue. He was not a patient man. He was a slave to no one's schedule or whim. Normally he would remove an employee who made him wait so much as a minute for a report, but this was a special informant, who could not be so easily replaced and thus Nemo allowed him some tardiness.

So, he had kept busy watching the antics of Yolanda, Scabbs, and poor Derindi. What an oaf. Nemo almost felt like keeping the weasel around after all this was done, just for the entertainment value the little man provided. But he could not be seen as going soft, so Derindi would have to be removed along with Kal Jerico and his cohorts once the item was safe in the spymaster's hands.

The light from the numerous monitors glinted off Nemo's glassy mask as he turned his head this way and that to watch the various spycams he had in place throughout the Underhive. Every once in a while he would flip a switch and cock his head as he listened in on a whispered conversation or some nefarious business transaction. Then he would make notes for his less devious employees, like the twins, about whom to shake down for tribute or purloined items.

Time passed quickly. Nemo truly enjoyed his work and he had almost forgotten about the call when a light blinked on a special panel and an alarm buzzed within his visor. The spymaster touched a switch next to the blinking light, which completed the connection and began the decryption process. A moment later, he heard the voice in the ear jack inside his helmet.

The voice sounded mechanical, a by-product of the encryption and decryption necessary to get vocal information out of the Spire without detection. But Nemo knew who was on the other end. Nobody else had access to this particular circuit.

'He's left the Spire,' said the voice in Nemo's ear.

'Is he alone?' asked the spymaster.

'No. He travels with a royal guard in disguise.'

'Will there be any repercussions if this guard should not return?'

'None that I cannot handle.'

'Where are they headed?'

'That I do not know,' replied the mechanical voice. 'They are being taken to the cargo entrance in Hive City. They should arrive within the hour.'

'That's not a lot of time.'

'I'm terribly sorry. I could not contact you earlier. I was not alone.'

There was a pause. For his part, Nemo was done with the conversation and had already flipped several switches to put plans into motion to follow Kal Jerico, but he knew the informant had one final question. 'Is there anything else?' he finally asked.

'Y-Yes,' came the tentative response. 'About my payment…'

'Believe me,' said the spymaster. 'When this is over, you will be able to buy and sell Gerontius Helmawr.'

GRUNN AND THAG trudged across the White Wastes on their way toward Hive City. Both Goliaths carried twin hundred gallon cisterns of slime that swayed back and forth on great yokes slung across their shoulders. The slime, harvested from beneath the dust that coated the floor of the Wastes and gave the area its name, would fetch a high price in the City markets.

Each thundering step Grunn and Thag took drove their broad feet deep into the dust. The Wastes were a huge void inside the Hive between countless different domes. Dust had accumulated for centuries, blown into the void along with ventilation exhaust from the surrounding domes. Beneath the dust could be found deposits of the valuable green slime. A few hardy individuals, like the Goliaths, lived in the Wastes as slime farmers.

Goliaths were seen as barbaric, even amongst the residents of Hive City who toiled amidst harmful chemicals, dirty water, and poorly recycled air. The Goliaths survived on the periphery of this harsh world, in the deepest and most toxic regions, performing gruelling tasks no other Hivers could or wished to perform.

For all this, they had grown larger, stronger and meaner. The toxins in the air and the sludge they harvested had killed all but the hardiest amongst them and today they were giants, and practically revelled in their role as the grunt workers upon whose backs the mighty Hive had been built.

Grunn and Thag, though, were an oddity even amongst House Goliath. They had turned their backs on the mines and slag pits to live and work in the Wastes as slime farmers. Thag, a large brute of a ganger in his youth, had risen quickly in the ranks of the Sligan gang. Using his heavy stubber, he'd demolished entire raiding parties, turning Sligan's gang into the one of the most feared in the Underhive, and winning him a position of respect and power, as well as the enmity of Uglar, another heavy fighter in the gang, who coveted the power of leadership.

Through Uglar's treachery, Thag found himself with a bounty on his head and was sold into the pits where he was forced to fight for his freedom. There he met and fell in love with Grunn. They fought side-by-side for two years to earn back the price on their heads. Thag vowed he would never again work for anyone but himself, so he and Grunn left the pits and made a home in the White Wastes.

Thag and Grunn had been walking the Wastes half the night and most of the day without rest when a shadow passed over them. Light in the wastes came from fungus growing amongst the gridwork and pipes lining the voids between domes. Warmed by power coursing through the conduits, the fungus phosphoresced, giving the Wastes an eerie bluish-white daytime all its own.

Nothing lived in the Wastes except the few lone farmers like Thag and Grunn and bands of roaming scavvies. Thag would have welcomed the diversion of a good scavvy battle, but knew of nothing in the Wastes that could fly. He glanced up in time to see a large black shape dropping on them from a hole in the metal sky. Warrior instincts launched the Goliath into action.

Thag whipped his shoulders around to launch one of the cisterns off the end of the yoke into the air toward the descending attacker. A chainsword whined to life above him, and Thag saw the cistern explode in a torrent of shards and slime. A moment later, the dark shape splashed through the green cloud, the chainsword still blazing in its hand.

Thag sloughed off the yoke and drew his own weapon; a massive, two-headed axe with spikes extending out between the twin blades. Beside him, Grunn dropped her cisterns onto the white dust, ripped the inch-thick chain from the yoke, and began swinging it over her head.

As their assailant hit the ground, it rolled forward and came back up before Thag could react. Not quite as broad

as Thag, the incoming attacker was nearly as tall as the
Goliath and powerfully built. It appeared to be scaled or
perhaps covered in strange, black-plated armour. Tubular
vessels snaked their way up from its arms and chest to the
base of its hideous head. Glowing, red eyes looked out
from a featureless, black face with no mouth.

Thag swung his axe across and down as the attacker
moved in, trying to cut off the beast's angle of attack,
but it simply ploughed through the Goliath's weapon,
taking the curved edge of the axe against its chest. Thag's
arms quivered as the axe bounced off the armoured
plates and he barely had enough time to fall backward
onto the dust to avoid the buzzing chainsword.

The beast stood above him. The chainsword plunged
down again from the top of its arc, but Grunn's chain
flashed over his head, wrapping around the creature's
wrist and pulling it aside. Thag rolled out from under
the attacker, right into the slime from his dropped cistern. He tried to rise, but slipped to his knees, just as the
black beast grabbed Grunn's chain and gave a mighty
yank.

Grunn tried to hold her ground but the huge creature
pulled her off balance. As she stumbled forward, it spun
around, sweeping the chainsword around in an arc at
chest height. Grunn fell to the dust, cut in half by the
powerful swing. Thag, finally back on his feet again,
rushed forward in a blind rage and right into the
rounded tip of the still-buzzing chainsword.

The Goliath could feel his organs shredding inside of
him as the chain ripped through his body. He fell to his
knees once again and then toppled over onto the white
dust next to his beloved. Unable to move with his bow-
els turned into so much ground meat, Thag was helpless
to stop the beast as it bent over Grunn's sliced body and
plunged the fingers of one hand into her throat.

The last thing Thag saw before the darkness took him was blood-red liquid coursing through the tubes up toward the beast's mouthless, black head.

# 4: THE GANG'S ALL HERE

VALTIN STARED OUT the window. He hadn't said a word since they left the Palace in the two-seat transport. They were currently circling the top of the Spire on autopilot, their pod bathed in sunshine, as they waited for clearance to descend into the perpetual grey cloud cover some five miles below.

'Never been outside the Spire, eh?' asked Kal.

'It's just so incredible!' said Valtin.

'Well enjoy the view now,' he said, 'because once we get into the clouds, your world will disappear, and then we'll step out into a whole new world that's not quite so incredible.'

'You've been out here before?'

'Outside the Hive?' asked Kal. 'Once or twice.' He saw Valtin forming the obvious next question and cut him off. 'I don't like to talk about it. Ever!'

But Kal had to admit the view was amazing. It was one thing to bask in the sun's rays with the walls of the Palace around you and the entire Spire beneath your feet. It was an entirely different matter to be in the sunshine looking back at the ten-mile tall conical Hive; to know that there was nothing between you and the ground but air, clouds, and a three-mile thick layer of noxious fumes.

The Hive wasn't exactly beautiful, though. It was simply impressive. Some effort had been made to make the exterior visually pleasing, certainly. Towers were attached here and there, complete with ramparts. Huge balconies stretched around the cone in places, overlooking the clouds. But the sheer size of the Hive itself dwarfed such architectural embellishments. They might have been impressive up close, perhaps even beautiful, but the ten-mile-high cone that seemed to float on a sea of clouds simply dominated the scene.

Valtin looked as though he wanted to push the question of Jerico's previous excursions outside the Spire, but instead turned back to the window. Kal took another look at the guard's outfit and snorted. He had changed out of his uniform into what he must have thought was Underhive casual attire. This consisted of a leather coat with silver buckles down the front and silver chains hanging over each shoulder, black leather chaps with red silk piping running down the seams, and a pair of knee-high, floppy leather boots with silver buckles that matched those on the coat.

'We'll have to do something about that before we get too far,' Kal said to himself. It wasn't so much the garish ornamentation – which would have to go – it was the fact that the leather practically glistened in its newness. Valtin would stand out like a bright red target the moment they set foot in Hive City.

The outfit was simply outlandish, made with the Spire mindset that everything looked better shined to a bright sheen, with a few baubles attached. It reminded him of the spear Valtin had presented to him before they left. It looked like a decent weapon, and in fact it was a fine piece of real wood, which itself was worth at least ten times the bounty on Svend they'd tossed down the incinerator, but the craftsman had ruined the weapon by encrusting the shaft with gems, and inlaying graceful swirls of gold along the entire length. He could sell the various parts for a fortune, but as a weapon it was worthless. All that extra weight threw off the balance. Unfortunately, he would have to carry it with him until he could sell off the valuable bits and pieces.

Kal glanced at Valtin again. He didn't really seem a bad sort. The kick to the groin had been all but forgotten. The guard hadn't even brought it up, and he seemed genuinely enthusiastic about accompanying Jerico on the hunt, but there was something oddly familiar about the palace guard. He had a certain air of confidence, a slight twinkle in the eye, and a particular sharpness of the chin that Kal suddenly recognised.

'Are we related?' he asked. Kal often found that bluntness cut through people's defences, but the question hardly phased Valtin a bit.

'My father was Major Geraint Lee Helmawr, a former commander in the House Guard, and son of our lord Gerontius Helmawr.'

'That would make you my…'

'Nephew, yes,' replied Valtin.

'Well half-nephew, probably,' said Kal with a laugh. 'Dear old dad has never been a one-woman man.' He turned to face his new-found relative. 'So, what happened to your father?'

'That bastard Armand killed him.'

'Ahh, so this is family business for you, is it?' Kal asked. 'I had thought that little bureaucrat Clein had simply ordered you to go.'

Valtin's eyes flickered away from Kal for a moment before he answered. 'I have my orders,' he said. 'But I volunteered for the mission, as did several others.'

'All relatives, I assume,' said Kal.

Valtin simply nodded, and Kal noticed the same introspective look in the guard's eyes again. The look passed and Valtin smiled. 'What about you?' he asked.

'What about me, what?' replied Kal, not willing to make anything easy on his nephew.

'Why are you doing this if not out of family obligation?'

Now it was Kal's turn to smile. 'Ahh, I see I have a lot to teach you, nephew,' he said, wagging a finger at Valtin. 'I don't do anything except for love or money, and the only person I love is Kal Jerico.'

'You mean to say you have no interest in the family?' asked Valtin. 'Don't you want to return to the Spire?'

'Only so far as it impacts me,' said Kal. 'I've lived in the Spire before. It's boring and it's political – two things I can easily live without. Sure, I'll take Dad's money, and if that means I have to live up there for a year, so be it, but I can then take that hundred grand stipend and live out the rest of my life where you know who your enemies are because they're pointing a gun at your head.'

'Sounds lonely.'

'No. I've got friends, and I can always buy love, or at least rent it,' said Kal with a smirk. He stopped and shook his head. 'No. Lonely is sitting in a dark room surrounded by advisors you can't trust and family who all want you dead.'

'I don't want Grandfather dead,' said Valtin, and Kal could tell the kid actually meant it.

'Then you may be the only one,' he said. 'Look, it's obvious that the only thing holding the house together right now are Father's advisors and the power of Gerontius Helmawr as a figurehead. They need him and he needs them, but as soon as a suitable replacement shows up or anyone gets evidence that Helmawr is a house of cards, it'll all be over for dear old Dad, and maybe the house. At that point, the safest place for any Helmawr will be the Underhive, thank you very much. So, I'll take my reward for turning on my brother, and then turn tail and do what I always do when the going gets tough…'

Valtin gave him a blank look.

'Hide, nephew, hide.'

Valtin fell silent for a time and eventually turned to look back out the window. The transport had finally begun its descent and they were now surrounded by roiling grey clouds. 'You know those scribes you saw behind Grandfather, back in the safe room?'

Kal wasn't sure what this had to do with anything, but bit on the question anyway. 'The ones that wrote down everything the old man said?'

'Yes.' Valtin didn't even look at Kal as he spoke. 'When he's… not quite himself, they write down everything that happens around him, and then read it back to him later.'

'Okay,' said Kal, still not sure where this was going. 'Seems reasonable.'

'Afterwards, all the records are burned.' He stopped for a minute and continued staring at the clouds swirling past the window. Jerico could tell that his nephew was getting up the nerve to say something more, and left him alone. 'If a scribe gets fired or leaves the house for any reason, we have standing orders to shoot them. They will go to any lengths to keep Grandfather's failing mental abilities a secret.'

'Interesting.'

The two Helmawr relatives spent the rest of the trip in silence, each with his own thoughts about what the future might hold.

* * *

LYSANNE MOTIONED THE two Escher juves on ahead. Tay and Tor were their names. Tay was tall and statuesque, the model of an Escher, with long, blonde hair. Tor was shorter, with almond skin and slightly slanted eyes, giving her a mysterious look. They'd been Lysanne's first recruits after getting promoted by Vicksen. Now she was leading her first mission and wanted everything to go just right. It was a simple patrol. She and the juves were heading down to Dust Falls to search for Yolanda.

She knew that Vicksen didn't expect any trouble, otherwise she would have sent more experienced gang members, but you could never be too careful, especially with that Underhive vampire on the loose. Themis said that reports of vampire attacks had been coming in from all over the Underhive in the last few days.

Tor indicated the all clear, so Lysanne and the others jogged towards the corner. Lysanne's cropped, mousey-brown hair bobbed as she ran. She was dressed in loose-fitting black pants and a wraparound top that tied at the sides, providing free motion when fighting. Two ornate symbols were painted on her back, spelling out 'sister' and 'friend,' which to Lysanne were one and the same. She pulled out her plasma pistol as she ran forward, just in case. You can't be too careful.

Tay stood at the door to The Dusty Hole, the main merc drinking hole in Dust Falls. Tor was crossing the street to join her. The Dusty Hole was usually full of ratskin scouts for hire. They led gangs over the Falls on the one-mile trip down to the Hive Bottom. The risk was great, but so was the reward, if you survived. If anyone had information about Yolanda, they'd be in here and should be willing to part with the info for the right price. And if not, well, that's what the plasma gun was for.

Lysanne was just about to cross the street to join Tay and Tor when the front of the bar exploded, sending the two juves flying into the air. 'Spread out!' yelled Lysanne to the rest of her gang jogging along behind. 'Find cover!' The young ganger ran into the street, grabbed Tor by the collar, and started pulling her back toward the corner.

She looked over at Tay, but knew it was probably too late. The blast had shredded her body. Worse than that, though, was the site Lysanne beheld at the end of the street. 'Spyrers!' yelled Lysanne. She redoubled her efforts to get Tor to safety as laser blasts slammed into the ground all around her.

A five-member Spyrer team, decked out in their impressive mechanical rigs, marched down the street. The looked more like robots than men in their power armour. These were noble-born gangers wearing the latest and greatest innovations in armour, with weapons you'd normally expect to see mounted on a tank attached to their arms and backs.

'What in the Hive are they doing here?' asked Ashya from the corner.

'How should I know?' replied Lysanne. She'd finally reached the side street, and laid Tor down next to Ashya. 'Why don't you go ask them nicely?' she said with a sneer. Looking at Tor, bleeding and burnt beside her, and Tay lying unconscious, or worse, in the street, Lysanne wasn't in the mood to talk.

She peered around the corner again. 'Damn. They're on the move and one of them is missing!' Luckily, the big brute with rocket launchers for hands was lagging behind, but there was one with a wicked-looking filament sword and a shield that glinted strangely in the light, along with two others with some strange tubes attached to their back. The fifth one had just disappeared.

'Ashya, Ginger, Ellie and Jenna,' she called out. 'Cover me. I'm going after Tay.'

'Bu-' said Ashya.

'Just do it. I'm not leaving her here to become an ornament on their armour.'

Jenna sent a line of flame down the street while Ashya and Ellie shot laser blasts through the fire with their laspistols. Ginger cocked her grenade launcher and pumped a couple of plasma grenades down the street.

Lysanne knew their weapons would have little effect against the heavily armoured Spyrers, but they might distract them just long enough, if she was quick. She sprinted back into the street, dived and rolled up next to Tay. Laser blasts burned holes in the ground all around her. The Spyrer with the monofilament sword advanced on her. She shot a blast from her plasma pistol at him, but he blocked it with his shield. The blast just seemed to get sucked into the jewelled surface. She didn't know what to make of that until he pointed the shield at her and the plasma bolt streamed back at her. Lysanne threw her arms up, but a jet of flame from Jenna intercepted the plasma, which exploded between Lysanne and the Spyrers.

'Get out of here or you're dead,' Lysanne yelled at Jenna. She lifted Tay onto her shoulders and ran toward the blasted front of The Dusty Hole, calling back, 'I'll meet you at the rendezvous point. Go, go!'

Lysanne got just inside the bar when another explosion rocked the building. Chunks of stone and metal beams fell all around her, and then her world went black.

LYSANNE OPENED HER eyes, but couldn't see a thing. Her head throbbed and she still felt a little dizzy, but she didn't think she'd broken anything. There was a weight on her back and she couldn't get up. She reached back. Whatever was on top of her was cold, but soft. She pulled her hand back immediately and tried to crawl forward. She moved a few inches and then a few more. Something shifted and creaked behind her, but nothing more fell. Dust rose up around her, making her cough.

A few more inches and her legs were clear. She sat up to get out of the dust and noticed some dim light seeping into the room. She got up carefully, testing her legs and the floor as she stood, and then felt her way around the debris toward where she had entered. Light was coming from a window that had not been totally covered with debris. She pushed through the opening and fell out onto the street.

The street was empty. There was no sign of the Spyrers or her Wildcat sisters. Lysanne had no idea how much time had passed, but decided to make her way to the rendezvous point anyway. They were supposed to meet just outside the settlement by the Dust Falls – a huge hole caused by a waterfall of chemical waste that had eaten its way right through to the bottom of the Hive. All that was left now was the hole and the dust that followed the waste, giving the settlement its name.

Lysanne checked her gear as she jogged toward the Falls. Her plasma pistol was gone and her pack had been crushed. Tay was dead now. She was sure of that. The body had been ice cold on her back. Tay's body had probably saved her life back there. 'I'll make those Spyrer scum pay,' she said quietly to herself.

The Falls were just ahead, but it was strangely quiet. She slowed down and crept forward to the edge of the last building before the hole. There were the Spyrers at the edge. The one that had disappeared was hovering over the hole. Her hunting rig incorporated huge wings that Lysanne hadn't noticed before.

The flying spyrer was carrying a human body, holding it under the arms and dangling it over the hole. It was

Ashya! She was kicking and screaming, but Lysanne recognised her straight black hair and the tight-fitting grey pantsuit she'd been wearing earlier. Lysanne went for her weapon, and then remembered it wasn't in her holster anymore.

She looked around for the rest of her gang, but didn't see any of them. The Spyrer with the filament sword was saying something.

'We know he was here!' he screamed. 'We found one of his weapons in the settlement.'

'Who?' Ashya yelled. 'The vampire?

'Vampire? What vampire?' asked the Spyrer leader.

'It attacked someone here a few days ago,' said Ashya. Now let me go!'

'First tell me about this vampire.'

'I don't know anything,' said Ashya. She'd stopped squirming but looked horribly frightened. Lysanne couldn't do anything but watch. 'It's supposed to be huge. Three metres tall. And it can fly. And it sucks blood. I don't know what you want!'

'Where is this vampire now?'

'The last I heard, it was in Glory Hole,' she answered. 'That's all I know. Please let me go.'

'You heard the lady,' said the Spyrer. 'Let her go.'

Lysanne stifled a scream as Ashya plummeted down into Dust Falls. Her scream could be heard for a long time.

'What in the Hive do we want with some mutant vampire, Jonas?' asked the Spryer with the rocket launcher arms.

'That's just Underhive superstition,' replied Jonas. 'I'm sure it's our quarry. The timing is right, among other things. Pack it up folks. We're headed for Glory Hole.'

Oh scav, thought Lysanne. That was where the rest of the Wildcats were headed. She loped away from the

Spyrers, trying to think where she could get a weapon big enough to cut through that power armour.

MARKEL BOBO WAS having a good day. He was on a simple R and R mission – reconnoitre and report. Even better, his target was currently on an inbound transport, there was only one access point to observe, and the subject was easily recognisable. Bobo had been able to spend an extra hour at the gaming tables before sauntering down town and holing up in one of his favourite duck blinds.

It was a sweet set-up. He entered Madam Noritake's House of Fun, paid for a room, and sat in a comfy chair in a darkened room with a full view of the Hive City docks. If the transport bringing his duck into town was delayed, his day could get even better. He *had* paid for the room already.

Bobo was well suited to his line of work. He was short, slightly built, and fairly nondescript. Most people who passed him on the street didn't give the little man a first glance, let alone a second, and Bobo liked it that way. He could disappear in plain sight or in the shadows. Anyone who underestimated Markel Bobo usually wound up dropped into Dust Falls.

His clothes were nothing remarkable. A simple cloth shirt and pants, not too clean, but not dirty either. He wore no visible weapons, and anyone who cared to worry about whether he was armed wouldn't be able to detect any under his clothes without stripping him bare. But Markel had access to no less than a dozen lethal weapons, not counting the ones he had stashed under the chair before sitting down.

So there Bobo sat in his comfy chair, eating a bowl of real soup courtesy of Jenn Strings, one of Madam Noritake's girls who was sweet on Markel, and enjoying his easy R and R mission, when his day went totally to hell.

Bobo resettled his visor over his eyes and focused on the roof of the House Cawdor warehouse where he'd seen a glint of light where it didn't belong. Yes, there it was again. The unmistakable shine of glass or metal reflecting a bit of light. Bobo wouldn't have even noticed it, except a group of dock workers were busy loading a shipment. The crane lights were at just the right height and angle to reflect whatever was on the roof of the warehouse into Bobo's room.

He focused in further and found what he was looking for. There, tucked between an air duct, heading up toward the top of the dome, and a group of conduits that ran the length of the docks supplying power to all of the warehouses, sat K W Dutt with a pict camera pointed down at the docks.

Bobo had always thought Dutt was far too tall to make a competent spy. That was one of the reasons he had never tried to recruit him as an agent. He was almost freakishly tall, especially compared to Bobo's one-point-five metre frame, wore rumpled, almost too large clothing, and had a shock of sandy hair that seemed to constantly fly around his head.

Where Bobo lived by remaining uniquely unremarkable and unmemorable, Dutt stood out like a peacock. His appearance almost demanded people to notice him as soon as he walked into a room, but somehow it worked for Dutt. He was so tall and so obviously dishevelled that people took pains to get out of his way and forget him as soon as he was gone.

But his height had given Dutt away today. If Bobo had used the Cawdor warehouse blind, he'd have been completely hidden behind the pipes. In fact he might have needed to stand on a box to see over the conduits. Bobo checked the time. The transport was due in fifteen minutes. Just enough time to check in and get guidance on how to proceed. No matter what, though, Bobo's easy mission had just gotten complicated.

It took a few minutes to set up a secure line. Bobo opened the case that Jenn kept for him and had placed under the bed before he arrived. Inside was a portable jammer that would shield the room and a closed-circuit pict-caller. With the click of a button, a tripod extended from the bottom of the case. He set it in the middle of the room and placed the jammer on top. When Bobo turned on the device, he could feel his short, stringy hair stand up as the power field ionised the air. No matter what he thought of House van Saar, he couldn't help but be impressed by their technology, especially when he hadn't actually paid for it.

He took the pict-caller over to the bed and opened a hidden panel in the wall behind the headboard. Inside was a conduit that had been cut open to expose the copper wire inside. It took just fifteen seconds to splice the device into the wiring. Bobo always timed it. He pressed a familiar series of buttons on the pict-caller, activated his personal encryption key, and then retired to his chair to keep one eye on Dutt while he waited.

A few minutes later the pict-caller beeped. Dutt hadn't moved yet and the transport was still ten minutes out. Bobo flicked a switch and stood to attention.

He heard a voice say, 'What is it, Bobo?' a moment before the image of Hermod Kauderer appeared on the screen. 'The transport hasn't even landed yet.'

'There's been a development, sir,' Bobo said. 'Nemo has sent a man to the docks as well. One of his best agents.'

'I see,' said Kauderer. Even from the small pict-screen placed on the low bed, the hawkish master of intrigue seemed to be looking down at Bobo. 'That was to be expected.'

Bobo was specially trained in the art of reading people. He had to know within seconds whether a person was trustworthy or not, whether they were telling the truth or lying, whether they should live or die. He could not read Kauderer at all. 'Should I dispatch him sir?'

'Whatever for?'

'If Nemo has put his best agent on this,' said Bobo, getting a bit flustered by his master's nonchalance, 'he must be taking a personal interest in Jerico's mission. It would seem prudent to keep the spymaster in the dark.'

'And alerting him to the fact that we know of his involvement seems imprudent to me,' said Kauderer. 'Proceed as ordered. Monitor Jerico's mission and report only if he succeeds. All else is being handled.'

'And what about Dutt, sir?' said Bobo. 'Um, Nemo's agent.'

'Take him out for tea for all I care,' said Kauderer. 'Just do not lose sight of Jerico.'

Bobo could read his master's tone easily now and kept his mouth shut, except for a quick 'Yes, sir,' before cutting the connection.

He stared at the blank screen for a moment longer before packing up the case and sitting back at his window. Dutt was still at his post, and the transport was now five minutes out. Nothing to do but wait; wait and think about the conversation with Kauderer. After a while, just before the transport was scheduled to dock, Bobo came to a decision. He stood at the window in full view of the docks, and turned on the lights. Just for a moment, just long enough to catch sight of Dutt staring at him from the warehouse roof.

This mission just got much more interesting, he thought.

* * *

YOLANDA STOOD ON the roof next to the hole where she had found Beddy's decapitated body. She had struck a pose, with her fists on her hips and one leg slightly forward as if she were an ornament on the prow of a ship. Of course, if she were Kal Jerico, she realised, a ventilation fan nearby would produce a stiff breeze to make her leather jacket and loin-cloth flutter in its artificial wind.

She straightened up and peered down into the hole. 'Find anything?' she called down.

'Yeah,' said Scabbs, his voice the only evidence of his presence in the darkness below. 'Lots of rats.'

'Well you should feel right at home then,' Yolanda said with a chuckle. 'Ask them if they saw which way the vampire went,' she added. 'You're practically family, right? You probably dated one of their sisters.'

As Yolanda laughed at her jokes, she saw Scabbs's torch stop moving in the darkness below. At first she thought he was just mad about the rat jokes, but after a minute the torch still hadn't moved again.

'Scabbs?' she called. 'Are you all right?'

There was no answer.

'Scabbs? Stop fooling around. You're starting to scare me.'

Still no answer. Yolanda listened, but all she could hear was her heart beating in her ample chest. She pulled out her laspistols, triggered the torches atop each one and jumped down into the hole. Standing with her arms outstretched in either direction, Yolanda slowly rotated, throwing light around the room. She finally found Scabbs, crouched on the floor next to his torch.

'What's wrong?' she asked, creeping over toward him but still waving one gun around the room to make sure they were alone. When she got close enough to see the floor around her partner, Yolanda screamed. 'What in Helmawr's name are you doing?'

Scabbs, surrounded by dead rats, was on his knees leaning down with his face almost touching the ground. At first, Yolanda thought he might be praying for the souls of his dead family members lying around him. Then she noticed that one of the dead rats was directly beneath the scabby half-breed's face. That was when she screamed.

Scabbs looked up. 'What?' He looked back down at the rat and suddenly realised what Yolanda was thinking. 'No,' he said dismissively, 'I was checking for puncture wounds.' He grabbed his torch and stood up. 'All of these rats have been completely drained, just like Beddy.'

'Helmawr's rump,' said Yolanda. 'They were alive yesterday.'

Scabbs nodded. 'It fed on them after Beddy. And if Beddy didn't fill it up, these rats sure didn't do the job.'

'It's out hunting right now,' she said.

Scabbs nodded again. 'Well, it should be easy to track. All we have to do is follow the trail of dead bodies.'

Yolanda realised something else as well. 'Come on,' she said as she put out the torches and holstered her pistols. 'It's time to leave Glory Hole.' She headed back to the hole and motioned for Scabbs to give her a boost.

'Why?' Scabbs asked as he waddled over to Yolanda. He interlocked his hands and looked up at her. She scowled at him in the dim light streaming through the hole and pointed at the floor. A moment later she climbed onto his back, as he crouched on the floor and jumped up to reach the edge of the roof.

When they were both back on the roof, Yolanda observed. 'It drained the rats instead of finding another victim. Why?'

Scabbs shrugged.

'Rats won't be missed like people,' she said. 'It could have been days before anyone found these drained rats. She was pacing back and forth across the roof now, barely even noticing that her loin cloth and leather jacket were flapping in the breeze she created with her long strides. 'But another person? With all these bounty hunters in town?'

She stopped in front of Scabbs, who still wore his normal stupid expression. 'Don't you get it?' she asked, thumping him on the top of his head with her fist. Nothing. She wanted to scream.

'Why did it eat again so soon after Beddy?' Another shrug.

'It was gorging itself to prepare for a trip, but didn't want to leave any more dead bodies behind for us to follow. The vampire left town last night.'

Scabbs raised his hands in submission. 'Fine. Let's say you're right,' he said. 'How do we find it now? There's no trail of bodies. We're at a dead end.'

'Are we?' asked Yolanda. 'We have you, the greatest half-breed ratskin tracker in all Glory Hole.' Scabbs smiled at the left-handed compliment and a few flakes of skin fell off his cheeks.

'It ate its last meal here,' she said. 'It can't have left through the settlement gates. So, where did it go? What secret exit do you know about that it could have used from this rooftop?'

A light bulb finally flared into life in the dark recesses of Scabbs's brain. He scanned the settlement, apparently getting his bearings. He looked up and down each street, did a few high-level calculations on his fingertips and then smiled. He pointed almost straight up without even looking.

Yolanda followed the finger up to the top of the dome, where a wide shaft extended at a forty-five degree angle out of the settlement into the vast wilderness spaces between domes. Yolanda clapped Scabbs on the shoulder, raising a dust cloud that coated her fingers. 'Fantastic,' she said. 'Now, how do we get up there?'

Scabbs produced Beddy's grapnel, which he had obviously purloined, and handed it to Yolanda.

KAL SAUNTERED UP the docks, breathing in the stale air, heavy with a multitude of odours. To the right was the sharp stench of spoiled meat coming from the Cawdor warehouse. To the left he got a thick, oily whiff of petrol from the fuel station and straight ahead was Hive City itself, with all those odours plus the bitter smell of Wildsnake and the pungent musk emanating from Madam Noritake's.

He was nearly home. So Hive City was quite the tumultuous life-in-your-own-hands place that the Underhive was, but he found it a damn sight more palatable than the Spire, all the same. The only thing ruining Kal's day now – other than being forced to work for his father and the fact that Nemo seemed to be after him again – was that he had that stupid spear strapped across his back.

'Welcome to Hive City,' he said to Valtin.

'It's not clean,' admitted the Helmawr guard, 'but it's not nearly as bad as I imagined.'

The two left the dock area and walked down a short street between squat, square buildings made of grey stone and metal. Variety, colour, and ornamentation were nowhere to be seen down here. Down in the real Hive, practicality and functionality were all that mattered.

'Remember,' said Kal. 'This isn't the Underhive.'

'What's the difference?'

'Spoken like a true Spire brat,' Kal laughed. 'For one thing, most of the buildings are still standing and occupied. For another thing, the air gets recycled once in a while and you can find your way around without a flashlight, assuming we knew where we were going. Plus you can walk for blocks without a gang war erupting around you. There are laws here against that sort of thing.'

'Not so in the Underhive?'

'The only law in the Underhive is the kind you carry strapped to your waist.'

They came to an intersection and Kal looked to the left and right. The connecting streets didn't run straight. They both curved away from the dome walls. Kal remembered that one direction had a bunch of cutbacks and dead ends; relics of generations of rebuilding due to hivequakes. Unfortunately, he could never remember which way had the more direct route into the main part of the city.

'Which way is it to that shop?' he wondered out loud.

While Kal tried to remember if he should turn left or right, Valtin asked, 'But I thought we were supposed to head down into the Underhive. Isn't that where nobles go to hide from the family?'

'Technically true, dear nephew,' said Kal. 'But there are one or two tasks we must accomplish here first.'

'What? Get drunk and find some women?'

Kal laughed again. 'You forgot gambling,' he said. 'That comes between the drinking and the wenching. No, we need to fix your clothes and get my dog.' With that, Kal made a decision and turned left.

An hour later, hopelessly lost in Hive City, he decided that left was probably the wrong decision. 'Damn Scabbs,' he muttered. 'Where are you when I need you? Probably still sitting in Hagen's Hole drinking on my tab.'

* * *

'KILL ME IF you want,' said Hagen. 'I can't tell you where they went because I don't know where they went.'

Themis tossed the big, hairy bartender into the corner as if he was nothing more than a sack of laundry. He lay there, his beard matted with blood and his left eye swollen shut. He was pretty sure that at least three ribs were broken. He landed in a puddle of Wildsnake, but it really didn't matter, since his clothes were already drenched with blood, sweat and spit. Only the spit didn't belong to him.

The Wildcats had taken Hagen by surprise while he was napping on the gaming table. It was the only table in the place sturdy enough to hold his huge frame. The bar had been packed with mercenaries for two full days and nights and Hagen had been beat. Everyone had finally left to hunt the vampire, so he decided to take a rest.

Then the Wildcats stormed in. The door was gone, lost to a frag grenade. The explosion woke Hagen and he had immediately rolled off the table into a corner. The lousy Escher women then shot up the front room and most of his stock behind the bar. They didn't seem to care that no one was in the bar. In fact, it seemed to make them even madder.

Hagen had tried to crawl to the storeroom door. If he could make it down the stairs, he might have a chance of getting to the escape hatch, but the one they called Themis saw him and shot another frag grenade over his head toward the door. Hagen dived back over the gaming table just as the door exploded. The fragments ripped through the table and cut the bartender in the head and shoulders.

They were on him before he could crawl out from under the remains of the table. The next hour had been a blur of kicking, beating, spitting, and screaming. They didn't even bother to ask questions until after he'd regained consciousness the second time. Hagen didn't hold back any information. He told them about the vampire, the dead mercenaries, Yolanda, Scabbs, and Kal: everything. But it didn't seem to matter. The torture and the spitting continued. He'd heard that Escher women hated men. Now, he knew it for certain.

The black cloud of unconsciousness threatened to take him again as the gang members moved into the front room. Hagen feared he wouldn't wake up this time so fought to keep his head clear. He heard Themis speak. She was a tall, powerfully-built blonde who Hagen could have gone for in any other circumstance (he loved a strong woman who could toss him around a little).

'He doesn't know where she went,' said Themis. 'Or if he does, he'll take it to his grave.'

'Kill him,' said another voice Hagen knew to be Vicksen Colteen, perhaps the scariest Escher woman in the Underhive, which was really saying something. 'Send a message to the shopkeepers that we are the Wildcats no matter who leads us.'

A dozen weapons cocked in a rapid staccato of clicks.

'We don't want to step over that line,' said Themis. 'A physical interview is one thing, but murdering Hagen? That puts a bounty on our heads and ticks off every mercenary from here to Dust Falls. Leave him alive and everyone knows that the Wildcats took on Hagen's Hole and won!'

'Fine,' said Vicksen. 'He lives. But we're no closer to Yolanda than we were a day ago.'

'Then we'll just have to interview a few of the fine folk in Glory Hole. Someone must have seen where she and the little scab-faced half-breed went.'

The next sound Hagen heard was the scuffling of feet on the metal grate floor and then silence. Minutes passed and they didn't return. Each breath sent an explosion of pain through his chest, and he wasn't sure if he could even move. He had to find help before the darkness took him again. He didn't want to let Themis down and end up dead anyway.

Hagen began to pull himself across the grate toward the shattered front door.

SEVERAL HOURS AFTER leaving the docks, Kal finally found a familiar landmark. They were only a few streets away from Fewell's armoury now. Valtin had been quiet most of the way, but as Kal picked up the pace, he asked, 'Do you know where you are now, or are we still lost?'

'Lost?' said Kal, putting on his best innocent bystander face. 'We weren't lost. I was just trying to confuse those trying to follow us.'

'Were we being followed?'

'Stands to reason,' said Kal. 'Seems like somebody's always watching me and somehow getting to where I'm going ten steps ahead of me.' In a way, Jerico was glad they had taken such a circuitous route. If anyone had been following them, he'd certainly made them work for it. And, it had given him time to notice something odd about Hive City.

'Did you notice anything strange while we walked the streets?' he asked.

'No,' Valtin looked a little disgusted. 'Just that there seemed to be an awful lot of them that ended in brick walls.'

'Have you heard any screams in the last few hours?'

'No.'

'Any lasblasts?'

'No.'

'Sirens? Claxons? Explosions?'

'No,' said Valtin. He grabbed Kal by the shoulder to stop him. 'Why? I've gone days without hearing any one of those things.'

'But as you said, this is not the Spire,' replied Kal. 'Sure, it's peaceful here in Hive City compared to the Underhive, but in three hours time we should have at least witnessed a mugging or seen an enforcer rousting a burglar. It's scavving quiet around here, and that ain't normal.'

They had arrived at Fewell's armoury. The sign by the door showed a suit of body armour with two crossed swords that appeared to be piercing the armour. Kal had never gotten up the nerve to ask Fewell if that had been intentional or if some disgruntled client had altered the image.

'This is the place,' said Kal.

'I have body armour,' replied Valtin. He looked closely at the sign. 'And mine doesn't have any holes in it.'

'The owner's been watching my dog,' said Kal, 'and fixing a few busted plates on his back.'

'Fixing a few whats on his where?'

'Just come on.'

They walked into Fewells. It was almost a home away from home for Kal, which was quite a trick since he had no home. Racks of body armour in various stages of creation or repair littered the cramped shop, making it tough to walk through to the counter. Hung on the walls in a haphazard fashion were metal weapons of all shapes and sizes from little rib stickers for the up-and-coming midget assassin to massive, crush-your-head-with-one-blow axes sized for a Goliath.

'Fewell,' called out Kal. 'Is Wotan ready to g–'

He never got a chance to finish the sentence. A huge creature flashed over the counter and bounded through the shop. Rack after rack fell to the floor, creating a cacophony of clattering metal. Valtin yelled an exclamation as the beast burst through the last of the racks and leapt into the air toward them.

'Wotan!' cried Kal as the metallic hound drove him over backwards and landed astride his chest. Wotan was easily a metre tall at the shoulders and almost two metres long from the point of his metal teeth to the tip of his tail. His head had been moulded to resemble a real dog with ears that stood up and a little bulb of a nose on the end of his snout. But he was all metal, with extra plating at the shoulders and joints, and long metal spikes for claws.

He barked, which sounded a lot like bones breaking. 'This is your dog?' asked Valtin.

'Yep.' Kal pushed Wotan's nose aside to make the dog move off his chest and then stood up. He patted Wotan on the head.

'I don't want to know where you got him, do I?' continued Valtin.

'And I don't want to tell you,' Kal replied.

Fewell was coming through the racks, picking each one up as he made his way through the store. 'I'm glad you're here, Kal,' he said. 'I'm getting tired of picking up these scavving racks.'

Fewell was a mountain of a man. He stood well over two metres tall and had a broad chest to match, but his comically oversized head seemed all the bigger thanks to his short-cropped, sandy hair and smooth chin. Kal had never seen so much as a whisker on Fewell's face, let alone the stubble most men sported at this time of day, which gave him the look of an overgrown adolescent.

'I'll take him off your hands,' said Kal, 'But…'

'I know, you'll have to pay me later,' finished Fewell. He rarely smiled, and he spoke in a constant monotone, which made it almost impossible to tell when he was joking and when he was really mad.

'Um, not only that,' continued Kal, 'but could I bother you for a sharp knife, some heavy pliers, and a little information?'

'What's mine is yours,' replied Fewell. 'You'll take it anyway.' He went back to the counter to retrieve the items.

'What do you need those for?' asked Valtin. He shied away from Wotan, who was busy sniffing the guard's boots.

'They're for you,' said Kal. 'We need to make some changes to your outfit.'

'Who's your pretty boyfriend, Kal?' asked Fewell when he returned with the tools.

'See what I mean?' said Kal. He took the pliers from Fewell, and said, 'He's my nephew. I'm teaching him how to fit in down in the Underhive.' Kal reached out with the pliers, grabbed hold of one of the silver buckles on Valtin's coat, and pulled. The leather ripped away, leaving a gash where the buckle used to be.

'You'll take these in trade, won't you Fewell' asked Kal as he grabbed the next buckle in line.

SCABBS LOOKED AT the drained bodies of the two Goliaths. 'I knew these two,' he said. 'That's Thag, or at least it was. He was one of the strongest pit fighters I'd ever seen. Cost me a hundred credits the first and only time I ever bet against him.'

'And the female?' asked Yolanda with a sigh. She was tired. Tired from trekking across the dust and tired of finding dead bodies. The two Goliaths upped the body count in the Wastes alone to twelve. A bloody dozen, she thought. No. A *bloodless* dozen.

'Grunn,' replied Scabbs. 'She's who I bet on with those hundred credits. It was their first match. Thag got her down in a chokehold and the crowd was calling for her death, but Thag wouldn't do it. He refused to kill her and forfeited all of his earnings to that point. Took him another two years to get out of the pits, but he took Grunn with him and they've lived in the Wastes ever since.'

'It's a beautiful story, really,' said Yolanda. 'But is there a point?'

'Nothing could beat Thag,' he said. 'Nothing! Not if he knew it was coming. And, look! His axe is still in his hands, and he was skewered through the chest. Thag was facing the vampire, weapon in hand, when it killed him.'

'So?' asked Yolanda. 'It's just like Beddy. Just like those Scavvy warbands we found out here earlier. It kills, it eats, and it moves on. Why is this one any different?'

'Thag was a powerful fighter,' insisted Scabbs. He was getting pretty agitated. The scabby skin on his face flaked off as he shook with emotion. 'I doubt you and Jerico could have taken him together on a good day. But Thag doesn't have a mark on him except the death blow. The vampire killed him with one hit! One hit! How in the Hive are we supposed to kill it if Thag and Grunn together couldn't beat it?'

'I don't know,' said Yolanda. 'Maybe we can starve it to death. Maybe Thud and Grunzilla here wounded it and we'll find *its* corpse over the next rise. I don't care. We're bounty hunters. We track killers and bring them in, dead or alive. It's what we do.'

When she was done talking, Yolanda noticed Scabbs staring at her. She glanced down at her clothes to make sure nothing was showing that shouldn't be showing. 'What?' she asked, finally. 'Do I have dust in my hair?'

'Starve it to death,' muttered Scabbs.

'Huh?' asked Yolanda. She began to worry that her scabby partner had succumbed to waste fever. Too much time under the phosphorescent light, breathing in the hive dust made people go a little off. She figured people who lived in the Wastes were probably a little off to begin with.

'You said, "We could starve it do death,"' said Yolanda. 'Have you noticed the vampire is feeding a lot more often? It drained Bester the first night, the shop-keeper and Beddy the next day, and then today, it's fed at least twelve times.'

'Unless there are other bodies we don't know about.'

'Maybe,' agreed Scabbs. 'But you have to admit that today has been a banner day in the bloodsucking business.'

Yolanda shrugged. 'Okay. It's eating more. What's that mean?'

'I don't know,' said Scabbs, 'but if its appetite is growing, you know where it must be headed.'

Yolanda wasn't listening anymore, though. 'Um, that's really great Scabbs, but we should go now.'

'What?' asked Scabbs. 'We can't just leave Thag here. We need to give him and Grunn a proper burial, or at least look through his pockets to see if I can get back my hundred credits.'

'Now, Scabbs!' urged Yolanda. She'd pulled out a pair of binoculars and was looking at the Wastes behind them. 'We have company.'

'Scavvies?' asked Scabbs. It was almost a squeak.

'Worse,' said Yolanda as she began to run. 'Wildcats!'

# 5: CAT FIGHT

SQUATZ'S LIFE WAS finally getting back to normal after that trouble a few months back. His bar, The Breath of Fresh Air, had been home territory to no less than three gangs. It was a sort of neutral ground where all the gangers could enjoy a drop of Wildsnake or his House Special along with the freshest air for miles around, thanks to the huge fan at the junction of no less than three ventilation shafts that sat above the square outside his door.

But then a strange little man came through looking for some lost bit of archeotech, sparking a gang war the likes of which Hive City had not seen in generations. Sure, the Fresh Air was situated amongst the lowest levels of the city, but this wasn't the Underhive, and the rule of law still applied. At least that's what Squatz had thought, but even the enforcers had proved powerless to stop this particular turf war and before you could say 'Did you spill my Wildsnake?' pretty much all his regulars were dead.

The loss of the three gangs left a nervous void as every gang within three domes wanted to lay claim to that fan and the fresh air it produced. Squatz's gold mine turned into a money pit overnight. Brawls were constantly broken up by the enforcers, rogue gangers menacing his more law-abiding patrons and the occasional shootout in the street had all driven his more respectable, hard-working patrons away and racked up a huge repair bill for Squatz. At long last, a Van Saar gang led by a runt named Quill had finally taken control. They often hung out in the bar after working their Underhive territories. They kept to themselves for the most part, and kept the other gangs out of the district. A sort of peace had returned to the Fresh Air.

Quill and his boys were in the back room, whooping it up over some big victory. Squatz stood on the plank behind the bar and watched them while cleaning glasses. He was a short man with only one eye. Some people might call him a dwarf. Those people wouldn't live to apologise. He scratched at the patch over his empty eye socket. He hated wearing it, but Quill had made it very clear that he had no alternative. Squatz loathed owning a one-gang bar, but it was better than the alternative.

Quill and his gang headed toward the bar from the back. Quill wore brown body armour with long barbs attached to the shoulders and upper back, making him look a little like a porcupine. Squatz figured it was the best joke the ganger's brain could come up with. He opened a bottle of House Special as they approached, but Quill flicked the back of his hand at the barman. 'Important business. We'll be back later. I don't want to catch you with that patch off again,' he said as they left.

Squatz took a long draught from the bottle, wiped his hand over his mouth, and then raised the bottle in a mock salute. He hopped off his plank and went around the end of the bar to go clean up the table. A moment later he heard lasblasts coming from the square. 'Not so damn close to my bar!' he yelled and ran to the door.

Squatz arrived just in time to see a huge beast of a man, with wild tangles of hair streaming around his face, land in the middle of Quill's men. He towered over the Van Saar gang, his huge black shoulders reaching the top of their heads. And there were tubes coming out of his chest and arms that snaked their way over his shoulders. It had to be the vampire, but Squatz was certain that he was wearing some sort of power armour. *The vampire was a Spyrer.*

Squatz backed away from the doorway, so as not to be seen, and watched. The vampire grabbed a juve named Kenner by the top of his head and tossed him into the air. Kenner slammed into the fan, which screamed in protest as it cut through the foreign body jammed between its blades.

'That's going to cost me business for a month,' said Squatz.

The rest of the gang reacted quickly, fanning out and diving for cover. A couple of them headed for the Fresh Air, but Squatz didn't want the vampire following them in, so he slammed the door closed and slid the bolt into place. He then moved to a window so he could see the rest of the battle.

The two gangers he'd just locked out turned, but the vampire was right behind them. He now wore some sort of mirrored helmet with glowing red eyes. The tubes that had been slung over his shoulders were attached around the base of the helmet. One of the gangers at the door got off a plasma bolt shot. It exploded on the vampire's chest. When the flames died away, Squatz could see that the explosion had done nothing more than chip away at one of the black plates on the armour.

The vampire swung a huge fist at the ganger, hitting and shattering the plasma gun. The resulting explosion knocked Squatz to the floor. When he got back up, the vampire was moving away. The two gangers lay in a bloody heap outside his door. The rest of Quill's gang opened fire from around the square. Laser blasts, shot-gun rounds, and stubber shots all rebounded off the armour, doing little or no damage.

One of the Van Saar, a tall, bull-headed ganger named Domerud, stood his ground on the other side of the square, unloading clip after clip from his autogun in rapid fire that bounced off the vampire's armour. With blinding speed, the vampire sprinted across to Domerud and grabbed the weapon from his hand. The vampire spun the weapon around, jammed the barrel through Domerud's sternum and pulled the trigger.

The resulting spray of bullets shot clean out of Dom's back and took down two gangers stood behind him. The vampire hoisted Domerud's limp carcass over his head and tossed him toward Quill. The Van Saar ducked, but by the time he'd straightened up the vam-pire was right above him. Quill stood his ground, aimed his heavy plasma gun at the vampire, and fired.

Squatz gave him credit. The gang leader must have known what would happen, but had obviously decided in that split second that it was the only way to save the rest of his gang. The explosion engulfed both the vam-pire and Quill in fire and black smoke that roiled up toward the roof of the square in a billowing cloud. That ought to alert the enforcers, thought Squatz. Not that they could do anything about the rampaging vampire. Enforcers would be no match for a Spyrer.

The huge fan that gave the Fresh Air its name dis-persed the smoke after a few moments. Quill's body lay in a charred heap on the ground, but the vampire was still standing. He wasn't moving; just standing and per-haps swaying a little. Squatz wondered if the gang leader had succeeded where all others had failed. Then the vampire turned. Squatz could see a small hole in his rig where a chunk of armour plate had been blown off, but that was the sum total of Quill's sacrificial act.

Hauk, Quill's second-in-command, an imposing figure standing well over two metres tall and broad across the chest, called for a retreat. The tattered remnants of the gang ran toward the exits from the square, while Hauk and two juves named Wat and Baddy laid down covering fire. The juves both fired laser blasts that hit the vampire in the head. The shots seemed to get absorbed by the mirrored material, and then red beams shot out from the eyes, burning both juves on the spot.

Hauk dropped his weapon and ran, pushing his way past two enforcers who were running toward the square. They took one look at the carnage and the imposing figure of the Spyrer-rigged vampire and turned to chase after Hauk. Funny thing is, thought Squatz, if they catch Hauk, he'll probably get charged with murdering his own gang. The peace has to be kept, no matter the cost.

The vampire didn't pursue Hauk or the enforcers. Squatz watched in amazement as the vampire picked up several bodies and jumped onto the horizontal ventilation shaft coming out of the fan housing. He scaled the vertical shaft above the fan and disappeared into the darkness.

A while later, as Squatz was about to go out into the square to see if anyone was still alive, he heard a noise from above the fan. The vampire was coming back down. Squatz closed the door and slunk back to his window. The vampire picked up the rest of the bodies and climbed back into the darkness.

Squatz decided to stay inside for the rest of the day, and perhaps the next few as well. He could live on synthnuts and House Special if he had to, but he wasn't opening that door for anyone or anything.

'THIS IS FINE looking silver, Kal,' said Fewell. He held all of Valtin's buckles in his meaty hands, along with the two silver chains from his jacket. The front of Valtin's jacket was in shreds as were the tops of his boots where Kal had ripped off all the buckles. 'This'll make a nice dint in what you owe me for the last five years.'

'Now about that information,' said Kal. He was kneeling next to Valtin with the knife, using it to rip off the silk piping.

'That'll cost you extra.'

'Add it to my tab,' said Kal with a chuckle. 'As always.' He was done with the silk piping and was now scratching and cutting at the too-clean and too-perfect pants and coat.

'Ow!' cried Valtin. 'Watch that knife.'

'Spire baby,' said Kal. 'It's not even all that sharp.' When he was finished, Kal tossed the knife toward one of the armour racks. It stuck fast. 'Okay. It's a little sharp.' A broad grin swept across his face. Kal turned to Fewell. 'I'm looking for another relative of mine.'

'Another fancy pants Spire brat like this one?' asked Fewell. He pulled the knife out of the rack and pushed his way back to the counter through all the armour that Wotan had knocked over.

Kal motioned to Valtin to pick up the armour, but Wotan just knocked them over again as he padded after Kal. When he got to the counter, Kal continued. 'No,' he said. 'This relative is older, more experienced. I don't think this is his first trip down here.'

'What's he look like?'

Kal realised he didn't know and didn't have a picture. 'Well, probably a lot like me,' he said, smiling. 'You know, dashing good looks, regal chin, full head of hair.'

Fewell raised his eyebrows and stared at the bounty hunter. 'Well, if you don't know what he looks like and he knows how to blend in, it'll be awfully hard to find him. The Underhive's a pretty big place.'

'He, um, has a bit of a temper,' added Valtin. He'd replaced all the armour and joined the conversation. 'Any, er, murders in the last few days?'

Now Fewell gave Valtin the same incredulous look. 'Murders in the last few days, you say, huh? Well, gee, I dunno. Just maybe a dozen or so. You boys ain't heard of the Underhive Vampire?'

'Oh that,' said Kal. 'I heard about that down by Glory Hole. Killed Bester.' He stopped and stared at Fewell. 'A dozen? All in Glory Hole?'

'Nah! All over the Underhive and even in Hive City.' The armour maker picked up a small hammer and a rounded sheet of metal and began tapping out some dents. 'All the way down to Dust Falls, I hear.'

Valtin pushed Kal out of the way to get closer to the armourer. 'When did you say all this vampire business started?'

'I didn't say.' Fewell looked at Valtin and then back down at his work. Tap. Tap. Tap.

Valtin glanced at Kal, who sighed. 'Lesson number two, nephew: down here everything has a price.' Valtin stared at Jerico, still not getting it. 'You'll have to pay him for the info.'

'But he was giving it to you for free.'

'He knows I don't have any money,' said Kal, 'and he'd just add it to my tab later, anyway.' He looked at Fewell. 'I really ought to look at that tab sometime to keep you honest.'

'Says the pot to the kettle,' replied Fewell.

Valtin ignored the two of them and dug into his pants for some credits. He looked at Kal again, wanting to ask how much to pay, but decided to chance it on his own. He laid down a five-credit chip. Jerico jerked his thumb into the air. Valtin took the five chip back and dropped a 100 credit bond. Jerico gasped, but Fewell had snatched it up without even missing a beat with his hammer.

'The first murder was here in Hive City three nights ago. After that, it's hard to say, but it seems like they were strung out from here to Dust Falls and then up to Glory Hole. Don't know after that.'

'The timing is about right,' said Valtin. He turned to Kal. 'There's something else you should know,' he said.

'What now?'

'Armand is most likely wearing his Spyrer rig.'

'You've got to be kidding me,' said Kal.

Valtin nodded.

'And you just thought to tell me this now?'

Another nod.

'Hey Fewell,' said Kal, sarcasm dripping off his voice. 'You wouldn't happen to have a spare monofilament sword in the back, would you?'

'No, but I know where you might get one,' he replied in the same monotone droll he'd used when answering Valtin.

Kal's mouth dropped open. 'Where?'

Fewell hesitated, looked over at Valtin, obviously wondering if he could get any more credits out of Kal's nephew, but then looked back at Kal's face, which was now stewing red. 'Out of the Spyrer team that's tracking your vampire!' he replied, finally.

HAGEN WINCED AS Skreed wrapped a sheet around his torso to help stabilise the broken ribs. He and Dungo had come into the bar just as Hagen was about to pass out again. They'd poured the better part of a bottle of

Wildsnake down his throat, which had shocked his system enough to keep him conscious. Then Dungo went to Hagen's place, which was just a spare room in the basement, to fetch bandages and a fresh shirt for the bartender while Skreed helped Hagen wash the blood and spit out of his beard.

The Wildsnake was taking effect, spreading its warmth through his beaten body and numbing the pain for a while. He didn't even complain when Dungo opened two more bottles for himself and Skreed.

'What in the Hive happened?' Skreed asked finally.

'Wildcats came looking for Yolanda,' replied Hagen. He groaned. Just talking made his ribs ache.

'We should take you to Hive City and find you a real doc,' said Dungo. He took a long pull at his bottle, as if worried they might leave right away.

'Nah,' said Hagen. 'It's just cracked ribs and a cracked head. Nothing the docs can do that a little rest won't cure.' Fact was, Hagen was afraid of only two things in life. One was spiders. He'd nearly been eaten by a giant hive spider once and was now skittish around all eight-legged creatures. The other thing was doctors. You couldn't trust a person you had to pay to cut you open. It just didn't seem right.

The three drank in silence for a while. Hagen wondered if the Hole would ever be the same. The vampire had driven off or killed most of his business. All of Glory Hole had been scared into their homes. It would take months to pay for all the damage the Wildcats had caused. By then, the mercenaries would have found a new hole to hang out in.

The silence was broken by an explosion down the street. 'Not again,' said Hagen. With nothing left to lose, he pushed himself out of the chair with a groan and hobbled over to the door, which Skreed had propped against the opening. He peeked through the crack between the door and the frame. 'Helmawr's rump,' he cried. 'Spyrers.'

A rocket exploded outside the Hole. The concussion blasted the door into Hagen. He flew across the room, hit the far wall, and fell to the floor. A second later the door landed on top of him. Hagen tried to push the door off, but his ribs screamed at him. Then he heard Dungo scream as well, and he decided to stay put.

Several lasblasts echoed through the room and then Hagen heard a whistling noise that he'd only heard once before in his life, followed by another scream and a dull thud. The whistling was the sound a monofilament sword made as it ripped through the atoms of the air and pretty much any object in its path

A commanding voice said, 'Where's the vampire?'

Skreed, his voice halting and choking as he spoke, answered: 'It… left Glory… don't know… where it went.'

'What's the closest settlement?'

'Nothing close. Just the Wastes and then Hive City.'

Hagen heard a sickening crack and then the unmistakable sound of another body hitting the floor.

'We head straight for the City,' said the voice. 'He has to eat.'

The Spyrers left, but Hagen waited a very long time before crawling out from under the door. As he suspected, Skreed and Dungo lay dead on the floor. Dungo lay in a bloody mass while Skreed lay next to his severed arm, his head lying at an awkward angle to his body. Hagen, moving very slowly, went downstairs and packed a satchel and then cleaned out the cash box.

First, he was going to go see a medicae, and then head out to take on those damn spiders again to get at their treasure. That had to be safer than running this place.

* * *

DERINDI POKED HIS head farther out of the hive dust to see what Yolanda was yelling about. She seemed to be looking his way and he feared that the statuesque bounty hunter had spotted his hiding spot. It had been tough following them across the White Wastes, but his small stature and willingness to cover his entire body with dust had kept Derindi hidden for the better part of a day. Of course, his whole body itched.

Now she was looking right at him through her binoculars. But he'd been almost completely buried! How could she have seen him? He glanced over his shoulder to see if there was something else she might be excited about. 'Oh, crap!' he said and ducked back under the dust just as the Wildcat gang thundered past.

He felt lucky that only two of the large Escher women had stepped on him as they ran past. He stuck his head back up a moment later, only to have it kicked from behind by a straggler. The last thing Derindi saw before losing consciousness was the bouncing bottom of a young Escher wearing a black outfit with some strange red writing on the back.

YOLANDA GLANCED BEHIND her. She'd been running for only a few minutes, but already Scabbs had fallen a full dust dune behind. The Wastes were inside the Hive, but the strange ventilation-spawned wind patterns from the surrounding domes that had brought the dust to this area in the first place, also produced dunes that looked almost natural.

The Wildcats were maybe two dunes behind Scabbs and would start firing soon. Yolanda could see the curved wall of a dome ahead, but she knew the Eschers would be on top of her before she could find the entrance tunnel, and would reach Scabbs before he even made the wall.

They had to make a stand. The question was, did she make it before or after Scabbs got shot? Better to have a wall behind her, but by then Scabbs would be dead. 'Helmawr's rump,' she said. 'I'd better save the little scabber.'

Yolanda dived to the ground at the bottom of the next dune, and then crawled back to peer over the top. When Scabbs crested the dune, she reached out and tripped her partner, sending him rolling down the dune. 'Get up here,' she hissed and then pulled out her laspistols.

As the Wildcats reached the top of the dune behind her, Yolanda fired two blasts that slammed into the hive dust, melting it into slag under Vicksen's feet. 'That's far enough!' yelled Yolanda. 'Speak your piece and leave, or I'll shoot you where you stand.'

Yolanda could just see Vicksen's head and shoulders and the tops of two or three Wildcats behind their leader without exposing herself too much. Vicksen turned and said something to one of the girls and then turned back and cupped her hands around her mouth. Yolanda watched the other ganger as Vicksen spoke.

'We need your help, Yolanda,' she called. 'Let me come over there – alone – and we'll talk about it.'

The ganger Vicksen had spoken to had her head bowed, like she was working on something. Whatever, it was, it made Yolanda suspicious. That, and the fact that Eschers were not known for talking out their problems. 'I don't believe you,' she said and punctuated the statement with another blast from her laspistol that went right past Vicksens's ear. 'The next one goes between your eyes. Now leave!'

'I've got a better idea,' said Vicksen. 'You leave – in pieces.'

The other ganger turned, with a grenade launcher in her hands. Yolanda pushed away from the dust and rolled sideways down the dune as the top exploded, sending a cloud of dust and metal fragments raining down around her. She slammed into Scabbs, who had made it half way up, and both of them rolled, bumping and jostling each other, all the way to the bottom.

By the time Yolanda and Scabbs got themselves untangled and stood up, the Wildcats were coming over the top of the blasted dune. Yolanda looked for her guns and saw them sticking out of the dust near the top of the dune. She pulled out her sword instead.

The sword was a jet-black katana. Its metal reflected the pale, blue light emanating from the rafters above the Wastes, giving it a eerie green shine. Yolanda struck a fighting stance and glared at the Wildcats, daring them to move within range. Upon seeing Yolanda standing there with her powerful arms and legs, wicked sword, and death in her eyes, anyone but an Escher woman would have hesitated.

In fact, the younger Wildcats stopped at the top of the dune, but Vicksen, Themis, and several others ran down the dune and encircled the bounty hunters. Yolanda moved to put herself and Scabbs back-to-back while keeping her eyes on Vicksen. 'Too afraid to fight me woman to woman?' she asked, staring straight into the Wildcat leader's eyes. 'Worried you can't take me alone?'

'No,' said Vicksen smiling. 'That's exactly what I want, in fact.' She snapped her fingers and said, 'Now!' The gangers surrounding Yolanda and Scabbs all fired at the same time. But there was no explosion, just a mass of sticky webs that hit them from all sides, gluing the two bounty hunters together and sticking them fast to the ground.

Vicksen walked up, grabbed Yolanda's sword by the blade, and yanked it out of her webbed hands. 'Just not here,' she continued. 'Not now. We're going to do this in as public a place as possible.'

'Why?' whined Scabbs. 'What do you want?'

'She knows,' said Vicksen. She was now staring deep into Yolanda's eyes with a big smile on her face. 'We never fought for control of the Wildcats, and until one of us is dead, the Wildcats can have no leader.'

'But why me?' asked Scabbs. 'What have you got against me?'

'You're the reason she left in the first place,' sneered Vicksen. 'You and the wretched Kal Jerico. For that you will both die, once I am crowned the true leader of the Wildcats. But that must happen in front of an audience so the entire Hive will know that I have beaten the great Yolanda. So, you both get to live a little longer. Well, at least until we reach The Breath of Fresh Air. The court-yard will make a fine arena for our battle.'

'Aren't you worried about the enforcers?' asked Scabbs.

'What, me worry about men with weapons?' sneered Vicksen. 'Hardly.'

BOBO SNUCK UP behind Dutt, who was crouched behind a rubbish pile in an alley across from the armourer's place. He'd thought it over and over, and had decided that something wasn't quite right. There was more to this mission than a simple R&R, and he hated working in the dark. It was time to compare notes.

He was amazed at how close Dutt had let him get. He could have killed him ten minutes ago if he'd wanted, but that was why Bobo worked for the Spire and Dutt worked for Nemo. The next part would be tricky, though. Dutt still had his pict-camera trained on the shop. If he turned and caught Bobo in the recorder's field of vision, Nemo would have a record of this meeting.

He took another step forward, ready to drop to the ground and roll if Dutt should turn around. Before

Bobo could take a second step, Dutt lifted a needler and pointed it right between Bobo's eyes without even turning his head.

'Impressive,' said Bobo. He slid to the side a few steps, and Dutt tracked him with the needler. Nemo's spy still hadn't turned. 'Very impressive. I'm not here to take you out. If I was, you would already be dead.'

Dutt turned, leaving the pict recorder on the pile, pointing at the shop. He spread his arms, palms up, although Bobo noticed that the barrel of the weapon never wavered. He wasn't sure what the shrug was supposed to suggest, so he just continued. 'I'm here to talk. There's something not right about this mission. So I thought – it sounds crazy now that I'm saying it, but it's been a crazy few days, huh? – I thought we should talk. You know, compare notes. Okay, if you don't say something soon, I'm just going to shoot you for spite.'

Bobo watched in fascination as Dutt raised his empty hand to his mouth. He opened up and reached inside with two fingers and his thumb. The fingers twisted slightly, and Bobo could swear he heard something click. When he brought his fingers back out, he was holding a tooth. Dutt reached down and jammed his hand into the rubbish heap up to the elbow, then brought his muck-encrusted arm back out, and spread his hand to show that it was empty.

'Now I can talk,' Dutt said. 'Nemo's subvocal implant. It transmits everything I say right back to Nemo. I had it modified, so I could remove it whenever I want.'

'Interesting boss you have there.'

'It's a living,' replied Dutt. 'I saw you at Noritake's.'

'Only because I wanted you to see me,' said Bobo. 'I saw you first.'

'Whatever.' Dutt glanced over his shoulder to make sure that Jerico was still in the shop. 'Say what you have to say. They'll be coming out soon.'

'How do you know?'

'Nemo's had the armourer bugged for ages,' said Dutt. 'It's one of Jerico's favourite haunts. Spill it. Why are you here?'

'I just got a bad feeling about this one. Too many big things happening all at once. There's the vampire, and now I hear that a Spyrer team is hanging round these parts and we're both watching Jerico for our respective masters. It seems that everyone knows that something big is about to go down, but nobody's telling us what it is or how far away from ground zero we need to be when it happens. And I don't know about you, but I hate working in the dark.'

He watched Dutt as he spoke, trying to pick up any clues from body language that would tell him how much the other spy knew. From his expression, Bobo was fairly certain Dutt was just as in the dark about the objectives of this mission as he was. That at least was comforting.

'So, what do you want to do, work together?' he asked.

The remark dripped with sarcasm. Bobo didn't need to read his face to figure that one out. 'Not work together so much as share information,' he said, matter-of-factly, in an effort to disarm his fellow spy.

If it worked, Dutt didn't show it and he was better at hiding his emotions than Bobo thought. 'You first,' was all he said.

'Fine. I did seek permission to eliminate you, but I was denied,' he said. 'Either my boss doesn't care if Nemo gets there first, which I don't believe, or he's working with Nemo on this, which I can't believe.'

'Maybe there's another explanation,' said Dutt with a smirk. Bobo just stared at him, unable to think of anything. 'My boss happens to know that your boss, Hermod Kauderer, is the one who sent the Spyrers down here. We're just witnesses. They'll be doing all the heavy work.'

'Does my bo… does Kauderer know that Nemo knows?'

'Sorry, I'm done sharing,' he said as he reached into the refuse pile for his tooth. Before he pulled it back out, he cocked his head slightly. Bobo suspected he was listening to some transmission in his ear. He still hadn't pulled the tooth out of the trash.

'Wait,' said Bobo. 'What was that?'

Dutt left his arm in the pile of refuse and smiled at Bobo. 'You first.'

Bobo wondered what he had that Nemo might be interested in knowing. It came to him like a laser blast. 'You know the noble travelling with Jerico?' he asked. Dutt nodded. 'He has orders to eliminate any witnesses once the mission is completed, including Kal Jerico.'

Dutt couldn't hide his pleasure at that nugget of information. 'Well then, you might want to know that the vampire just took out an entire Van Saar gang at The Breath of Fresh Air,' he said. Bobo gave him a blank look, although he'd already guessed the rest. 'That's where your boss's Spyrers will be headed next.'

KAL WAS DUMBSTRUCK. 'There's a Spyrer unit chasing Armand as well? What in the Hive did he steal – the old man's brain?' Kal looked back and forth from Fewell to Valtin. Fewell continued hammering, obviously pretending he hadn't heard the part about stolen merchandise. Valtin, on the other hand, glanced at the ceiling and wouldn't look Jerico in the eyes.

He knows something, thought Kal, but he was wise enough to know Valtin wouldn't spill it here in front of Fewell. He turned back to Fewell, and made a big show of being upset. 'Great. Just great!' he said. 'Not only do I have to defeat a Spyrer-suited vampire, but I have to take on an entire team of Spyrers on the way.'

Fewell and Valtin just stared at him. Kal took a few deep breaths to try to show that he was calming down, and then asked, 'Any idea where I can find these Spyrers?'

Fewell shook his head, and continued tapping on the armour. Kal couldn't tell if the armourer was buying his act or not.

'I think I might know someone who can help us,' said Valtin.

BOBO WATCHED FROM behind Dutt as Jerico and Valtin left the armour shop. He let the rival spy, and his pict-camera, leave the alley first, and then stepped onto the street and simply followed his targets. Bobo had a very practiced saunter. He looked like any other person out for a walk, even when he was the only one on the street. It was a gift. His short stature, coupled with a calm self-confidence, was quite disarming and nobody ever suspected he could be capable of doing anything wrong.

This natural ability allowed Bobo to tail Jerico and Valtin back across the city to the docks. He wasn't sure where they were going and wasn't all that worried about it until they entered Madam Noritake's. Bobo didn't know if he should follow them or not, but he knew three secret ways out of the pleasure house and assumed Jerico knew of at least one of them.

He chanced it and slipped inside, ducking behind a large urn that always stood next to the door. Kal and

Valtin were talking to Madam Noritake. She was a short woman with straight black hair that didn't quite reach her shoulders. You wouldn't call her pretty, but you also wouldn't call her plain – at least not to her face or any-where within ear shot. Madam Noritake could be a vindictive little woman.

Could they possibly be looking to score a little plea-sure at a time like this? The vampire was in the city, the Spyrers were on their way, and these two were going to go off and have a little cuddle? Bobo had to get closer to hear what they were saying.

Both Kal and Valtin had their backs to the door, so he slipped out from behind the urn and dropped into a comfy chair in the little sitting area across from Noritake's desk. He couldn't see Madam Noritake, but he could hear her squeaky voice. 'He's not here now,' she said.

'Do you happen to know if Mr Bobo will return later today?' asked Valtin.

A ringing began in Bobo's ears as his heart pounded faster. They had come looking for him? What in the Hive was that about?

'Maybe. Maybe not,' said Noritake. 'I'm not his mother. I just rent rooms. Ten credits gets you half an hour. You want a room while you wait?'

Bobo heard Kal say 'Why ye–', but then Valtin cut in. 'No, thank you. We'll just wait down here.'

Bobo's heart pounded even harder and faster. They would be coming toward him in mere moments. He glanced around for some escape and then caught sight of Jenn Strings, wearing her customary string outfit, coming down the stairs. She saw him and smiled. He motioned toward Jerico and made the talk signal with his other hand.

Jenn was a smart girl. That was one of the things Markel liked about her, along with that string outfit. She walked right up to Kal, flipped her long, blonde hair away from her face and pressed her lithe body against him. 'Hi there,' she said. 'This is Madam Noritake's House of Fun. Want to have some fun?'

Bobo didn't look back. He took his chance and ducked back behind the urn and then out the door. From there, he made his way around to the alley and climbed hand over hand up the ventilation shaft to the roof. The panel at the top lifted off: one of the three secret exits. He'd never used it to actually break in, but a few moments later, Markel Bobo was walking down the stairs toward Madam Noritake's desk.

'I shall return later, madam,' he said. 'Please keep my room ready for me.'

Madam Noritake just stared at him. He could tell she didn't have a clue as to where he had come from or how he got there. Best not to push it, he thought. She's not the brightest bulb in the house. Besides, Valtin was already headed toward him. Jenn was still talking to Jerico. They were on the couch now, and her hair flips looked more like she was genuinely flirting and less like she was protecting his escape. He'd have to talk to her about that later.

Valtin spoke. 'Mr Bobo, I believe?'

'Yes,' said Bobo. 'Do I know you?' His face remained calm, despite the pounding heart that was now finally quieting back down.

'No, but I know you,' said Valtin. 'Or rather I know of you. We have a common acquaintance. A Mr Kauderer?'

'Yes, I know Kauderer,' replied Bobo. 'Are you a friend of his?'

'Not exactly,' replied Valtin. He looked around the room and then dropped a hundred credit bond in Markel's hand. 'Is there somewhere we can talk privately? We need some information about another group of mutual acquaintances.'

Bobo looked at the bond. Perhaps this day was turning out alright after all. He suppressed the smile that endeavoured to cross his face. 'We can speak in my room if you'd like.'

'DROP HER IN the middle of the square,' yelled Vicksen as they entered the courtyard in front of the Breath of Fresh Air. The large fan spinning in its housing above the square provided a cool breeze and the only sound other than Vicksen's voice.

Vicksen's auburn ponytail swung back and forth as she scanned the empty square. 'Where in the Hive is everyone?' she asked. 'Lysanne, go into the Fresh Air and announce the battle. We need a crowd for this.'

As the young ganger ran off across the square, Vicksen tossed her shotgun to an Escher with black, spiked hair, named Brandia, and then unbuckled her bandolier and handed it along with her dagger to a juve standing nearby. She grabbed her chainsword from its sheath as the juve moved off. 'Themis, drop Yolanda's sword on the ground and then pat her down for hidden weapons.'

She walked toward the middle of the courtyard where Yolanda lay, bound hand and foot. 'This is a sword battle,' she said. 'Me and my chainsword versus you and your little knife.'

'That's hardly fair!' said Scabbs. Two Escher women, Kirsta and Suzeran, held the squirming little half-breed between them near the back wall. Scabbs looked pitiful and small compared to the tall Escher gangers. He barely came up to their breasts, and had no chance of breaking their hold on him. Vicksen smiled as she thought what this victory would mean to the gang.

'It's a katana,' spat Yolanda. 'I don't need machinery to add power to my sword arm.'

But her insult fell on deaf ears, for Vicksen was looking at Lysanne, who had returned from the bar with a dour look on her face. 'What's wrong?' asked Vicksen.

Lysanne cast her eyes down to the ground, which irritated Vicksen even more. 'Look at me when you speak, girl!' she roared. 'You are a Wildcat. Act like one.'

'Ma'am. Yes, ma'am.' said Lysanne, now standing straight and tall and looking Vicksen in the eye. 'The Fresh Air is closed, mistress.'

'Closed?' asked Vicksen. 'How can that be?'

'The door is locked and the lights are out,' said Lysanne. A small pout played across her lips and she crossed her hands over her black-clad chest. 'I'm sorry, ma'am.'

'Don't be sorry!' screamed Vicksen. 'Just go find me a crowd. Bang down doors if you have to. What the hell is wrong with this place?' Vicksen stood in front of Yolanda and seethed. Her blue hair spikes vibrated above her bright red forehead.

'Guess we'll have to postpone our little group hug,' said Yolanda with a smile.

Themis stepped over the prone and bound bounty hunter and grabbed her leader by the shoulders. 'Get hold of yourself,' she whispered. 'This is your day. Control it. Don't let it control you. We are your audience. Once the Wildcats know you've defeated Yolanda, everything will change.'

Vicksen took a deep breath to calm her temper. 'Of course, you're right, Themis,' she said. She turned and looked at her gathered gang. 'Today you will witness the turning of a new page in the Wildcat lore. Today we will close the door on the old rule and open the pathway to a better future. Today, Yolanda Catallus, former Wildcat leader shall fall in the field of battle to Vicksen Colteen, your present and future leader.'

The assembled crowd roared like a hungry mob as Vicksen finished her speech. 'Cut her loose, Themis,' she said. She pulled the cord on her chainsword and began circling, looking for an opening as Themis backed away from Yolanda. The former leader waved her katana back and forth in front of her. 'After today, no one will even remember the great Yolanda,' yelled Vicksen above the metallic whine of her chainsword. 'You're going to die with only your 'Cats as witnesses.'

UNSEEN IN AN alcove high above, one other creature had been watching the events unfolding in the square below. The two buxom Escher women weaved and danced around each other, waving their weapons as the gathered Wildcats cheered from the sidelines, while Armand Helmawr, the Underhive Vampire, watched with the eye of a hungry predator. He grabbed hold of the ventilation shaft and started climbing down toward the fan to get a better look at the action.

SCABBS WATCHED IN horror as the battle began. He knew Yolanda was good. He even knew she was crazy enough to believe she could take on a chainsword-wielding Escher with nothing but her katana, but this was the leader of the Wildcats she was fighting. He had to do something to help, and do it fast.

Vicksen rushed forward as Yolanda's sword dipped. The Wildcats leader swung her buzzing chainsword across at chest height, but Yolanda was no longer there, having dropped down and rolled forward, slicing at Colteen's exposed legs. Vicksen sidestepped just in time, but Scabbs could see a rip in the leader's pants and a tiny trickle of blood running down her inner thigh.

That round went to Yolanda, but all she got for her nifty move was a nick. Once Vicksen connected,

Yolanda would lose more than a little leather and blood. Scabbs looked at the two Escher women holding him. Their biceps were larger than *his* thighs. They each had him by a forearm and had wrapped their meaty arms around his skinny limbs, holding his elbows against their torsos. His wrists and ankles were bound tight. There didn't seem to be any escape.

Vicksen had backed off a little after her failed attack and was circling Yolanda again. 'What, no sharp retort now?' asked Yolanda. She reached out and ran her fingers along the tip of her katana and then licked the blood off her fingertips. 'I've tasted first blood, and it's sweet.'

'You'll be tasting your own blood when I rip out your intestines,' said Vicksen, holding her chainsword up high.

In that instant, Yolanda dashed in and jabbed the point of her blade into Vicksen's ribs. Vicksen screamed and swept her arm down, but Yolanda raced on past the Wildcat leader after her attack and was well behind Colteen before the chainsword even came close.

Kirsta and Suzeran groaned at Yolanda's deft move and Scabbs could feel their grip loosen slightly. Now he had a chance. For what the Escher women didn't know was that his skin flaked off easily. One good twist now and he'd be free. Of course, there was still the matter of the ropes on his ankles, but he spied Vicksen's shotgun and bandolier on the ground nearby. Lying atop the bandolier was a wicked, curved blade. He had a plan.

Yolanda's stab had caught Vicksen just below her leather half-vest. Blood streamed down her flat belly and spread across the top of her leather pants. She dabbed at the blood with her free hand and growled at Yolanda. 'That little toad sticker won't save you now.' She pulled a grenade off her vest and lobbed it over

Yolanda's head, rushing in with her buzzing chainsaw to cut off the bounty hunter's escape route.

All of the Wildcats seemed to be holding their breaths, but Scabbs tensed for action. As soon as the grenade exploded, he yanked his arms up in the air, twisting them as Kirsta and Suzeran tried to hold on. Then he was free and running as best he could in his bonds. He half expected one of them to shoot him in the back, but when he glanced over his shoulder he knew he had much bigger troubles. They all did.

The vampire stood between Scabbs's former captors, holding the burly women up in the air by their hair. He slammed their heads together, and the resulting crack resounded through the square, getting everyone's attention.

Scabbs didn't question his amazing good luck in choosing just that moment to run. Living with Kal Jerico, he had almost come to expect it. So, of all the people in the square, he was the only one not taken by surprise; the only one still moving as the vampire dropped his first two victims and moved toward the next 'Cat in line.

# 6: CHAOS THEORY

'WE ARE ABOUT to enter Hive City, sir,' Jonas said through his rig's portavox unit. The Spyrer commander held up a hand to halt his fellow Spyrers as he made his report.

'Excellent,' replied Kauderer's voice in his ear. 'I have new information for you from my agent in the field. The most recent sighting has Armand somewhere near a bar called The Breath of Fresh Air. It is not far from your current location.'

'I know the place, sir,' replied Jonas. 'We will find the renegade.'

'Belay that order,' snapped Kauderer. 'I must still make my report to Lord Helmawr, and I do not want to have to include a Hive City riot in that report.'

'Sir?'

'You are to proceed with all due caution,' ordered Kauderer. 'We cannot afford any enforcer involvement. Remove your rigs before entering the City. This is still a covert operation. You must not cause any incidents inside Hive City. Neither the Enforcers nor the City Houses must be alerted to your presence.'

'Remove our rigs, sir?' asked Jonas. 'That would be most unusual, these aren't really the kind of thing that one just *removes*.' He sounded indignant.

'What's the matter with you, Jonas?' said Kauderer. 'What are you, some kind of Green Hunter? Your rigs have been configured for this mission, and this mission alone. You might lack some of your customary power boosts, but I'm sure you'll find the preparations I ordered have made your devices rather more flexible, than usual.'

Jonas snorted. He wasn't convinced it was such a good idea and wasn't going to let it rest quite so easily. 'How are we to take down Armand without our rigs, sir?'

'That has all been taken care of,' replied Kauderer, curtly. 'There's a weapons stash in the city.'

'Very well!' said Jonas grudgingly. He turned to his squad and relayed the news. 'Leoni, Grell,' he called to the two Spyrers wearing Malcadon rigs. They had tubes running from their gauntlets to a large device on their backs that produced thick, viscous webbing. They saluted. 'Climb into the rafters and use your webs to attach all of our gear away from prying eyes. We're going into the city, in street gear.'

'I'll fly up there with them?' said Chimone. Jonas thought that the Spyrer wearing the Yeld rig, was a whiny, little hive brat, but he'd been forced to accept her as part of the team due to her political connections.

'No,' said Jonas. 'You will keep your rig. I want you to fly on ahead of us and then use your rig's camo to stay out of sight until we need you.'

Chimone smiled. He hated giving her the plum assignment, but he had no choice. Without their rigs, they would be vulnerable. He needed eyes on the inside. Chimone flew off, but the rest of the squad just looked at him. 'You heard your orders. Now move.'

\* \* \*

'You know where this Breath of Fresh Air is located?' asked Valtin as they walked through the city. Even he could feel the change in the air now. The entire dome seemed deserted. It seemed everyone had heard about the vampire attack earlier.

'Yeah,' said Kal. 'It's not far.'

'Not far by real reckoning or by Jerico reckoning?' asked Valtin, remembering how long it taken them to get to the armourer.

'It's right around the corner, okay?' asked Kal. 'Yeesh, everyone's a critic. Okay, so I'm no pathfinder, but I have other skills and attributes.' He squirmed and tried to scratch in between his shoulder blades. 'Damn this spear,' he cried. 'The gems keep poking me in the back.'

They turned the corner and were met by an explosion that almost sent both of them to the ground. 'I thought you said gang violence was rare in Hive City,' cried Valtin.

'Rare enough to make me think that my brother is probably involved. Come on!'

Kal sprinted into the square with Wotan padding along beside him. Valtin followed but stopped to stare at the scene, completely unprepared for the chaos of a gang battle.

In the square, Yolanda was rolling on the ground as shrapnel rained around her. A large Escher woman with spiky blue hair and a long red ponytail stood over her with a chainsword. In the background, the rest of the Escher gang was running and screaming, and then the newcomers saw the reason. Their quarry, Armand.

Just as Scabbs was about to dive onto the weapon pile, he thought he saw Kal running into the courtyard. He dismissed it as wishful thinking and worked at grabbing the hilt of the knife with his teeth so he could hold the blade steady while cutting through the bonds at his wrists.

He glanced at Yolanda. She'd survived the explosion, but now Vicksen stood above her, slashing down with the buzzing chainsword. Yolanda rolled to the side but couldn't get away from the crazed Wildcat leader. All hell was breaking loose around them, but Vicksen still seemed intent on winning the duel. Scabbs gave up on the ropes and grabbed the shotgun. He hoped Vicksen had left a cartridge chambered because he couldn't cock it with his hands tied.

Scabbs fumbled with the weapon, trying to get a firm grip, aim and pull the trigger while bound. Luckily, his scabby arms moved a little within the bonds. Yolanda rolled back and forth beneath Vicksen as the gang leader slammed her sword down over and over again. As she raised the buzzing blade above her head for the next blow, Scabbs fired.

The shot hit the chainsword, knocking it out of her hands. It clattered on the ground and began spinning with the chain still buzzing. Yolanda rolled away, sweeping her legs through Vicksen's ankles, knocking the Wildcat leader to the ground.

As Yolanda rolled, Scabbs saw Kal again. The swarthy bounty hunter, a huge grin on his face, ran up to Yolanda, grabbed her unceremoniously around the waist and half-carried, half-dragged her over to Scabbs. Jerico fell next to Scabbs as he dropped her to the ground, flipped his wayward blond braids out of his eyes, and said, 'Are we having fun yet, kids?'

'What battle were you watching?' asked Scabbs as he finally cut himself loose from the bonds on his wrists.

VICKSEN SEETHED AS she watched Kal drag Yolanda away. 'Bring her back here, you interfering son of a–'

'Themis, Vicksen! Help!' called Lysanne.

Vicksen looked behind her and, for the first time, saw the carnage being wrought on her gang. Four girls were already on the ground, bleeding and broken behind a huge armoured beast of a man with burning red eyes, who was now advancing on Lysanne. She knew in an instant that it was the vampire. 'What have I done?' cried Vicksen. She looked down at her spinning chainsword lying on the floor and realised she had no weapon.

Themis opened fire with her heavy stubber. The recoil made the chains hanging from the epaulets on her shoulders rattle, but the hail of bullets had little effect on the vampire. Lysanne was rooted to the spot in fear and unable to move out of the way of the advancing vampire.

'Grenade,' called Themis to Vicksen.

The Escher leader didn't think a single grenade would even faze the beast. She looked at Themis, about to argue, but saw that her second in command had unslung one of her chains and looped the end around her heavy stubber. Vicksen understood. She pulled a grenade off her vest and waited for Themis.

Themis swung the cannon around her head at the end of the chain once and then let it fly. Vicksen took aim and tossed the grenade, and then ran toward little Lysanne. Both weapons hit the vampire's chest at the same time. As the grenade exploded, Vicksen jumped toward Lysanne, hitting her and pushing her to the ground.

A huge fireball erupted behind the two Escher women and bullets ricocheted around the courtyard as the heavy stubber's ammo ignited. Vicksen held onto Lysanne as the two of them rolled away from the explosion.

When the smoke cleared, the vampire was still standing, but Vicksen could swear the fire in its eyes had dimmed a little, and it wasn't moving – for the moment. She pulled Lysanne to her feet and pushed her away from the beast, but before she could follow, the vampire's eyes regained their brilliance and it looked right at Vicksen.

'I SEE YOU two found the vampire,' said Kal as Valtin finally joined the bounty hunters. They were all huddling behind a stone bench near the edge of the courtyard.

'More like he found us,' said Yolanda. 'So, what do we do now?'

'I vote for the Sump Hole,' said Scabbs. He'd draped Vicksen's bandolier over his shoulder and hugged the shotgun to his chest.

'Tempting,' said Jerico. 'But we can't let the vampire get away.'

'And we should help these poor women,' added Valtin. The other three just stared at him.

'I would agree,' said Yolanda, 'if they hadn't just been trying to kill me.'

'Look, we stay low and we stay alive,' said Kal. 'If we can help the Wildcats, great, but our lives come first and capturing the vampire comes second.'

'How in the Hive are we supposed to do th–'

A huge explosion rocked the courtyard behind them. They all peeked over the bench to see a black cloud of smoke where the vampire had just been standing.

'Now may be our chance,' said Kal, but then the smoke cleared and the vampire moved in on Vicksen. 'Maybe not,' he added.

\* \* \*

LYSANNE HIT THE wall and rolled around. She'd never been so frightened in her life. That monster was huge, and those eyes. She wanted to close her eyes, but kept her resolve. She pulled out the new laspistol Themis had given her earlier that day. As the vampire advanced on Vicksen, she stepped out and shot at one of its glowing, red eyes.

The shot hit, but it didn't penetrate and didn't bounce off the mirrored surface either. It just seemed to get absorbed. She'd seen the same thing happen with the Spyrers at Dust Falls. She knew what was going to happen next.

'Duck!' yelled Lysanne.

CHIMONE SAT ON the ventilation shaft next to the fan and watched the battle, cloaked by the chameleon-like properties of her rig's wings. She had seen no reason to interfere so far. Let the little gangers soften him up for us, she thought. Then we can follow him back to his lair and attack when his defences are down.

She'd pulled strings to join Jonas's team to show everyone that a female could be as tough and as strong as any Helmawr male. In that respect, she had a lot in common with the Wildcats, but she felt no pity for them. They were gangers. They were outside the law and lived or died by their weapons and wits. Today they would likely all die. It was just that simple. Just like it had been back at Dust Falls. They were Hivers. They were hardly human after all.

A voice crackled in her ear. 'Chimone, we're coming in now. What's the situation?'

'There's a contingent of Escher gangers between you and Armand,' she reported. 'Jerico and his cronies are huddled on the other side of the square. The rest of the Escher are rushing to help their leader.'

'Lay down some cover fire for us in thirty seconds.'

'Got it.'

VICKSEN DOVE TO the side just as the vampire's red eyes emitted a laser blast at the Wildcat leader. The blast burned a ten-centimetre hole through the thick metal plates that made up the ground in the courtyard. That could have been Vicksen's head, thought Lysanne. Or mine!

The Wildcat leader came back up and sprinted away from the beast. Lysanne was about to run as well, when she saw the flying Spyrer that had dropped Ashya down the Falls appear above the square and soar down toward the battle. As she glided over the heads of the Eschers, blasts from the Spyrer's twin lasers shot out in a rapid fire into the gang's ranks. Several Wildcats dropped. The rest scattered as the new threat entered the battle.

Hatred and vengeance surged inside Lysanne as she saw Ashya's killer, but she knew her little laspistol was no match for Spyrer armour. She needed something more powerful. She got an idea – a crazy, Yolanda type of idea – but someone had to do something, and Yolanda was still huddling with her new friends across the square.

Lysanne calculated the angle she needed and ran out into the square. 'Hey, beastie!' she yelled. 'Over here.' As she ran, Lysanne shot several laser blasts at the vampire's head. The black, mirrored surface drank in the power. The eyes flashed and Lysanne jumped high into the air.

The first blast hit the ground behind her. The second sizzled through the air just behind her as she reached the top of her arc. The laser beam burned a hole in the Wildcat's fluttering black top, before continuing on through the air, right into the body of the flying Spyrer.

Lysanne landed hard and her ankle crumpled under her as she fell to the ground in a heap. She looked up just in time to see the Spyrer, a hole burned clean through her chest, falling to the ground as well. But her moment of victory was short-lived. She could hear the vampire moving up behind her

Lysanne tried to stand, but screamed as she put weight on her shattered ankle. She fell back to the ground right in front of the vampire. Before he could reach her, another set of explosions rocked the square and four more gangers entered the battle.

The vampire fell back and Lysanne took advantage of the moment to crawl away, trying to get as much space between her and the vampire as possible. As she crawled, Lysanne got a look at the new gang and recognised one of them as the Spyrer leader who ordered Ashya's death. He wasn't wearing his rig anymore, but his face had been burned into her memory.

'WHAT THE HELL's going on downhive?' bellowed Helmawr, as Hermod Kauderer walked into the darkened chamber. He seems to be spending all of his time in here lately, considered Kauderer. He had been told that the darkness helped regulate the man's moods, but there had been no evidence of that so far as he could tell.

Kauderer nodded to the other advisors as he stepped into the glaring light in front of their master's desk.

'Well?' asked Helmawr. 'Report. I hear that work has all but stopped in Hive City. Explain yourself, Kauderer.'

Kauderer had also been informed that Helmawr was lucid but livid today. It was always a coin flip whether you would get the angry and efficient master or the forgetful and childlike one. But Kauderer had never seen Lord Helmawr quite this manic before. He decided to accommodate the old man as much as possible. He smiled at his lord, or at least tried to smile. On him a smile always looked more like a snake about to hiss than anything a warm-blooded animal could muster.

'Sire, the Hivers are afraid because Armand has been terrorising them,' replied Kauderer. Best to couch the lies in as much truth as possible. 'Once the matter has been handled, production will return to normal, and no one has linked the attacks to House Helmawr. Everyone believes the deaths have been caused by a mutant from the Hive bottom. They call him the Underhive Vampire, sire. There has been nothing to suggest any connection to House Helmawr.'

'That's not completely true, sire,' interjected Obidiah Clein. 'I have reports that describe Spyrer activity in the Underhive as well – Helmawr Spyrers to be exact. The entire place is turning into a war zone.'

Kauderer glared at Clein. Where was he getting his reports from, he wondered. Kauderer thought that perhaps he ought to put an agent on Clein as well. But first, a little misinformation to cloud the issue. 'It is not terribly surprising that some in the Hive have seen Armand's Spyrer rig for what it is, and were not fooled into thinking him some sort of monster,' he replied. 'But the prevailing story is still that an Underhive Vampire has come up from the Hive bottom to feed. Lacking any physical evidence, any other theory will soon be forgotten.'

He turned to Obidiah and spoke directly to the wily politician. 'And as for the Hive being a war zone, that is the common state for Hivers. Their reality is one of daily terror and death – a state you should become more familiar with very soon.'

The thinly veiled threat seemed to have an effect on Clein. Certainly the other advisors took note of it, for they all had taken this moment to stare at their shoes. Kauderer turned back toward the desk. 'The matter will be taken care of quite soon, my lord,' he stated. 'And rest assured there will be no physical evidence left behind to implicate this House.'

'Be sure I do not hear otherwise,' said Helmawr. The lights went out on his desk, leaving the advisors in a completely black room.

'I RECOGNISE THEM,' said Valtin as they all turned toward the new arrival. 'Jonas, Cyklus, Leoni, and Grell. That's the Spyrer team, minus their rigs.'

'What, more relatives?' asked Kal.

Valtin nodded.

'Great. We'll have the reunion later.' Kal looked around. The Escher were regrouping around Vicksen in the middle of the square. Armand had one exit street blocked, but had stopped for the moment. The Spyrers now had the other exit street blocked, and were advancing.

'Where in the Hive are the enforcers?' asked Scabbs.

'Holed up with the rest of Hive City,' replied Kal. 'Would you want to face that vampire if you didn't have to?'

'I have to and I don't want to,' whined Scabbs as he scratched at the red skin on his wrists.

'Fine,' said Jerico. 'We'll take out the Spyrers and get out. Let the Eschers deal with Arma… the vampire. Then we'll come back when it's calmed down and pick up the trail.'

Scabbs nodded. Yolanda looked briefly at Vicksen and then nodded as well. Valtin patted Kal on the shoulder and said, 'I'll meet you at Fewell's later,' and ran off toward Armand.

'What in the Hive is he doing?' asked Yolanda.

'Being a fool,' replied Kal.

'Or a hero,' added Scabbs as he pumped a shell into the shotgun.

'Same thing,' said Kal. He pulled out his laspistols and jumped over the stone bench, laser blasts leading the way. 'Wotan, attack,' he called back. The metal dog leaped out and quickly overtook his master, bounding toward the incoming Spyrers as Kal ran to keep up.

VICKSEN AND THEMIS stood back to back in the middle of the square. Both had re-armed with weapons from fallen Wildcats. Vicksen had a plasma gun while Themis had picked up a spare stubber and was loosing a hail of bullets at the vampire. A dozen Wildcats were on the ground, at least half of those from the last set of explosions. The rest, mostly juves, had fled before the second gang showed up.

'Who in the Hive are they?' asked Themis. She was keeping the vampire at bay with the constant stubber barrage, but her ammo wouldn't last forever, and when it ran out, Lysanne was its next victim.

'They look too clean to be Hivers,' said Vicksen. She shot an incoming grenade out of the air with a plasma bolt. The explosion sent the two women sprawling to the ground. 'Must be the Spyrers Lysanne told us about.'

'Then they must die,' said Themis as she scrambled back to her feet.

'Watch after Lysanne,' cried Vicksen.

Without Themis's constant rain of bullets holding it off, the vampire had regained its composure. It leapt the distance to the injured Wildcat before Themis could raise her weapon to fire. The vampire grabbed Lysanne by the waist and hoisted her up in the air. Holding her like a human shield, he advanced on the last two Wildcats.

* * *

SCABBS STAYED BEHIND the stone bench, pumping and firing the shotgun as fast as he could to provide covering fire as Kal, Yolanda, and Wotan charged into battle. Kal's twin lasguns fired in quick succession back and forth in his hands as he raced into the fray, and Yolanda followed close behind him, using the black-mirrored surface of her re-acquired katana to ward off incoming laser blasts.

The big brute holding the grenade launcher fired a shot toward Wotan, but the dog leapt to the side and the grenade sailed past, landing right in front of the bench. Scabbs kicked the bench over, falling backward at the same time, but the explosion still left the half-breed dazed and lacking cover.

VALTIN STEPPED IN front of the vampire as he advanced on the Wildcat leaders. 'Armand,' he said. 'It's time to end this.'

The muffled sound of maniacal laughing emanated from behind the mirrored helmet. 'Look,' said Armand. 'It's the nephew all grown up. How cute. Are you here to save these pitiful Hivers from the big bad vampire?'

'No, I'm here to take you back,' said Valtin, 'dead or alive.' He palmed a device in his pocket. It was nothing more than a little black box with a button and two antennae at the top.

'Back where?' said the muffled voice. 'Back to the tainted world of our fathers and their fathers before them? I think not.' He raised his armoured fist as if to strike Valtin dead on the spot.

Valtin was faster. He pulled the device out and pushed the button. Armand screamed and froze in place. His arm quivered as he tried to slam it down on top of Valtin's head, but moved only an inch at a time, as if he was forcing it through molasses.

'Neat device, huh?' asked Valtin. 'A small magnetic field drains the nearest power cell. You're under your own power now, uncle!' Valtin pulled out a power maul and slammed it into Armand's shoulder, causing the screaming Helmawr to drop his Wildcat hostage. Valtin grabbed the injured girl by the forearm and thrust her toward Vicksen and Themis. 'You three should leave,' he said to them. 'This is my fight now.'

OBIDIAH CLEIN STOPPED at the exit from the secure room to scratch at his chin as if deep in thought over some critical matter. In truth, he was waiting for Hermod Kauderer to get a head start down the hall so he could follow him from a safe distance.

Following a spy – am I crazy? He asked himself. But Clein knew that Kauderer and Katerin had been conspiring. Years of service in this web of intrigue had fine-tuned his ability to read people and their motives. Kauderer was a blank slate. The spy knew well how to hide his emotions and motives, but the military man was much easier to read. He'd been nervous at the meetings lately and giving Kauderer quick, sideways glances. Plus their constant bickering had all but stopped since the Armand business had begun.

He decided he'd waited long enough and sauntered through the antechamber out into the connecting hallway. There were no windows or doors here. They were too deep inside the palace to get natural light, and this hallway only existed as access to the secure room. But Kauderer had already disappeared, somehow. Colouri, the guardian of the coffers, Chancellor of the Spire Prong, Croag, the lawyer, and even Katerin were all there, walking in a loose bunch, ahead of him, but Kauderer was nowhere to be seen.

Clein decided to follow Katerin instead. He'd be easier to tail, and the two of them had to be meeting somewhere. Clein vowed to put someone on Kauderer, but he didn't know who he could trust in the palace.

As they all climbed toward their respective offices in the upper levels of the Spire, a buzzing in Clein's ear gave him a start. The others looked at him, but he just glared back. His ear buzzed again, and Obidiah knew he had to hurry. He pushed his way through the group and then jumped two steps at a time the rest of the way up the steep staircase.

'Forgot another meeting,' he called back.

Once safe in his office, Obidiah locked the door and sat at his desk. He touched a series of switches on his desk that erected a security screen around the office and opened a direct channel to the person who buzzed him.

'What took you so long?' asked Nemo.

'Excuse me,' said Clein into the vox. 'We were meeting with Lord Helmawr about the Armand situation.'

'Fine,' said Nemo. 'But if I should ever be forced to buzz three times, our relationship will be terminated.'

Clein appreciated the significance of Nemo's choice of words as well as his intonation. 'Understood.'

'Report.'

'Kauderer and Katerin still run the palace for all intents and purposes,' said Clein. 'Only now, they seem to be working together.'

'That is not good,' said Nemo. 'You must break up their alliance somehow. Together they are too powerful.'

'I have tried,' replied Clein. I know Kauderer sent the Spyrers down into the Hive against Helmawr's orders, but I have no proof. I think I can get Katerin to crack, but I will need leverage in order to give him a final push.'

'Then find proof and start pushing,' said Nemo. 'This is too important. Once I have the item, Lord Helmawr will no longer be an obstacle, but working together these two could find a way to keep the House from crumbling around him. They must be out of the picture before then.'

KAL DODGED UNDER Jonas's power sword and feinted with his sabre toward the Spyrer's thigh. Jonas bit on the feint and Kal brought the hilt up hard on his opponent's chin, knocking him back a step.

'You can't dodge my sword for long, Jerico,' spat Jonas as he rubbed his sore chin.

'I can the way you swing it,' Kal replied. He had to admit that Jonas had pretty good stamina. They'd been dancing for several minutes now, and Kal had gotten in several good hits, but the Spyrer hadn't slowed a step.

He glanced at Yolanda, who was taking on the brute with the grenade launcher. She'd cut off the end of his weapon with her katana and the muscle-bound Spyrer had dropped it in favour of a power axe. Kal didn't know what bothered him more: how Yolanda got her sword so sharp or where these Spyrers had gotten such good weapons.

At least he didn't have to worry about Wotan. Kal's dog had his opponent, a dark-haired and dark-skinned man that Jonas had called Grell, on the ground fighting for his life. Wotan stood on Grell's chest, trying to get his metal jaws around his fleshy neck. The Spyrer had one hand on Wotan's upper jaw and the other on the lower jaw, but he was losing ground fast.

Kal had lost sight of the female, but Scabbs was firing the shotgun at something, so he assumed he would at least get some warning if she came up behind him. Besides, Jerico didn't have time to worry about anything except the power sword shimmering in Jonas's hands. If it did connect, the family reunion would get cut short by exactly one family member.

'GET LYSANNE TO safety,' said Vicksen. 'Break down the door to the Fresh Air if you have to.' Sweat glistened on her cheeks, neck and cleavage. She swiped at the blue spiked hair, which had gone limp and kept getting in her eyes, but it just stuck to her forehead, so she gave up.

'Where are you going?' asked Themis. She cocked her heavy stubber and nestled it in the crook of one arm and then reached down and pulled Lysanne to her feet, supporting the injured Wildcat with her free arm.

'I'm going to finish what we came here to do,' growled Vicksen. 'I'm going to kill Yolanda Catallus.' The new-comer was keeping the vampire busy and Kal's people were fighting the Spyrers. Now was her only chance to get to Yolanda.

She ran across the square, scooping up her chainsword. Ahead, she saw Yolanda standing toe to toe with a huge brute of a Spyrer. He had a barrel chest and a wide, round face topped by short-cropped, brown hair. The epitome of a jar head. They were wrestling, each one holding the other's wrist just below their respective weapons.

The muscles in Yolanda's arms and legs rippled as she used all her force to try to push the brute away, but Vicksen could tell that even as strong as the bounty hunter was, the brute would wear her down eventually. He simply had more mass to throw into the equation.

They twisted and turned in their clench, bringing Yolanda around to face the oncoming Vicksen. The Wildcat leader made a snap decision and fired her plasma pistol at the brute. A ball of highly charged plasma slammed into the Spyrer's back and exploded, sending both combatants sprawling to the ground.

Vicksen was mildly upset that the blast hadn't killed the Spyrer, but there would be plenty of time for that later. His armour lay in pieces and the power axe had gone flying out of his grasp. Vicksen ran up and gave him a swift kick to the head, and then turned to the prone Yolanda.

'Get up,' she yelled. 'It's time to finish this.' Vicksen tossed her plasma pistol to the ground and revved up her chainsword.

VALTIN TURNED BACK to Armand, who seemed to be try-ing to retreat but was moving in slow motion. The younger Helmawr raised his power maul over his head and slammed it down on top of Armand's helmet. The mirrored dome cracked slightly. He brought the maul around for another blow, but Armand was able to turn enough that the weapon just glanced off the side of his head, ripping out several of his feeding tubes.

Armand turned his torso and swung his arms around in a slow arc. Valtin easily stepped back out of reach. Then, ducking under the massive arms of the vampire rig, he swung the maul. Blue energy swirled around the legs of the power suit as the maul struck, chipping and breaking the interlocking plates of armour. Armand's knees buckled and he fell to the ground.

'It's over, Uncle,' said Valtin. He jumped on top of the fallen vampire. 'Now I will kill you as you killed my father.'

'Kill me and you'll never find what I took from Stiv,' Armand wheezed, his voice barely audible through the cracked helmet.

'You think I care about that?' demanded Valtin. 'This is for my father.' He slammed the maul down on

Armand's chest. The power coursed through the armour, cracking several more metal plates. 'You are a blight on House Helmawr, and you must be removed before you bring down the entire House.' Valtin could see the hole in the armour from Armand's earlier battle in the courtyard. He aimed his next shot at that weak point.

'I am but a symptom of the sickness,' said Armand, his voice oddly calm now. 'The whole House stinks of decay and disease. I am the fever that will root out the evil virus within and burn it with holy fire. Only then will the House be cleansed. Only then can I rest.'

'Too bad you won't live long enough to see that day come,' Valtin replied.

He swung the maul down toward the tiny hole in Armand's armour, but the weapon was halted in mid-swing. Valtin looked down. Armand had grabbed hold of the shaft with one hand. The arm of his rig coursed with energy from the maul.

'Wrong, nephew,' said Armand. 'You won't live to see it.' He grabbed the power cell draining device from Valtin's other hand and threw it against the wall of the Fresh Air, and then stood, still holding onto the young Helmawr's arm. 'By the way, thank you for the borrowed power.'

KAL DODGED AND weaved, trying to find an opening for his sabre, but Jonas had grown a little more conservative since the sock to his jaw. Kal had to admit that the Spyrer leader was well-trained. When he concentrated on defence, Jonas was nearly flawless. He was going to need more time to get the better of his well-trained opponent.

Next to them, Wotan had gotten past Grell's flailing arms and had his jaws around the struggling Spyrer's neck. Grell screamed, 'Help! Jonas. Help!.'

Jonas turned toward his comrade and Kal, seeing the opening, moved in. He grabbed the leader by the wrist and slammed the pommel of his sabre on the back of his hand. Jonas dropped his sword. Spinning around, Jerico kicked Jonas in the gut, sending him flying. He then turned to his faithful robot companion. 'Wotan, sit!' he commanded. But the dog continued to apply pressure to Grell's exposed neck. 'Damn!' cursed Kal. 'Wotan! Obey!'

Kal heard a sickening crunch of metal jaw on bone. He reacted instantly, diving at Wotan and pulling him off the prone Spyrer. Grell screamed again as Kal and Wotan tumbled to the ground. By the time Kal got himself untangled from Wotan's scrabbling legs, he was flat on his back and looking up at an extremely upset Grell.

Blood trickled down the front of Grell's shirt from four matching puncture wounds on either side of his neck. He held a plasma pistol pointed at Kal's head. 'Good-bye, cousin!' said Grell.

Jerico looked to the side. He'd dropped his sabre when he tackled Wotan, and it was well out of reach. He raised his hands in protest. 'But I just saved your life!'

'Bit of a mistake for you, then, wouldn't you say?' said Grell as he pulled the trigger.

A blur of motion passed Jerico as he rolled to the side. Grell screamed and Kal heard him fall to the ground just before the plasma ball exploded somewhere behind him. Kal rolled to a crouch and looked back toward Grell. Wotan sat atop the Spyrer, bits of flesh and bone hanging from his mouth. Grell's neck was gone and his head lolled at an angle that made Kal a little queasy.

Being sick wouldn't bring Grell back and there was still Jonas to deal with. Time was running short. The enforcers wouldn't stay away forever. The Spyrer leader, still looking a little dazed from landing on his head, crawled toward his power sword. 'Wotan!' called Kal. 'Fetch!' The dog leapt off Grell's body and scooped up Jonas's sword in his still bloody mouth.

Kal stood and faced Jonas. 'Time's up,' he said. 'Rules change.' Standing with his legs apart and slightly bent, he raised his sabre into attack position, and curled his free arm up over his head. Once again, his positioning was perfect. The wind from the fan across the courtyard blew his long leather coat around his legs as he struck the pose.

'Nice move,' said Jonas. 'But killing me won't save cousin Valtin!' He pointed behind Kal.

The bounty hunter knew it was a trick, but when one of the Escher women screamed, 'Help him! Somebody help!' Kal had to turn and look. As soon as he did, Jonas barrelled into him and they both went sprawling on the ground. In that instant, Kal saw Armand jump onto the ventilation shaft above the fan and disappear into the darkness, carrying Valtin over his shoulder.

# 7: BAD BLOOD

KAL AND JONAS wrestled on the ground in the square outside The Breath of Fresh Air. They rolled back and forth as both men tried to gain an advantage over the other. Jonas had obviously been trained, because he knew moves that Kal had never seen before. He locked his legs around Kal's ankles to take away the bounty hunter's leverage and then snaked a hand under Kal's armpit, grabbed him by the hair at the nape of his neck, and flipped him over onto his back.

In an instant, Jonas had pinned Jerico. Sitting on his chest he pummelled the bounty hunter's face with rock-hard fists. Kal began to laugh in between the hits. First a chuckle, then a couple of snorts, followed by a near-hysterical fit that ended in a series of hacking coughs as he fought for air with the Spyrer sitting on his chest.

Jonas paused, holding his fist in the air as he stared at Kal's smiling face. 'What in the Hive are you laughing about?' he asked. 'You enjoy pain that much?'

Kal continued laughing as he spoke, 'Ha – I just thought of something funny – ha ha, that's all.'

'What?' growled Jonas. 'What's so damned funny?

'You – hoo hoo – stopping hitting me long enough so I could say: Wotan! Attack!' The last two words were barked loud and clear.

Jonas realised his mistake and swung his fist down toward Kal's face one last time, but it was too late. Wotan slammed into Jonas from the side, sending the Spyrer sprawling to the ground again. Kal rolled the other way, got his knees under him, and hopped to his feet. Wotan had landed on top of Jonas and was snapping at the Spyrer leader's neck with his massive metal jaws.

Kal felt his sore jaw and considered letting Wotan have his fun, but Jonas had called Valtin 'cousin', meaning he was yet another long lost relative. Besides, now that they knew the Underhive vampire was Armand in a Spyrer rig, Kal needed as much firepower as possible to get his bounty, and save his nephew.

'Wotan! Sit!' he commanded. 'Guard!' The oversized dog plopped his metal rump down on Jonas's legs, but kept his front legs on the Spyrer's chest. Jonas squirmed under the weight, causing Wotan to growl, which sounded like the buzzing of a chainsword, and chomp his teeth, which looked like a sump rat-trap snapping shut.

Kal looked around. Armand was gone, but the fighting in the courtyard continued. Yolanda and Vicksen were dancing around one another, waving their swords, while Scabbs was leading the last Spyrer on a wild Scabbs chase around the square. The oversized jar-head Spyrer was just coming around next to Yolanda, while the last two Wildcats huddled by the door to the Fresh Air.

This had to stop. If Kal was going to rescue Valtin and put an end to this Underhive Vampire nonsense, he would need a lot of help. To hell with working alone. Dad would just have to understand that sometimes you had to improvise; sometimes you had to go with plan W.

'Everybody!' he called. 'I need your attention! Listen up! Hey! Everybody!'

It was no use. Kal walked over to where he'd dropped his lasguns, picked them up, twirled them in both hands once, twice, three times, and then struck his pose – legs splayed wide and arms outstretched to either side. Somehow the fan across the square knew to speed up and send his coattails flying behind him.

He shot twice with his left hand and twice with his right hand in quick succession.

'Hey!'

'Ow!'

'Yikes!'

'What the–?'

Four perfect shots had disarmed the last four combatants. 'Now that I have your attention, I would like to propose a truce!'

'Now THAT'S AN interesting development,' said Dutt.

Bobo nodded. The two spies were sitting on either side of a window inside one of the abandoned shops on the square. With this entire sector of the city practically shut down due to the vampire scare, the spies pretty much had the run of the district. It kind of took the fun out of it for Markel, who had insisted on entering the shop through the ventilation shaft while Dutt just picked the lock and walked in.

They'd given up all pretext of skulking around each other and had decided to work together for the time being. Dutt just had to watch where he pointed the pict camera and he could only speak freely if he removed the transmitter tooth.

'He's got to realise that Jonas will kill him and the others once they recover the item,' remarked Bobo. He munched on some synthnuts that Jenn had packed for him before he left Madam Noritake's. They still had to talk about her flirting with Jerico, but the food took the edge off of that concern for now.

Dutt grabbed a handful of nuts and munched on them. 'Undoubtedly,' he said through the nuts. It was almost unintelligible, which Bobo realised was exactly what he had been going for.

'Plus, he's going against orders,' continued Bobo. 'Kal was supposed to do this alone. Now he's not only bringing in his friends, but a rival gang, and the Spyrer unit sent to kill him and take the item back.'

'You know what you always say, Nemo,' said Dutt, speaking both to Bobo and to his master, 'Kal Jerico is freaking nuts. This just goes to prove it.'

'They've stopped arguing and are going into the Breath of Fresh Air, well, breaking in.' Bobo looked at Dutt. 'Nemo wouldn't happen to have the Fresh Air bugged, would he?'

Dutt just smiled and nodded.

Markel sat back and tossed a fist full of synthnuts into his mouth. This day hadn't turned out so bad after all, and it had been fun working with Dutt. A spy's life was usually pretty solitary. You might get a little female comfort now and again, but you never made friends; at least not the type you could talk to about work. It was a shame he'd have to kill Dutt before this was over.

KAL ENTERED THE Breath of Fresh Air after the jar-head, Cyklus, busted through the door. 'You didn't have to do that,' he said. 'I've got a key.'

'And where did you get a key from?' asked a voice from behind the bar. 'I never gave you no key.'

'Squatz!' called Kal. 'I'm glad to see you alive.' He walked up to the bar and peered over the top. 'You can come out now. It's safe.'

Squatz climbed onto the step behind the bar and looked at the assemblage in his bar. 'Safe, am I?' he asked. 'With a broken door, three rotten Spyrers in my bar, a blood feud brewing in my front room between two Wildcat leaders, and a vampire on the loose?'

Kal thought for a moment, 'Well, yes,' he said. 'Because now I'm here.'

'Well that makes it all right than, doesn't it,' said Squatz. 'Two things, though. First, you're going to pay for that door.'

'And second?'

'Hand over the key!'

Kal dropped the key on the bar. 'Bring a tray of House Special when you get a chance,' he said, dropping a small pile of credits on the bar. He turned back toward the motley crew he had brought into the bar.

'It'll stunt your growth,' said Squatz.

'You should know,' replied Kal over his shoulder.

It was an interesting scene in the front room. Vicksen and her last two Wildcats stood against one wall, weapons pointed at the Spyrers and at Yolanda. The three Spyrers stood against a second wall, pointing their weapons at the Wildcats and at Kal. Scabbs and Yolanda had taken a seat in the middle, their weapons on the table within easy reach. Wotan sat by the door, wagging his metal tail, which threatened to knock a hole in the wall.

'Now, isn't this more comfortable?' asked Kal. The gangers all glared at him. 'Okay, listen,' he started again, pulling his lasguns out and pointing one at each group. All six gangers levelled their own weapons at Kal. 'I'm not asking us all to be friends, but we will have to work together to stop Ar… the vampire.'

'We care nothing for your so-called vampire,' spat Vicksen. 'It's a Spyrer like these three, and they can all die for all I care.'

'Look,' said Kal. 'Yolanda tells me you want clear rulership over the Wildcats. If you work with us to get the vampire, she will publicly bow to your superior battle skills and declare you the rightful leader.'

'I'll do what?' asked Yolanda. Kal waved his pistol at her and shook his head.

"We'll never work with them,' cried Lysanne, pointing at the Spyrers. She was leaning against the Escher named Themis, and Kal could see she was in a great deal of pain. But there was still a fire in her eyes. 'They killed Ashya, Tor, Tay, and half a dozen other 'Cats.'

'Fine,' replied Kal. 'You can work with Scabbs. Yolanda will work with Jonas's people. We all need to pull together if we're going to defeat Armand.' He looked at Vicksen when he said the name. 'Yes, he is a Spyrer… or was, anyway. But right now, he's a menace to Hive City and the Underhive, and it's up to us to stop him.'

Jonas shook his head. 'You talk nobly, Jerico, but we all know why you're doing this – bounty, pure and simple. Helmawr is paying you handsomely to retrieve the item Armand stole, and you're planning to use us to help make you rich.'

'That was true up until about ten minutes ago,' said Kal. 'But then I saw my nephew pay the price for doing the job I should have been doing.' He tossed his weapons on the table and began pacing. 'I have family I never even knew about. You're my cousin or nephew as well, as are these two, I guess.'

Jonas nodded.

'Well, family never really meant much to me. My mother abandoned me when I was just a baby and it wasn't until a couple of years ago that I found out that Lord Helmawr was my father. Scabbs and Yolanda are the closest I had to family and we take care of each other. Well, now it's time for me to take care of my real family. I'm going to save Valtin, and when we find Armand, you can take the item back to Helmawr. That was your mission, anyway wasn't it? The old man is good at covering his bases, huh?'

'You expect me to believe that you want nothing out of this but a warm, fuzzy feeling for helping out your nephew?'

'That plus the two thousand credit bounty on the vampire's head. That will belong to the three of us.' He sat down with Yolanda and Scabbs and took a long sip of his House Special. It burned his throat.

The room fell silent. All the weapons still pointed at Kal – which he figured was better than firing at him, or each other – but they were beginning to drop lower and lower.

Vicksen was the first to speak. 'What do you want us to do?' she asked.

Kal looked at Jonas, who nodded. 'Your terms are acceptable. We will allow you to help us locate and neutralise Armand.'

'Excellent!' Kal smiled. 'Squatz! Another round of House Special. My cousin Jonas is buying this time.'

Jonas looked like he was about to argue, but dug into his pocket and tossed some credits on the table instead.

Kal's smile grew even larger, but before he could continue, Lysanne moaned and slipped to the floor. Vicksen put her weapons away and motioned to Themis to help her get the injured 'Cat to the table. 'Before we go anywhere,' said Vicksen, 'we need to do something about Lysanne's ankle.'

Kal looked at Jonas. 'I'm certain you didn't leave home without a medi-pack,' he said. 'Why don't you get it out and help our partners deal with their wounded?'

Jonas motioned to Leoni, who produced the medi-pack from her gear. She set it up on the table and began scanning Lysanne's ankle. Lysanne glared at the Spyrer, but with Themis supporting her she relaxed and let Leoni do her work.

Satisfied that the truce would hold up for now at least, Kal picked up his pistols, twirled them, and slammed them home into his holsters. 'Well now, here's what we need to do next,' he said. 'First we need to find Armand. Scabbs will take Wotan and the two Wildcats back into the square to search for clues. Second, we need more firepower for when we do find Armand. Yolanda, you go with...' He pointed vaguely at the Spyrers.

'Cyklus and Leoni,' said Jonas.

'Go with Cyklus and Leoni to get all the rigs and bring them back here,' finished Kal.

'And what will you be doing?' asked Vicksen and Jonas together.

'I need to sit and think,' said Kal. 'And I do my best thinking in a bar with friendly company. I'd prefer to be in the Sump Hole with Scabbs and Yolanda, but you two and this place will just have to do.'

'Thanks,' said Squatz. 'If it's all the same to you, you can all go to the Sump Hole. In fact, any sump hole will do.'

VALTIN'S HEAD POUNDED with a steady rhythm that felt like a spike driving deeper and deeper into his eyes. At first he thought the drumming was his own heart, driving blood and pain into his brain with every beat, but after a time he began to realise that the pounding was external. There was a banging sound outside his head that went along with the vibrations pounding in his brain.

Of course, pain meant that he was alive, which came as a bit of a surprise. The next step, he decided, was to open his eyes and find out why. When he slid his eyelids open, precious little light seeped in, which was good, for he feared that bright light would make his head explode with even more pain. What little light there was came from work lamps that seemed to be attached to railings by the wall.

Where was he? That was what Valtin really wanted to know, as well as the nagging question of why he was alive. He was afraid to broach that other question, though, because he was still a little worried that the answer might be that he wasn't alive at all. Had it not been for his first brief glimpse of Hive City earlier, Valtin could easily have believed it was hell.

He couldn't move, so his field of vision was pretty narrow. There was the wall, which looked slightly curved. It was difficult to tell because of the intertwined mass of pipes, conduits, cables, and wires attached to the wall. There was also a floor, although to call it a floor gave it more credit than it really deserved. It was no more than metal mesh laid across support beams. In fact, looking down through the floor at the jumble of pipes disappearing into the darkness, made Valtin feel like he was floating. Or falling. The sudden vertigo caused his stomach to heave. Very little came up, though, as he hadn't eaten since leaving the Spire.

As Valtin's body shook with dry heaves, new pains flared around his wrists and ankles. His mind seemed a little less cloudy now with the rush of adrenalin that the retching brought with it and he realised the reason he couldn't move was that he was bound hand and foot; trussed up like a calf on its way to slaughter.

He also realised that the banging had ceased, although that did little to lessen the pain in his head. A moment later a pair of bare feet and two hairy legs came into his view. He rolled over a little to get a better look, wincing at the cutting pain in his wrists and ankles.

Towering above him was Armand, naked, carrying a large dagger.

He certainly looked the part of an Underhive monster. His wild hair, all matted and tangled, grabbed at his sweaty neck and shoulders. Fresh cuts covered his filth-covered, half-naked body, some of which looked quite deep. Blood trickled down his stomach from an open wound and Valtin could see blood on the tip of the dagger in his hand.

'Good,' said Armand. 'You're awake – and alive. I was worried, worried, worried. Your blood will stay fresher if you're alive. Good. Good.'

Armand's eyes glowed with almost the same intensity as the artificial eyes in his Spyrer suit.

'Where are we?' asked Valtin. His voice was raspy and hoarse, and the effort of talking made him cough, which brought on another spell of dry heaves.

'High up,' said Armand. 'Very high up. Don't fall. Not as high as dear old father, though. His fall will be much greater. Much greater indeed.'

He's gone completely insane, thought Valtin. I'm being held prisoner by an insane man who drinks blood.

He decided to try again, anyway. 'Why are we here?' he asked.

Armand laughed. It was not the laugh of a man enjoying a joke, but of a man on the edge, a man driven to the brink of hysteria by some horrible personal demons. 'That is the question,' he said, finally. 'We're here to serve. We're here for the greater glory of House Helmawr, the unholy House of Helmawr!'

'I mean,' started Valtin again, his throat finally clear enough to speak more than just a few words. 'Why are we here now? What are you going to do with me?'

'Why, feed off your blood, of course, dear nephew,' he said, a smile blooming on his face. 'I have much more work to do, but your uncle, the other uncle, wants to stop me, so I need time. Time. Time to sleep. To rest. To fix my rig, which you broke. Such a bad boy you are, nephew. But you'll be good inside me. Good noble blood. Better than that wretched Hive scum blood. Even the Goliaths have no strength in their blood… blood… blood…'

He plopped onto the mesh floor and looked right through Valtin, as if the young Helmawr wasn't even there. 'Bad blood. That's the problem you see,' he continued, but he was now speaking to himself. Valtin was sure Armand didn't even realise he was there anymore.

'Tainted. Yes, tainted, that's the word. All of House Helmawr. Tainted by evil. Tainted by all that we've done. Can't get rid of the evil. New blood for old blood. New in, old out. Still tainted. Got the proof. Every evil deed. Every stain on the House from Hell. Ripped the proof right out of the chamber pot. So much evil. So many dead. So much ruined. All for the greater good.'

He looked back at Valtin again. 'That's why we're here. The greater good. But the taint won't wash away. Can't be cut out. Can't be drained away. Goes much deeper. Right down to the soul. How do you cleanse the soul of a House? How do you cleanse the deeds of the past?'

And then he was silent. Valtin stared at his uncle. His other uncle. Wild hair and dirt didn't hide the square jaw and high cheeks; the marks of Helmawr nobility that Armand, Valtin, and Jerico all shared.

Valtin wondered what it was that had finally driven him totally and murderously insane, what House secrets the wayward son had ripped from the chamberlain's head. Then, as he lay there, he noticed that Armand had fallen asleep. Sitting not three metres away,

Armand slept, holding his dagger in his lap, blood trickling down his chest and mixing with dirty sweat. A lone tear hung on his noble Helmawr chin.

'THIS IS WHERE they fought,' said Lysanne. 'Kal's friend and the vampire.' She stood with one leg slightly bent, obviously not trusting her full weight on the injured ankle just yet.

'You sure?' asked Scabbs.

'Do you call her a liar?' accused Themis. She towered over the scabby bounty hunter, glaring at him.

Scabbs shrunk back slightly. 'No,' he said. 'I just… It was chaotic out here. I'm just, you know, making sure she remembers everything.' He turned and started searching the ground. 'Yeesh,' he grumbled. 'She's as bad as Yolanda.'

'I heard that.'

Scabbs turned with a sheepish look on his face, but then tripped over Wotan. Both women began laughing. 'You're a big help,' he said to Kal's dog. 'Why don't you go bite her knee?' He got up and started searching again.

'What are we looking for?' asked Lysanne.

'I don't really know,' replied Scabbs. 'Clues. Anything unusual that might help us figure out why the vampire kidnapped what's-his-name.'

'The nobleman used some sort of device on the vampire's rig,' said Lysanne. 'Turned it off or something.'

'That would have been good to know,' said Scabbs. He stopped and scratched at his face as he stared at the young Wildcat. The sarcasm seemed to be lost on her. 'What happened to it?'

'I don't know,' she said. 'I'm sorry. I was scared.'

'That's okay,' said Scabbs, softening a little. She wasn't much older than a teenager after all. 'I'm scared all the time.' She smiled at him, and he almost tripped over

Wotan again. 'See if you can find that device. I'm sure Kal will want to see it.'

'This is pointless,' said Themis. She was standing over a fallen Wildcat. 'We should be putting our companions to rest, not helping Kal Jerico bag his bounty.'

Scabbs was examining a piece of black metal he found on the ground and only half-heard what Themis had said. 'That's fine,' he said absently as he looked at the odd metal. 'Have a good time.'

Scabbs was fairly certain it was part of Armand's Spyrer rig, but it almost looked like a large fish scale. It was rounded and bulged in the middle. Part of it was scorched and there was hole the size of a credit chip in the middle. He turned it over and found blood smeared on the inside.

When he looked up again, Themis and Lysanne were pulling Wildcat bodies into the middle of the square. 'What in the Hive are you doing?' he asked.

'Taking care of our sisters,' said Lysanne. 'Like you said we could.'

'I did?' Scabbs scratched his head, causing a cascade of dead skin to rain down on his shoulder. 'When did I do that?'

'Just now!' yelled Themis. 'Don't you even listen to yourself?'

'Fine!' said Scabbs. 'Whatever. Wotan and I will search the square.' He moved around toward the fan, looking for any more clues as to where Armand might have gone. He found Valtin's power maul just below the ventilation shafts. It was dead. He also found another body.

'Hey!' he called out. 'I found another Wildca–' He looked again. The body was of a male; Van Saar by the look of the clothes and hair. 'Never mind,' he called back. 'Now, what is this all about?' he wondered. He checked the pockets for loose credits and palmed the ganger's weapon, a beat-up laspistol. 'Hmmph. Guess I can leave it here,' he said. 'Let Kal sort it out later.'

'Hey!' called Lysanne.

Scabbs looked up. There was a big bonfire in the middle of the square. Black smoke rolled up from the pile of bodies. Luckily for Scabbs, he was underneath the fan and the smell was being blown away from him. Lysanne was running toward him.

'I found the gadget,' she said as she came up to him. 'Valtin's gadget. I found it. I found it.' Lysanne threw her arms around Scabbs and hugged him.

The stunned bounty hunter had no idea at all how to respond. 'Thanks,' was all he could think to say.

'DERINDI!' SCREAMED A VOICE. 'Answer me, you worthless pile of hive scum!'

He heard the voice, but it sounded like it was very far away, as if it was part of a dream. The voice seemed to echo in his head. Perhaps it was a dream.

'Derindi!' screamed the voice again. 'Answer me now or the last thing you see in this world will be Seek and Destroy!'

Well, that was an odd thing to say. It must have been part of his dream. He was the sultan of a desert planet; a hot, dry, sandy desert planet and he was on a pilgrimage. This must have been the voice of his god telling him to seek and destroy the lord's enemies.

Seek and Destroy. Very odd. But also somewhat familiar. He had heard those words somewhere recently. Where had he heard those names? Names? They *were* names. Seek and Destroy – the twins who worked for Nemo! Nemo. The voice was Nemo. Oh crap!

Derindi awoke with a start, hearing only the last part of Nemo's next message in his ear. '…one last chance. I can find you wherever you hide, you little weasel.'

He tried to speak but his mouth was bone dry and full of dust. All that came out was a raspy wheeze. Derindi sat up. He was covered in hive dust and itched all over, and something seemed to be crawling up his leg inside his pants. He tried to ignore the itch and the dread of what might be inside his clothes and concentrate on talking. He spat out as much dust as he could and then swallowed the rest in an effort to get some saliva moving.

'Yes,' he said. 'I'm here. Yes. Don't hurt me. I'm here. Yes. What do you need?'

'Okay,' said Nemo. 'Just shut up already and report. What have you been doing?'

Derindi wasn't sure which order he should follow. He took a guess and decided to keep talking. 'I, uh, I was knocked out during a battle with the Wildcats, sir.' He started. He wasn't sure how much of the truth he should really tell. 'I'm sorry, sir. I, um, lost Scabbs and Yolanda.'

'Yes, yes,' said Nemo in his ear. 'I know. They are in the Breath of Fresh Air with Jerico and the Wildcats. Get over there and don't let them out of your sight again. Bring me the item they are all after and you will be a very rich man.'

'Yes sir,' said Derindi. 'Thank you, sir. Right away. Thank yo–' The creepy crawly reached his crotch and bit down hard.

'Derindi!'

'Yes sir?' he squeaked, as he slapped at the bug in his pants.

'Shut up!'

'Yes sir.'

Later, after cleaning most of the dust and bugs out of his clothes, Derindi started walking toward the nearest dome entrance. It wasn't far, though he grumbled silently to himself the entire way there, staring at the white dust as he kicked it with every step. He happened to look up just as he reached the final rise in the dunes and saw several people standing near the entrance.

One of them looked familiar. Tall, leggy, spiked hair waving above her forehead and a katana sheathed at her waist. Yolanda. She was staring up into the struts above the Wastes. Derindi pulled out his pict camera and zoomed in. There were two people up there on grapnel lines, cutting something big out of some webbing.

'Nemo, are you getting this?' he asked so quietly he thought the transmitter might not pick it up.

'Yes, Derindi,' came the instant reply. 'Good work. Those are Helmawr's Spyrers. They're retrieving their rigs. Follow them and Yolanda.'

It didn't take the Spyrers long to get the rigs down. There were four separate rigs. The Spyrers donned two of them and looked like they planned to carry the other two. Yolanda argued with them for a few minutes, pulling her katana half way out of its sheath at one point. Finally, the female Spryer tossed her hands in the air and handed one of the spares to Yolanda. The male Spyrer carried the other and all three re-entered the dome.

Derindi ran the rest of the way to the entrance. He stuck his head in to make sure they had moved on, and then slipped inside and ran down the access tunnel to catch up.

YOLANDA WAS AMAZED at how comfortable she felt in the Spyrer rig. She had expected to feel claustrophobic and clumsy in the metal suit, but it felt no more binding than a tight set of clothes, which she was quite used to wearing. The rig's hydraulics responded to her muscle commands as well as, if not better than, her own arms and legs.

Ordinarily, no mere Hiver could wear a Spyrer rig. Each was carefully crafted to match its wearer's own size and requirements, and its operation was based on a variety of control systems so sensitive that only its original occupant could stand any chance of figuring them out. Still, Yolanda was no mere Hiver. She had once been a Catallus, not that she considered herself such anymore. Nonetheless, she had in her youth been fitted for a Spyrer herself and, more importantly, had received the basic subcutaneous grafts. Perhaps it was this preparation that now paid off unexpectedly.

By the time they returned to the square, Scabbs and the Wildcats had gone back inside the Fresh Air to show Kal and their leaders what they had found. Cyklus dropped Jonas's rig off and the three of them went back out to see if they could follow Armand's trail.

Yolanda and Leoni wore identical rigs. She had called it a Malcadon rig. Apparently, twin bulbs on each wrist could shoot out iron-hard and very sticky webbing. Armour plates and spines protected the web-producing hardware on her back. The pistons and hydraulics in the arms and legs gave her excellent mobility.

She and Leoni had no trouble at all climbing up to the fan housing. Cyklus was able to lumber his way up to the fan as well, but it was obvious his rig was made for power and defence, not mobility. There was no way he'd be able to scale the vertical ventilation shaft, which was where Armand had taken Valtin.

'I'll stay here and guard you,' he said. The missile launchers that encircled his wrists spun, bringing a new missile into firing position on each arm.

'Impressive,' said Yolanda. 'Very cool!' She looked at Leoni. 'How do I fire my web spinners.'

'No way,' said Leoni. 'I showed you how to climb and jump. That's all you'll need for this excursion. No weapons. I'll spin us some rope for climbing. You just follow me, and try not to fall.'

Yolanda watched as Leoni shot the webs high up onto the shaft. She just seemed to point her hands and the webs came out, but there was something odd about how she held her fingers. Must be a switch or sensor on the palm, thought Yolanda. She decided to experiment later while Leoni wasn't watching.

As the web hardened, it started to look like steel cable. Leoni grabbed hold of it with both gloved hands, braced herself against the ventilation shaft and climbed the web rope. She scooted her legs up the metal duct-work as she pulled her body up the rope. It almost looked like she was walking up the side of the shaft.

Yolanda let her get a fair way up before grabbing the rope. She didn't want to let the Spyrer get out of sight. But she did want the rope to stop swaying. And she wanted at least a little warning should Leoni lose her grip and plummet.

It took them several minutes to scale the entire shaft. It went quite a way up and Leoni had to shoot new strands several times during their ascent. They eventually reached a catwalk attached to the roof of the dome. When Yolanda pulled herself up over the lip she could see Leoni bending over some dark object off to the side. It was a body; Van Saar by the look of it, and as white as the dust in the Wastes.

Leoni looked up. 'What in the Hive happened to him?'

'Armand,' said Yolanda. She recognised the pale colouring and sunken cheeks. 'Check his neck. Do you see puncture marks?'

Leoni pulled the dead ganger's collar down, showing two red holes in his neck. 'What the–? He really is a vampire?'

'He drains the blood of his victims,' said Yolanda, matter-of-factly. 'We don't know what he does with it, but I doubt he's filling a pool.'

'Well, he went this way from the ventilation shaft once today,' said Leoni. 'It's a good bet he followed the same path with cousin Valtin.'

They trotted down the catwalk for some distance until they found another body. 'Van Saar again,' said Yolanda. 'He's been feeding more and more each day. I doubt Valtin has much time left.'

They ran on, but found no more bodies, and the catwalk ended not too far past the second one. They backtracked to the second body, checking above, below and to the sides of the catwalk as they went. Just before they got back to the body, Yolanda noticed something familiar along the ceiling some way out from the catwalk. All of the pipes, conduits and ductwork in the area converged on one spot, which from her vantage point just looked like a large dark spot on the ceiling.

'Is there a torch on this rig anywhere?' asked Yolanda. She leaned out a little to get a better look.

'No,' replied Leoni. 'But I've got photo contacts. What do you see?'

'Check out that dark spot right there,' said Yolanda, pointing at the convergence point. 'What is it?'

Leoni followed Yolanda's finger out toward the ceiling. 'It's an access shaft, I think,' she said. 'Must angle back toward us. I can't actually see into it, but all the pipes turn and run into the opening.'

'That's what I was afraid of,' said Yolanda. 'Armand's gone. He used one of those shafts to escape from Glory Hole. He could be anywhere in the Hive by now.'

KAL SAT AT the table and thought, with a bottle of Squatz's House Special in one hand and his lasgun in the other. He spun the weapon idly as he considered the evidence that had been brought in. Bodies of Van Saar (from a battle Squatz had witnessed earlier), information about two utility access tunnels Armand had used for his escapes, reports of attacks up and down the Hive; nearly two dozen in just a few days in many different domes. He was like a ghost, or a vampire with bat wings, able to fly off into the night without trace.

It all connected somehow, but there was still a piece missing from the puzzle. What wasn't he seeing? Where was the missing piece? Where had Armand taken Valtin?

Kal looked at the items Scabbs and the Wildcats had brought in. They were arrayed on the table in front of him. There was a broken and bloody piece of Armand's armour, Valtin's power maul, which was completely drained of power, and the device his nephew had used to incapacitate the Spyrer rig, which now lay in several pieces.

An argument had broken out by the bar. Again.

'He's dead already,' said Leoni. 'We just regroup and wait for the next set of bodies to show up.'

'Typical noble reaction to Hiver deaths,' spat Vicksen. 'Follow the trail of dead gangers to your precious brother.'

'Yeah, and you can kill a few yourself along the way, just for sport,' added Themis.

'We're just saving you the trouble of killing each other,' said Cyklus. He ducked as a bottle whipped past his head. A second one smashed on the front of his rig.

'Look,' said Jonas, stepping in between Cyklus and the Wildcats. 'It's our cousin he's taken hostage.'

'But it's our family lying dead in the square at his – and *your* – hands,' Vicksen retorted. She stood inches from Jonas, her blue hair waving above her head as she stared down the Spyrer leader.

'You'd better do something, Jerico,' said Lysanne.

He looked up at the young Wildcat and suddenly remembered something she had said. 'Lysanne, right?' he asked.

'Yes.' She nodded her head.

'You were closest to the vampire when Valtin showed up, right?'

She nodded again.

'You said, he pushed the button and the vampire stopped moving.'

'He – your nephew – said something about draining the power cell.'

'So, how did Armand get enough power back to defeat Valtin and carry him off?'

'I don't know, sir.'

Kal spun his weapon and thought. Drained the cell. He looked at the drained power maul. 'Lysanne, this is important. Did you ever see the vampire absorb anything?

'Absorb?'

'You know, suck up – not like blood – power, energy.'

She nodded her head, excitedly. 'Yes. Yes. That's how I killed that flying Spyrer. I shot the vampire and he reflected the blast at her. It was cool!'

The whole bar went silent. Kal looked up. Vicksen and Jonas were still standing toe-to-toe, but both had stopped shouting at each other.

'You killed Chimone?' yelled Jonas. 'Why you little bitch.'

Vicksen slapped him hard across the face. 'Your bitch deserved it. She killed several of my girls.'

Kal jumped out of his chair and rushed between the two leaders. 'Ladies,' he said, 'Both of you are pretty. Now, stow it. We can worry about who killed whom

later. I know where Armand has taken Valtin, and I'm
sure he's still alive. But we have to hurry.'

# 8: SHAFTED AGAIN

'MIGHT I HAVE a moment of your time, captain?' asked Obidiah Clein. He stood in the doorway to Katerin's office, a wan smile on his doughy face.

Katerin spread his hands apart to indicate the pile of paperwork cluttering his desk. 'I am quite busy, Clein,' he said. 'Can this wait? All these extra meetings in the secure room have put me way behind on requisitions for the month. If I don't sign them, the royal guard goes hungry. And believe me, you don't want hungry guards.'

'I'm sorry?' said Clein. His eyebrows wrinkled in confusion.

'Sorry,' said Katerin. 'Old military saying. Hungry soldiers make for angry villagers.'

'Oh. I see.' But it was obvious to Katerin that the young political officer didn't see. 'It is a matter of some importance. I think the men will get by for five minutes without their papers signed.'

Katerin pushed the pile of papers to the side. 'Of course, Obidiah. I'm always available for one of our lord's advisors.' He actually kept most of the sarcasm out of his voice.

Clein gave another little half-smile and then slipped inside the door, closing it after him. 'Can we speak privately?'

'You did close the door,' commented Katerin.

'I mean,' said Clein, his smile having disappeared, 'is this room secure?'

'Ah. Yes. Just one moment.' Katerin reached under his desk and touched a switch. Before returning his hand to the desk top, he hit a second switch as well. 'That should do it,' he said. A bead of perspiration formed on the top of his head. He hated this cloak and dagger stuff.

Clein pushed the papers back toward the centre of the desk and sat on the edge, forcing Katerin to look up at the short advisor. 'I have evidence that Hermod Kauderer sent Spyrers into Hive City to murder Lord Helmawr's son.'

'Is that right?' asked Katerin. He tried to look innocent, but the bead of sweat on his brow was already snaking its way toward his bushy eyebrows while other beads blossomed up top.

'And further,' continued Clein. 'I have reason to believe that you are working with Kauderer in a conspiracy to seize power in the house.'

'I – we, that is – I never intended… '

'Do you deny it?' asked Clein. He leaned forward, further invading Katerin's personal space.

The captain grabbed his handkerchief from the desk and dabbed at the sweat, which was now streaming down his head into his eyebrows and beard. He took a breath before answering. 'What is your proof?' he asked.

There was only the briefest hesitation before Clein answered. 'That shouldn't concern you right now,' he said. 'What should concern you is how you can get yourself out of this jam.'

The room fell silent for a long moment. 'I'm listening,' Katerin prompted finally.

'If you played an unwitting role,' said Clein, 'then you

might be saved the embarrassment and dishonour of losing your commission if you were to come clean immediately and help me expose this conspiracy. There's no telling how deep it runs.'

Clein leaned back away from Katerin and let the wan little smile cross his face again. The captain was amazed at the transparency of the political officer's interrogation tactics. After years of bantering with Kauderer, who was a master at eliciting information, these amateur attempts seemed as obvious as if Clein had come in with a cattle prod and a whip.

Still, he dabbed at the continuing flow of sweat before answering. 'What would I have to do?'

Clein slipped off the desk and took a seat on the chair. Katerin knew this was supposed to make him feel like they were equals again, working together to right the horrible wrong. 'Help me gather evidence, more evidence against Kauderer. Perhaps record your conversations with him.'

'Then we'll turn the evidence over to Lord Helmawr?'

'Yes,' said Clein. Again there was the slightest hesitation. 'We'll put all the evidence together, yours and mine, and present it to him.'

'I'll see what I can do,' said Katerin. 'Recording Kauderer won't be easy, and could be dangerous. He is a master spy after all.'

'Yes, but he trusts you,' said Clein. 'At least as much as he trusts anyone. You'll be fine.'

Yes I will, thought Katerin. But I have my fears about you. He let a worried smile cross his face as he got up and shook Clein's hand. After the little man left, Captain Katerin closed the door and returned to his desk. He wiped his forehead and then heard a panel open behind him.

'You heard everything?' he asked.

'Yes I did,' said Kauderer, as he stepped into the office. 'Very interesting.'

Katerin looked up at the spy who'd been in his closet. 'He knows what we're doing.'

Kauderer came around the desk and stared at the door. 'But has no evidence yet.' He turned to look at the sweating Captain of the Guard. 'You did well. I honestly thought he had you worried.'

'I was, a little,' admitted Katerin. 'At first, but the man is an amateur.'

'Still it is good to worry,' said Kauderer. 'We need to act quickly.'

Now he smiled at the captain, but Katerin could never read the man's hawkish face, so couldn't be sure if it was genuine compassion or an act to get his cooperation. At this point, it didn't really matter.

Katerin sighed. 'What do you need me to do?'

'How DO YOU know Valtin's not dead?' asked Yolanda. She sat at the bar, still wearing the Spyrer rig. She'd crushed three bottles of House Special in her gloved hand before getting the hang of controlling the rig's enhanced grip. Good job she hadn't had to contend with any intimate itches in the meantime, she thought to herself.

'It's simple, really,' said Kal. He paced the length of the bar as he explained, pausing at critical junctures for dramatic effect. With Kal it was always fifty per cent substance and fifty per cent performance.

'How many Hivers has Armand killed and drained?' he asked as he paced. He didn't wait for an answer. 'Two dozen, perhaps more now with the Van Saar? And how many has he dragged off? A few to drain in a less public place or to hide away and keep his secret safe.'

'So?' interjected Jonas. 'He's dragged some off, just like he dragged Valtin off.'

'Not exactly just like Valtin,' said Kal. 'Every single body he dragged off was already dead, and all were found within several hundred metres of where he killed them, drained and left to rot.'

He paused to let it all sink in, but the group seemed less than impressed by his oration. 'But where is Valtin's body?' He must have carried it out of the dome with him. Why would he continue to carry Valtin's dead body when he could have easily drained him on the cat-walk and left him with the other Van Saar bodies?'

Again, he was met with blank stares. Even Scabbs looked bored. He sat at the table, tinkering with Valtin's gadget and absentmindedly picking at the scabs on his arms.

'Quit the theatrics, Kal, and get to the point,' said Yolanda. She grabbed at her bottle, but accidentally spun a web around it instead.

Kal threw his hands up into the air in desperation. 'Armand carried Valtin out of Hive City even though we weren't chasing after him. He could have easily drained him before leaving, but opted to carry him instead.'

'Why?' asked Vicksen.

'Aha!' cried Kal. 'Exactly. Why would he do that? That is the question we need to ask ourselves...'

'Kal!' pleaded Yolanda.

'Because Armand's rig malfunctioned,' he said. 'Or, and this is the more interesting notion, Valtin somehow drained its power cell with that gizmo.' He pointed at the table just as Scabbs pulled two of the pieces apart. 'Try to fix it, Scabbs, not break it even more. We may need it.'

'Okay, fine,' said Jonas. 'Cousin Valtin is alive and well...'

'Until Armand can recharge the rig's power cell,' finished Kal.

'So how does that help us find him?'

'It doesn't,' said Kal.

'Then why in the Hive are we sitting here listening to you prattle on?'

'Because I do know where he went,' said Kal. 'I think Armand has a base of operations in the Underhive. That's where he's gone to recharge. That's where he's taken Valtin; probably for a snack later on. And that's where we'll most likely find the item.'

'Where is it?' asked Jonas.

Kal looked at the Spyrer and smiled. 'As soon as that gadget is working again, I'll take us all there.'

'HELMAWR'S RUMP!' EXCLAIMED Dutt. 'Tell us where he is!' He slammed his fist down on the window sill. 'I can't believe the luck of that bounty hunter. There's no way he knows we're listening. I could have gotten the jump on them all.'

Bobo just sat and smiled. For the moment, Jerico's luck was his luck. 'He doesn't trust the Spyrers any more than he trusts Nemo,' he said. 'Looks like it'll be a rat race all the way to the end, and I wouldn't have it any other way. Gets the blood moving, doesn't it?'

The little spy popped another handful of synthnuts into his mouth and stared through the window at The Breath of Fresh Air across the courtyard. With his photo contacts, he could peer into the dimly lit bar well enough to see the bodies moving around the front room. While Dutt sat and fumed about missed opportunities, Bobo enjoyed his synthnuts and waited for Jerico's uneasy coalition to get on the move.

Over the next half-hour, Bobo watched Scabbs working at the table. He couldn't tell what the little half-breed was doing at this distance, but he could hear him muttering and swearing through Nemo's hidden voxbug. The rest of the crew alternated between silent drinking and heated arguments over such trivial matters as life and death.

As he watched, Bobo noticed some movement at the other end of the square. He refocused his photo contacts and took a closer look. 'What in the–?' He looked again and started to laugh.

'What's so funny?' asked Dutt.

Bobo pointed and continued to laugh. He could hardly breathe, let alone speak, at the moment. Dutt stared at the spot where Bobo pointed with a puzzled expression for a moment and then broke out laughing as well.

In an alley at the far corner of the square, Derindi attempted to climb a water pipe attached to the building. There must have been decent hand and foot holds down low, but once he got about halfway he kept slipping as he tried to scramble up to the roof. The two spies watched in amazement as the snitch clawed his way up the side of the building.

'Pretty determined, isn't he?' asked Dutt.

'I wonder what he's doing here?' mused Bobo. He grabbed some more synthnuts and watched the show. The little weasel was far more entertaining than Jerico and his crew at the moment.

Dutt was oddly silent. Bobo glanced at him. 'He's working for Nemo? Why in the world would Nemo use that bumbling idiot?'

Bobo could see Dutt working through some inner turmoil. Finally, he removed his transmitter tooth and pocketed it. 'Okay, we're working together, right? Nemo told him to keep an eye on Jerico, but he was just supposed to be a diversion. We all assumed he'd get caught as soon as he started, which would allow me to work in secrecy. Funny thing is, he's pretty good at staying hidden.'

'Most snitches are,' agreed Bobo. 'At least the ones who live long enough to snitch on anybody.'

The both turned to watch Derindi again. He had gotten one hand on the lip of the roof, but had lost his footing and was just hanging there by his fingers while his legs flailed and kicked at the building.

'Now you owe me something,' said Dutt. 'I shared with you, you need to reciprocate.'

Bobo thought about it. 'Hmm,' he said. 'That was pretty trivial, but okay. I'll give you a nugget. Of course, you're going to owe me back after this one.'

'I'll be the judge of that,' said Dutt. He chuckled and pointed at Derindi. The snitch had both hands on the edge of the roof and had just slammed his forehead against the wall.

'Nemo's man inside House Helmawr is not what he appears.'

Bobo let the statement sit there in the silence that filled the room. It was a fishing expedition, pure and simple, but he didn't want to push too hard. Dutt was good, and if he tried to set the bait too soon, he'd lose him for sure. He'd wiggle it in front of him again later. He knew Nemo must have a man on the inside. Finding out who would not just mean a promotion, it might just answer some of the nagging questions he had about this whole mission.

Instead, he stared intently at Derindi, who had gotten one leg over the edge and finally pulled himself onto the roof. At that moment, the two spies heard Scabbs say, 'I got it!' In less than a minute, the gang of nine emerged from the Fresh Air, with Wotan the metal dog nipping at the Spyrer legs as they strode across the courtyard.

'Looks like we're on the move again,' said Bobo.

He glanced one last time at Derindi, zooming his contacts in to see the weasel's face. Along with his other talents, Bobo was a pretty good lip reader. Derindi, seeing Kal and company crossing the square, swore profusely and then headed toward the water pipe to climb down again. Bobo just laughed.

VALTIN SAT WITH his back up against the pipes. His head had cleared a little and Armand had been kind enough to prop him up, so now he could see more of his surroundings. He suspected that the only reason Armand had moved him was to keep an eye on his hostage.

Valtin sat on what appeared to be a service lift in an enormous utility access shaft. Pipes of all sizes lined the walls of the shaft, disappearing into the darkness above him and past the mesh floor below. He could just barely see the far side of the shaft in the dim light of the work lamps, which he could now tell were wired to the railings of the lift platform.

His ankles were bound tight with copper wire which dug into his skin every time he moved. His wrists were bound behind his back, and from the pain he felt, Valtin was sure Armand had used copper wire for that task as well.

The lift sat just outside an alcove or access tunnel. The back of the tunnel was pitch black, so he couldn't tell if it ended or not. Armand paced back and forth near the mouth of the passage, which he had lit with a few extra work lamps. At first, Valtin wasn't sure what the elder Helmawr was doing, but then he saw Armand holding part of his rig.

Tubes ran off the top and flopped around on the ground as Armand twisted it back and forth, as if looking for something. He finally found what he needed, and then grabbed a tool from a box at his feet. He worked the tool for several minutes and then dropped it back in the box and set the hunk of rig aside.

He came toward Valtin carrying a thick, grey disc about the size of a dinner plate. Valtin immediately recognised the object. It was the power cell for Armand's rig that he'd drained during the battle. Valtin pulled his knees up, hoping to get a chance to kick the cell out of Armand's hands, but his uncle never got that close.

He stopped at the edge of the lift, next to one of the work lamps. Casually, with the calm air that only the truly crazy attain, Armand yanked the lamp from its housing and tossed it over the edge of the lift, leaving nothing but bare wires. Valtin counted the time it took before the lamp hit bottom, but while he heard it bang against the walls, the clattering simply continued to grow fainter and fainter until he simply couldn't hear it anymore. It was a long way to the bottom.

Valtin looked back at Armand. It was hard to tell what he was doing now because of the missing light, but it seemed like he was trying to connect the live wires to the power cell. Valtin could see power jumping from the ends of the wires to Armand's fingertips, but there was no recognition of pain on his face. Once he finished hotwiring his power cell, Armand set it down on the handrail and turned to go back into the access tunnel.

They hadn't talked since Armand's manic rant about the tainted Helmawr blood. Valtin wondered if he could get any useful information out of his crazed uncle. He cleared his throat and said, 'Um.'

Armand twirled around and stared at Valtin, his eyes wide open in an honest look of surprise, as if he had no idea anyone else was there with him in the shaft. 'Nephew!' he said. 'Good to see you again. Don't worry.

Supper won't be long now.' He then turned and disappeared into the darkness at the back of the passage.

HERMOD KAUDERER SAT at his desk trying to determine the best course of action against Obidiah Clein. The hawkish Kauderer kept a spartan and tidy office. He had no personal effects, no books or bookcases, no files or filing cabinets; not even any desk drawers. He kept everything he needed in plain sight, and placed in positions precise to within a millimetre at all times. It would be next to impossible to hide anything in Kauderer's office that he could not spot at once and remove.

He had no pict terminal either, or any other device of any kind in the office (at least not visible to the naked eye). He distrusted any communication device that left a trace or record. Nor did he use paper and pen. Kauderer committed everything to memory and transmitted all messages verbally. He never left a paper trail and he could never get caught by means of eavesdropping in his own office, as it was well shielded from external listening devices at all times.

Kauderer did his best thinking at the desk. With no distractions calling for his attention, he could devote one hundred per cent of his quite abundant brain power to whatever task he set before himself, which at the moment was one Obidiah Clein. He could simply kill the odious little man in his sleep, but that was bound to bring repercussions from any number of sources. You didn't just kill one of Lord Helmawr's advisors and hope to walk away clean.

That, of course, was what currently kept Clein at bay as well. Clein needed hard evidence against Kauderer before he could move. He was trying to use Katerin to get that evidence, which would ultimately fail. The problem with Clein, thought Kauderer, is that he's too stuck in the real world. Why look for evidence when you can create it instead?

An idea began to form in Kauderer's mind. Evidence could point in any direction if handled properly, and it could find its way into any number of hands as well. An odd series of knocks at his door broke the intrigue master's concentration. He played back the sequence in his mind and translated the coded message. It was time.

Captain Katerin had set up a meeting with Clein, ostensibly to discuss how to gather the evidence against Kauderer. They were now in Katerin's office, which would give Hermod fifteen to twenty minutes of uninterrupted time in Clein's office, more than enough for a professional intrigue operative such as he.

He left his office and strode through the palace, making sure to be seen by a number of high-ranking officials on his way to the lower levels and the secure room. However, upon entering the antechamber – the darkest room in the entire palace – he made a slight detour to the side wall. He tapped a code into a pad concealed in the wall and entered a secret passage that opened before him.

Hermod now had complete access to almost the entire palace. He had the map of the secret passageways committed to memory, so it was a simple matter to make his way up to Clein's office and enter, the same way he had accessed Katerin's office earlier. Kauderer could have entered the passage from his office, but now had an irrefutable alibi should he need one. He was meeting with Lord Helmawr, whom he knew to be napping in his office at the moment.

Clein's office was a mess. Kauderer had no idea how he could find anything in the clutter. Papers were strewn everywhere on every single horizontal surface.

His desk was covered in a mound of papers, books and file folders. Messages were pasted on the walls, chairs and even on his pict monitor. The bookcases were stacked two and three volumes deep and crammed into every single pocket of space on every shelf. Boxes filled with even more books were heaped in every corner, some of which had fallen over and then been pushed out of the way to make a path from the desk to the door.

When Kauderer opened the panel access to Clein's office, a stack of boxes nearly fell over on him. He had to prop it up and sidle through the opening, and then close the panel behind him lest the boxes spill into the secret passage. He looked at the office and realised that fifteen minutes wouldn't be nearly enough.

'First things first,' he said, as he donned a pair of skintight gloves. He entered a few commands on Clein's control panel, sending a brief message that would appear on Katerin's monitor. It said, simply, 'stall.' A few more commands gave Kauderer complete access to all of Clein's files. He checked Clein's daily itinerary for the past week. Oddly, the file was empty. He checked the contacts file. Again, empty.

Was he covering his tracks? Kauderer glanced down at the mess on the desk. A scrap of paper sat on the top of the pile. It read: 'Meet Kat, Re. Kau' with a time and date. The time was now. The other scraps of paper had similar notes. Messages from subordinates, notes about calls, meeting schedules; they were all written on pieces of paper and then pasted on the walls or left lying on the desk.

'How does the man function?' Kauderer muttered. If Clein had kept his records in some kind of legible order like any normal person, it would have been a simple matter of accessing the files and comparing schedules to itineraries to find holes in his day, or combing through his data for hidden files or messages.

In an odd way, he and Clein were alike. Kauderer kept all of his information in his head to ensure against just this kind of data mining. Clein seemed to do it because he was a slob, or perhaps he was the classic absent-minded professor, spending too much time researching and too little learning how to function in the real world. Kauderer had to remind himself that up until just a few days ago, Clein was a junior political officer, toiling away in near obscurity.

'I just have to think like Clein,' Kauderer said to himself. He picked up a pile of folders from the man's chair and sat at the desk. He looked at the folders, assuming they would be the most recent additions to the mess. They all seemed to deal with political issues with other houses. It looked like he was getting himself up to speed on the current political climate in the Spire. He sat the folders on the floor.

Kauderer needed to think, but the clutter made it difficult for his ordered mind to concentrate. Clein was working for someone. There was no other way such a junior official could have risen so far so fast, unless he had gotten outside help. But from the look of this office, Clein was no spy, at least not a professional. That meant he would think like an amateur. He wouldn't hide his biggest secrets in plain sight where nobody would think to look. He would hide them in dark corners which were like beacons to thieves and agents alike.

He scanned the office again, this time looking not for items within the clutter, but at the structure of the clutter itself. When he saw it, Kauderer felt like kicking himself for not noticing the incongruity earlier. One pile of boxes in the back corner of the room, quite close to the desk, had been very purposefully stacked to look like a haphazard pile. But it was obvious to Kauderer's practiced eye that the boxes had been arranged in such a way that they could be moved without upsetting the pile.

He rose from the chair, replaced the folders to within millimetres of where they had been originally, carefully moved the chair back to its original position, and then stepped over a pile of books to get to the stack of boxes. He slid it out and looked at the floor. One of the tiles had minute scratch marks on the edge from where Clein had prised it up.

Kauderer pushed on the opposite edge and the tile flipped up. The floor below had been cut away, allowing access to the space between the floor joists. Kauderer reached in and pulled out a box. Inside the box he found about a dozen canisters used for sending messages via the Hive tube system.

'Perfect,' said Kauderer. He pocketed a single canister and then replaced the box, the tile, and the stack of boxes. He checked the room to make sure he had left no mark of his scrutiny, then opened the access panel and left Clein's office.

'WE SHOULD BE able to gain access just up ahead,' said Jerico. They were trotting down a large utility tunnel, like many that ran beneath and between the Hive City domes. Pipes carrying everything from power and water to message canisters and effluvium ran along one side of the tunnel. The one-metre diameter pipes were stacked five high and three deep on large metal racks.

The walkway next to the racks was only wide enough for the gang to walk two abreast. Cyklus actually had difficulty getting through some of the narrower sections in his bulky rig. Light came from circular lamps hanging from the ceiling, but these were spaced about ten metres apart, giving the tunnel eerie pools of light all along its length.

'That's what you said half an hour ago,' commented Vicksen.

'And half an hour before that as well,' added Jonas.

The entrances to these utility tunnels were hidden in the dark recesses of the sewers and locked at all times. Only maintenance workers were supposed to have access to the maze of tunnels, but maintenance personnel are notoriously underpaid and easily bribed, so most bounty hunters and many of the more prominent gang leaders all had keys and had mapped out the sections of the tunnels they used most often.

Kal had a map of the entire complex of utility tunnels under Hive City. It had cost him the credits of five bounties to get it, but it had paid off five times that amount over the years, in bounties he never would have been able to collect without the map.

Unfortunately, they had come into the tunnels through a different entrance than the one marked on Kal's map. It had been thirty minutes before he had realised his mistake and another thirty before he had asked Scabbs for help, but now Jerico was confident that they were near their objective; confident enough to finally tell his ersatz gang where they were headed.

'This time is different,' Kal said with a smile on his face. 'Scabbs has figured out where he went wrong–'

'Where *I* went wrong–' began Scabbs.

Kal continued. 'And you are all about to see something the likes of which very few alive today in the Hive have seen.' They had come to a spot in the tunnel where the pipes made a ninety-degree turn toward the wall, plunging through the wall and leaving a gap in the bank of pipes. The pipes seemed to emerge again from the wall five metres further on, where they once again turned and continued running down the tunnel under the pools of light as far as the eye could see.

Kal turned and scanned the bare section of wall. There was a double door set into the concrete wall, but it had no knobs nor any visible lock. Kal found what he was looking for on the far side of the door: a small panel set between two of the pipes coming out of the wall. Opening the panel revealed a key pad. Kal grabbed the map back from Scabbs and folded and unfolded it, looking for the access number.

'Where in the Hive are we?' asked Jonas. 'Tell us now or I'll kill you, take that map from your dead hands, and open the door myself.'

Every member of the group was nodding in agreement after this statement, even Scabbs and Yolanda, so Kal thought it best to finally reveal what he had figured out. 'The vampire, my own brother Armand Helmawr, has had unparalleled access to all levels of the Hive,' he said. 'There's only one way he could have gotten everywhere he's been in the last few days…'

Kal had found the code and tapped it into the panel. The doors slid apart, disappearing into the tunnel wall with a slight hiss. Beyond was utter darkness. Kal flicked on a torch and beamed its light through the door. The pipes from the tunnel could be seen intersecting other pipes that ran up and down in a huge vertical shaft. The torch light just barely licked the far wall of the shaft some fifteen metres away from the door.

'He followed the utility pipes,' finished Kal. He tossed the map to Scabbs, pulled a credit from his pants and flipped it into the shaft. The gangers listened to the credit bang its way down the shaft. It never hit bottom.

'He's in the shaft,' said Yolanda.

Kal nodded.

'You don't suppose he might have heard all that bang-ing just now?'

Kal gave Yolanda a sheepish grin. 'Oops!'

'Up or down,' said Vicksen.

Kal just looked at her, his eyebrows creased in puzzle-ment.

'Is the vampire up or down from here?' she asked again.

Kal shrugged.

'Up,' said Yolanda. They all looked at her. She pushed a few wayward strands of hair out of her eyes. 'He took Valtin up through that utility access tunnel at the top of the dome. Plus he seems to have a penchant for heights.'

'Comes from too many years living in the Spire,' said Kal, nodding his head. 'Okay. Up it is.'

Lysanne stepped up to the doorway and peered into the shaft. 'Um, how do we get there?' she asked. 'Hey, there's a couple of buttons here on the inside wall.'

'That would be for the service lift,' said Scabbs. He smiled at her and pointed at the map in his hands. 'It says so right here. Go ahead and push the up but-ton.'

'No.' said Kal. Everyone froze. 'Armand would surely hear the lift moving. We have to climb. There should be ladders on either side of the door as well.'

The entire group groaned.

A LITTLE WAY down the tunnel, there was another groan, unheard by Kal and his merry band.

'Looks like your day just went into the sump,' said Bobo.

Dutt nodded in the shadows. 'I have to go up there,' he said. It was almost a question, as though he were pleading with Nemo through their link. If he was, the answer wasn't good. 'Crap!'

'Lucky for me, the Spyrers are working on my side,' said Bobo. 'I can just sit back and wait to make sure they have the item when they come back down.' He decided to take another shot at getting the informant's name. 'You don't have that luxury. I mean you can't rely on what's his name up in the palace to hand it over to Nemo.'

'Clein or…?' asked Dutt, and then immediately clamped his hand over his mouth.

'Yeah, Clein,' said Bobo as smoothly as possible. He recognised the name and knew Kauderer would definitely be interested in this bit of news. He palmed a dagger while talking, just in case Dutt tried anything after letting the name slip. 'Like I said, he's only out for himself. You know how political officers are, they're… well, political. You can't trust 'em.'

Bobo smiled again, keeping a watchful but relaxed eye on his counterpart. He decided to change the subject. 'Buck up,' he said. 'Maybe it won't be that long a climb.'

Dutt remained silent. Bobo noticed a tenseness about the other spy's shoulders and elbows, as if he was preparing to strike. The Helmawr spy slipped the point of the blade in his palm into the crease between his middle and ring fingers and prepared to jab it into Dutt's neck. The anxious silence continued for several heartbeats, but was then broken by a shuffling sound echoing down the tunnel.

Dutt and Bobo dropped to their stomachs at the same moment and rolled under the racks of pipes. A moment later, Derindi tiptoed past them, doing his best to move silently, but failing miserably. Bobo stifled a snigger. Once the snitch was out of earshot, he looked at Dutt, whose face was no more than a metre from his own, and said, 'Maybe you won't have to follow them after all.'

Both spies heard a sharp metallic sound like bones breaking. It was Wotan barking. Of course, thought Bobo, the dog couldn't climb up the shaft. 'It's Jerico's dog,' he said. 'There's no way Derindi will be able to get past it.'

'Not without help,' said Dutt. He slid out from under the pipes and dashed down the tunnel.

Bobo wanted to go help. He enjoyed Dutt's companionship, and was just starting to get some good information out of him, but he knew he should take the opportunity to check in and send the name of the spy inside House Helmawr. He pulled out a small tablet and typed out a quick message, his fingers practically flying across the tiny keys.

He hit 'encode and send' just as Dutt returned. He slipped out from his hiding spot and stood up. Down the tunnel, steam erupted from a hot water main and he could hear the dog yelp, which sounded a little like metal scraping against metal.

'Derindi got away okay, then?' he asked.

Dutt nodded again. 'Derindi is on his way up the shaft,' he replied, telling both Bobo and Nemo at the same time.

Bobo smiled and pocketed the dagger. The diversion had eased the tension between them. 'You know you'll need more than a little steam to get the item away from Jerico – or the Spyrers – when they come back down.'

Dutt nodded, but remained silent this time. Something in his eyes told Bobo that he and Nemo already had a plan in place for when the time came. Now Bobo needed a plan as well.

KAUDERER HAD BEEN working on the canister for several hours when a signal alerted him to an incoming message. He ignored the signal for the moment. He was at a critical juncture with the canister. He'd attached leads to both ends. One set of wires led to a digital readout. The other set was connected to an input pad. He nearly had the password decrypted and would only have a few precious moments to key the sequence into the pad, before the sensors within the canister detected the worm working its way through the data and triggered any number of booby traps inside.

There it was! Kauderer deftly typed the complex set of digits and symbols into the pad and the canister snapped open. He sat back and shook his hands to release the tension and then smiled. He still had not figured out what message to send to Clein's employer. It would have to be a fairly vague message as he didn't know the name of his contact, but too vague a message would give the game away just as much.

He'd almost forgotten about the message when the signal buzzed again. Kauderer disconnected the leads from the canister, picked it up along with his code-breaking equipment, and stepped to the back of his office. He depressed three switches that were camouflaged as part of the decor on his wall and a section of wall opened up, revealing a pict phone, a terminal and a bank of monitors.

A light on the terminal blinked. He waited for it to repeat to make sure he'd gotten the correct pattern and then keyed in the corresponding code to accept and decrypt the incoming message.

'How timely,' said Kauderer. He deleted the message and then erased all traces that a message had even been received. Thoughts flew through his mind as he closed his monitor station and returned to the desk, with the open canister still in his hand. Clein was working for Nemo. That much he could have guessed, but confirmation was always a necessity in a high stakes game like this one. Bobo also had knowledge of a possible second agent in the palace. That knowledge might prove quite useful in the endgame. The last bit of the message had been even more intriguing. An idea crystallised in Kauderer's brain and he sat down to craft a message for the canister.

SEEK AND DESTROY stood in the doorway to Nemo's control room, waiting for orders. Nemo could see them out of the corner of his eye but had not acknowledged their presence yet. He'd found you could learn a lot about people by watching the way they handled the stress of torture; and for Seek and Destroy, waiting was the worst torture he could ever devise.

So he continued to check his monitors and issue commands, via his network of inner ear transmitters, to his agents throughout the Underhive, all the while watching Seek and Destroy get more and more agitated. With his eyes hidden behind the mirrored mask, he knew they couldn't even tell if he knew of their presence.

Nemo watched as they debated without words whether or not to speak and, if so, who should do the speaking. One (he thought it was Seek, but it was almost impossible to tell, and didn't really matter) pointed at Nemo and then pointed at his brother. The other shook his head and pointed back at the first.

This was obviously taken as some sort of an attack or an affront because the first one punched the second in the arm. This elicited a swift kick to the shins, which in turn brought a chokehold, which then quickly escalated into a wrestling brawl on Nemo's floor.

The master spy let the fight go on for several minutes to see if they would come to their senses or perhaps work it out themselves. They didn't, and it looked like the fight might go on forever. As soon as one got away, the other ran him down and it started all over again. It was truly amazing to watch; all the more amazing because neither one seemed to do any permanent damage to the other.

When the fight got a little too close to Nemo's chair, he finally spoke up. 'Boys,' he said in a soft, but stern voice. 'Stop. Now!' He'd learned long ago that yelling never worked with the twins. A quiet reminder of who held the power worked so much better. Fear was an excellent motivational technique.

The twins snapped back to attention as quickly as possible, but one accidentally stepped on the other as they got off the floor, which brought a quick jab to the kidneys once they were both standing. Nemo could see retribution brewing in the other's eyes, but they stood still, for the moment at least.

'It is time to get into the game,' said Nemo. 'You know what to do?'

'Yes sir,' they said in unison.

'Excellent.' He handed them a data pad. 'This map will lead you to utility access tunnel E2S. Gather our new friends and proceed there. I will monitor the situation from here and give you final instructions when all is ready.'

They saluted, turned and walked toward the door. At least three more punches were thrown before they made it into the next room. Nemo sighed. Luckily, they were just added muscle. The others he had hired would do the delicate work.

He was just about to get back to Derindi's monitor when the whoosh sound from above indicated an incoming message canister. Nemo held out his hand and snatched the canister from the air as soon as it dropped from the tube. He checked the ID indent. It was from Clein.

'Well, this should be interesting,' he said, glancing at the message he'd just received from Dutt. 'Yes, this should prove most interesting indeed.'

# 9: THE PRICE OF REDEMPTION

'GOOD. YOU'RE AWAKE,' said Armand. He stood over the bound Valtin once again. 'I was worried I might have drained too much blood. I wasn't exactly in my right mind earlier.'

Armand wore his Spyrer rig, but the helmet hung on his back, attached to the suit by tubes that connected at various spots around the collar. Valtin looked up at him, a questioning look in his eyes. He tried to sit up, but couldn't. 'I feel weak,' he said.

That's to be expected,' said Armand. 'You've lost a lot of blood. Although I guess I wouldn't say you actually lost it.'

'You seem to be feeling... better,' Valtin's breathing was shallow.

Armand had cleaned up a little once his head had cleared. It had been days since he'd gotten a decent transfusion, and his mania had left little time for personal grooming. His wild hair was pulled back into a ponytail, and he'd managed to scrape several days worth of growth from his face, opting to leave a budding goatee, mostly because of the difficulty of shaving around his mouth with nothing but a dagger.

He looked down at Valtin, who now looked much worse than when they had first met in the square.

Armand was worried that his nephew might die from massive blood loss, which would be a shame because he planned to live off Valtin for quite some time. 'You mean, I'm not a raving lunatic anymore? A side effect of the process, I'm afraid, but with you here to sustain me, I shouldn't get that bad again.'

Valtin looked even more confused than before. 'Ahh, youth,' said Armand. He kneeled in front of his pale, weak nephew. 'You'll begin to understand after you've lived as long as I have.'

'You're not that much older than I.'

Armand laughed. 'How old do you think I am?'

'Forty,' said Valtin. 'Perhaps forty-five.'

'Try doubling that,' said Armand, still laughing, but then the laughter died off as the joke really was on him. 'I'll be ninety-two next month, if I can survive that long on the crap that passes for blood down here.'

'How?'

'Rejuvenation therapy, of course, you idiot. How young are you anyway?' Armand didn't wait for an answer. 'We are the wealthiest family on the planet. Don't you think we can afford to keep ourselves alive?' He stood and started pacing around the edge of the lift, his metal boots clanging on the mesh flooring. 'Gene therapy, blood transfusions, organ replacements – you name it, I've had it. Father too, and even a few of his most trusted aides.'

'Why?'

'To live forever, of course,' said Armand. 'To rule forever.' He felt some of his mania returning and took a deep breath to calm his nervous metabolism. 'Father is over four hundred years old, did you know that? He has ruled the family for centuries, ruled Hive Primus for centuries. And I am the heir apparent, so I get to live forever as well – or at least until father chooses another heir apparent. As long as I stay in the Spire, and don't piss off Father too much, I am immortal.'

'Then why did you leave?'

'I had to, don't you see?' Armand stopped pacing and stared at Valtin. Emotions coursed through his body along with the fresh vigour of Valtin's blood. He was elated and depressed at the same time. Clear in purpose, but troubled by doubts of ever affecting any real change in the status quo. He didn't know why he was even telling his nephew all of this. Perhaps it was his subconscious telling him that it was time to pass the burden on to someone stronger. Perhaps he just needed to finally cleanse his soul.

'I had to leave because that place, that House, was killing me.' He slumped to the floor of the lift, his knees tucked up tight against his chest. 'I might live forever, but I would end up dead inside, my life purchased on the blood, sweat and tears of others.'

'I don't understand,' said Valtin.

'And I hope that you never will,' replied Armand. 'Father calls me "troubled", but troubled isn't the half of it. I have seen the devil, Valtin. I see him every day in the mirror and I see him sitting on the throne of Hive Primus. We are tainted, Father and I. Our very blood is tainted by every foul act this family has performed in the name of power; in the name of eternity. There is no hell, you see. Just the Spire.'

'Then fix it,' said Valtin. 'Restore the family's soul.'

'It's too late for me,' replied Armand. 'Far too late. My life is inextricably tied to the evil now. I can't last a day without a transfusion. I can't seem to last a scavving hour down here on the waste-polluted blood of these Hivers. But I can bring an end to the root of all evil, if I only have enough time.'

Armand jumped to his feet and disappeared into the tunnel next to the lift. When he returned, he was carrying the item that had half the Hive searching for him. 'I can take him down, Valtin. I can bring Father to his knees with this.' He held up the object to show Valtin. It was not much bigger than a grapefruit and slightly oblong, with a short tail coming off the narrow end.

'What is that?' asked Valtin. Armand could tell by the horrified look in his nephew's face that he had already guessed.

'It's the Royal Chamberlain's brain.'

'But it's mostly metal.'

Armand held the brain up to look at it. 'Why yes it is,' he said. The brain was dull grey with an array of tiny steel wires poking out from all sides. The tail, the brain stem, was housed in an accordion-like, metal tube that twisted and turned like a snake. The stem ended in an intricate set of prongs. 'This is just the housing, of course. What's left of old Stiv's brain, along with a series of cogitae valves, is held safely inside.'

'The chamberlain was a servitor?'

'No, just mostly augmetic pieces after all these years,' replied Armand. He held the brain in his palm and raised it up to his face, trying to imagine Stiv's face surrounding the five-pound hunk of metal and tissue. 'Father once told me that Stiv had been with him from the beginning. The only aide he trusted with all of his secrets. And they are all in here. Every dirty deal he ever made. Every enemy – and quite a few "friends" of the family – he ever had killed. Every single credit he ever bilked from the other Houses and failed to report to the tax inspectors. It's all in here.'

'If that fell into the wrong hands… '

'It would mean the end of Gerontius Helmawr,' finished Armand.

'And the entire house,' added Valtin.

'Perhaps,' conceded Armand. He looked at his nephew, lying on the mesh floor of the lift, pale and weak like a baby. 'But that is the price of redemption.'

'You won't live long enough for redemption,' said Kal Jerico as he pulled himself up onto the lift.

'AH, BROTHER,' SAID Armand. 'So good to see you again. And you brought the cousins and a few playthings. Looks like a party.'

'It's your going away party, brother,' said Jerico.

'Playthings?' added a female voice behind Valtin. He thought it sounded like the Escher leader from the fight in the square, but he couldn't see her.

Valtin couldn't see Jerico from his vantage point either, but he saw movement out of the corner of his eyes and noticed Yolanda, wearing a Malcadon Spyrer rig, pulling herself up onto the lift behind his homicidal uncle.

Valtin felt momentary relief that Kal had found him while he was still alive, and seemed to have brought a small army with him. More and more boots clanked on the metal mesh floor of the lift, but then Armand grabbed him by the collar of his leather coat and lifted Valtin up, holding him like a shield as he retreated toward the tunnel.

Valtin could now see everyone except Yolanda, and he hoped that Armand hadn't noticed the rigged-up amazon woman behind him.

'Watch your aim everyone or House Helmawr loses one of its youngest sons,' said Armand as he waved Valtin's body around in front of him.

'He's of no value to us,' said Jonas. 'Cyklus, blast that traitor.'

'No!' yelled Kal. He spread his hands and took two steps toward Armand. 'We can all get out of this alive.

Armand, just give Jonas what you stole from your father and everyone goes their separate ways. Nobody else needs to die today.'

'That wasn't the deal, Jerico!' yelled the leader of the Wildcats. 'He has to pay for the deaths of my girls!'

She rushed toward Armand, firing her shotgun as she ran. Armand swung Valtin's body toward the charging Escher. His feet smacked into the barrel of her weapon. It discharged, shooting the young Helmawr in the foot. He screamed in pain.

He heard a clatter beneath him and looked down to see the chamberlain's brain rolling around on the mesh. When he looked back up, Armand had grabbed the Wildcat leader by the neck. He snapped it with a quick flick of his wrist and then threw her body toward Cyklus.

The brute reacted, shooting a missile from his wrist, which exploded upon impact, blowing the dead Wildcat's body apart. The other two Escher women screamed and readied their weapons. Cyklus re-aimed his wrist rockets. They were now aimed right at Valtin's head.

Kal jumped into the middle of the stand-off. 'Wait!' he called out. 'Just wait a moment, everyone.' He took another step toward Armand, his arms still splayed wide. He kept talking, inching forward with every sentence. 'This is senseless. None of us wants to die today. Let's talk this out.'

Valtin thought he saw Kal's eyes dart to a point behind Armand as he continued to talk. 'You have something we want.'

'But you have nothing I want,' spat Armand. He slammed the helmet down on his head. It latched automatically.

'How about freedom?' asked Kal. Valtin noticed that the fingers on Kal's left hand were no longer splayed.

There were only three fingers out, then two, then one, then none.

Kal lunged forward. At the same time Valtin heard a noise behind him. He turned to see Yolanda spraying Armand with the web shooter from her borrowed rig. In a moment, Armand's arms were held fast against the body of his rig. Kal slammed into Valtin, grabbing him around the waist and pulling him from Armand's grasp. They both fell to the floor of the lift and rolled. Pain shot up Valtin's arms and legs from the wire bindings.

As Jerico and Valtin rolled to a stop near the tunnel, all hell broke loose behind them. Cyklus shot off two more missiles, which did little more than break Armand free of the webbing. Armand then rushed at Cyklus, who continued to fire missiles wildly. One of them exploded on Leoni's chest and another sent Yolanda diving for cover as Kal pulled his nephew into the tunnel and propped him against the wall.

When the smoke cleared, Valtin could see that cousin Leoni's face and part of her skull had been destroyed by the blast. The rig stood for a moment and then crumpled to the floor of the lift in a heap. Yolanda lay sprawled near the edge of the platform. Valtin couldn't tell if she was alive or dead.

Armand grappled with Cyklus as the Escher women and Scabbs shot at him from behind. Armand went down on one knee and leaned back, pulling Cyklus off balance. As the big brute fell forward, Armand stepped in and lifted him over his head. Cyklus screamed and shot off two more missiles, forcing everyone else to dive for cover. Armand stood and ran toward the edge of the lift platform. At the last second, he heaved Cyklus and his massive rig over the rail. Missiles shot up the shaft, exploding well overhead as Cyklus fell into the blackness.

Kal pulled out his sabre and cut the wire bindings around Valtin's wrists and ankles. Relief spread through his aching joints, but his foot had gone numb where he'd been shot. Kal then stood and turned toward Armand, who was surveying the carnage he'd wreaked.

'You whelps have no hope to defeat me!' came the bellowing voice from inside the domed helmet. 'I was ripping Underhive mutants in half with my bare hands before any of you were even born.'

'Kal, wait,' said Valtin. 'You can kill him. Armand has a weakness even he doesn't know about.'

'What is it?' asked Kal.

Before Valtin could answer, he saw Jonas rise and face off with Armand. 'I'm no Underhive mutant, you treacherous scum. See if you can rip me in half.' He stepped in and swung his monomolecular sword at Armand, who blocked it with his armour-plated arm. The sword bounced off the armour, but took one of the overlapping plates with it.

Armand raised his hand over his head and brought a fist down toward Jonas's unprotected head. Jonas got his shield up just in time, but the shield was made to reflect energy attacks, not physical ones. The force of the blow crushed through the reflective crystals and shattered the shield around Jonas's forearm.

Kal seemed to remember something. 'Scabbs, now!' he yelled. 'The device. What are you waiting for?'

Valtin glanced at Scabbs, who had his power cell disruptor in his hand. He pointed it toward the combatants and pushed the button just as Valtin screamed, 'No!'

Jonas's rig stopped moving. He had been between Scabbs and Armand, and the disruptor's field would seek out the closest power source. Armand grabbed Jonas by the arm, just below his now useless sword, and twisted. The armour and the arm inside snapped. He then casually tossed the Spyrer leader to the side and advanced on Scabbs.

'Quickly,' said Kal, 'What's his weakness?'

'His armour has a small crack that runs all the way through,' Valtin said. 'Middle of the chest, but it's tiny…' Kal was already running off and didn't hear the rest. '…only about the size of your thumb.'

Armand reached Scabbs before Kal. He grabbed the scabby little man around the waist and threw him over the edge of platform. 'Noooo!' yelled Kal as he charged in.

HERMOD KAUDERER SAT on the edge of Gerontius Helmawr's desk in the secure room. He could see the appeal that this little slice of rebellion had for Kal Jerico. Sitting on a person's desk was belittling yet playful. Normally Kauderer disdained playful, but he was in an odd mood. He even allowed a little smile to escape his lips, but just for a moment.

Of course, he would never sit on the Helmawr's desk if he were actually in the room. The ruler of the House was currently napping again. This time in the privacy of his own chambers. The stress of this Armand business had taken a toll on his health these past few days, and he had spent an inordinate amount of time asleep. Kauderer suspected that the palace doctors were keeping him drugged, as high stress tended to exacerbate his memory loss.

Kauderer sat on the desk in the dark room all alone, waiting. Everything was in motion. The message had been sent to Nemo. All of Clein's incoming messages were being monitored and Kauderer had also made sure that the return canister from Nemo had been routed to him first. He now held that canister in his hands and waited.

Finally, he heard voices in the antechamber. Two voices. Captain Katerin and Obidiah Clein. As they walked into the dark room, Kauderer reached out and flipped a switch, turning on the lamps that lined the large desk. Clein stopped for a moment in the shadows, looked back at Katerin, who had shut the door behind them, and then walked forward into the light, a large smile plastered on his face.

'Kauderer,' he said. 'You're already here. Excellent.' Kauderer sat right in front of one of the lamps, which forced Clein to stare into the light if he wanted to look Kauderer in the eye.

'Clein. Captain.' Kauderer nodded to both, keeping his face completely impassive.

'Captain Katerin felt it best we meet here,' continued Clein, squinting as he stared into the light. 'We're all professionals. No sense in this affair going public. A simple resignation will certainly suffice.'

'I couldn't agree more,' said Kauderer. He stood to gain just a little more height advantage over Clein. He stared down his hawkish nose at the political officer. 'Although I do have one or two extra demands.'

Clein chuckled, but Kauderer could tell it was a somewhat nervous laughter. 'You don't understand, my dear Hermod. I don't see how you are in a position to demand anything. Captain Katerin here has you on tape confessing the whole sordid affair. I've heard the evidence myself.'

Kauderer paced around to the other side of the desk and sat in Helmawr's chair. 'No, I'm afraid it is you who doesn't understand,' said Kauderer. 'You will be the one resigning.'

Clein shuffled his feet nervously. Kauderer could tell that this meeting was not going anything at all like Clein had thought it would. 'But the tape…'

'Erased itself as you listened to it,' finished Kauderer. 'Did you honestly think it would be that easy?'

Clein looked at Katerin, who wasn't sweating at all, for once. The captain shrugged his shoulders and said, 'I told you it would be difficult to tape him.'

'Now you will listen to me, you odious little man,' said Kauderer.

'I will not!' he said and turned on his heels.

As he strode into the darkness, Katerin called after him. 'That door is locked and guarded on the outside by four of my best and most loyal men.'

Kauderer stood behind the desk. 'Nemo can't help you now,' he said. 'You can't even get a message to him from in here.'

Clein stopped walking. A moment later Kauderer could hear his footsteps getting louder. He returned to the light. His shoulders sagged and he stared at the floor. 'Fine,' he said. 'You both got me. Well done. I'll resign and leave quietly. I'm sure neither of you want another scandal on top of the Armand debacle.'

'Oh, you'll do that and much more,' Kauderer stated. 'You see, I believe Nemo has another mole inside the palace. Before you leave, you're going to help us uncover your fellow spy.'

'But Nemo will… he'll kill me!' he stammered. 'I don't even know who the other spy is. This is the first I've even heard of it.'

Katerin clapped the dejected Clein on the back. 'From what I know of Nemo,' he said, 'he'll kill you just for failing.'

'Besides,' added Kauderer. He walked back around the desk and stared down at Clein. 'You have no choice.'

'What do you mean?' Clein asked. He looked up at Kauderer and then over at Katerin. 'What do you mean, I have no choice?'

'I took the liberty of sending Nemo a message earlier today,' said the intrigue master, 'using one of your special canisters.'

'You did what? How? How did you...?'

'Because I am who I am and you are who you are,' replied Kauderer. 'Now be quiet.' He paced in front of the desk as he spoke. 'The message itself was quite simple. All it said was: *Believe I have been compromised. Kauderer closing in. Please advise.*'

'Oh, dear lord,' said Clein.

'Yes, it is quite elegant, isn't it?' said the intelligence officer. 'Nemo, as our dear captain mentioned, doesn't tolerate failure, and obviously can't afford to let you get captured...'

'He is going to kill me.'

Katerin nodded. 'Most likely through the other agent he already has in place.

'Assuming there is one,' said Clein.

'I don't need to assume any longer,' said Kauderer. He stopped in front of Clein and tossed him the canister. 'Here is the reply to your last message. Go ahead and open it. I've already read it.'

Clein looked like he was about to ask how, but then decided not to. He tapped the code on the canister and snapped it open. He pulled out the neatly folded note and read it aloud. 'Stay put. Help is on the way. You will be taken care of.'

'So,' said Kauderer, pacing again. 'As I see it, you can help us locate the other agent before he kills you, or we can let him kill you and find him that way. As I said, you really have no choice.'

'You can't protect me.'

'The good captain and I will do everything in our power to keep you alive, even if we have to send you into hiding afterward.'

Clein looked at the two men, and said, simply, 'But what if one of you is the other agent?'

A long silence filled the dark room. 'Then, Mister Clein, you are royally scavved.'

YOLANDA WAS DAZED. She'd hit her head on the rail of the platform when that idiot Cyklus's missile exploded beside her. She was just coming around when she heard Kal scream. She looked up and saw Jerico rushing toward Armand. At the same moment, a blur fell past her. She thought she heard Scabbs's voice scream, 'Help!'

Yolanda's mind snapped to attention. She rolled over and peered over the edge of the lift and saw Scabbs falling down the shaft. Before she could react, his body had fallen out of the meagre light provided by the work lamps. She lunged forward and let her torso drop over the edge as she aimed her web shooters into the darkness. She could still hear him screaming.

She shot two streams of webbing down the shaft. At first, the webs just sprayed into the darkness, not impacting anything. Yolanda weaved her arms around in figure eights as she pressed her thighs and toes into the mesh floor of the lift to keep from slipping. Seconds seemed like minutes, but she kept spraying.

Finally, one of the web streams contacted something. She immediately aimed the second shooter at the same spot. It stuck as well. As the webs hardened, Yolanda continued spraying, but also looped the strands around her wrists. When she stopped, she had two long ropes of steel-strength webbing connected to the ends of her arms by what looked like huge balls of glue where her hands used to be.

Then the lines went taut, pulling Yolanda's legs over the edge of the lift.

'Scav me!' she cried as her knees slipped past the edge.

\* \* \*

Lysanne crept over to where Themis lay motionless on the floor of the lift. She tried not to think about the squishy bits on the wire mesh under her hands and knees. Vicksen was dead. Two of the Spyrers were dead. Now Scabbs had been thrown down the shaft. She sniffled and wiped her eyes and nose with her forearm. She just wanted to crawl away into a dark hole and forget this day had ever happened.

She reached Themis and took a breath before turning her over, afraid of what she might find. At first she was relieved; Themis's eyes were open and her lips were moving, but as she tried to speak, Lysanne knew something was wrong. Her voice was barely more than a whisper. 'I'm here,' Lysanne said. 'What's wrong?' She leaned over and put her ear next to the elder Wildcat's lips.

'Missile… lodged in… ribs,' she wheezed. 'Can't… breathe.'

Lysanne pulled open Themis's long, leather coat and saw the blood. Her vest was coated in red, the leather glistening in the lamplight. The tailfin of one of Cyklus's arm rockets stuck out a few centimetres, just below her left breast. It must have been a dud or the firing mechanism had jammed when it struck her ribs. Either way, it hadn't gone off.

'What should I do?' asked Lysanne. 'I don't know what to do!' She sniffled again. Her hands began to shake from the stress and she couldn't concentrate.

'Pull… yourself… together,' whispered Themis. 'You can… do this.'

'Do what?' Lysanne sniffled.

'Remove the… missile.'

'There's so much blood,' she said. 'What do I do about the blood?'

'One thing… at a… time.' She coughed and blood flowed out of the wound around the tailfin. 'Hurry!'

Lysanne reached out tentatively with both hands and grabbed the missile by two fins. She gave it a little tug. It didn't move. She pulled a little harder. The blood began to flow, but the missile stayed stuck. She looked at Themis for help. The new Wildcat leader had passed out. Blood trickled from her lips down her cheek.

KAL SLAMMED INTO Armand's stomach, leading with his shoulder, but it barely moved the elder Helmawr an inch. Jerico let his momentum spin him around the side of Armand, just as his brother's armoured fists swung down toward his head. He danced back out of reach and flipped his blond braids out of his eyes.

'Did that make you feel better?' asked Armand.

'A little,' said Kal. 'You're going to pay for Scabbs and everyone else you've murdered.'

'Why do you care about them?' asked Armand. 'They're insects compared to us. You have noble blood running through your veins, yet you choose to cavort with Hive trash.'

He rushed at Kal, swinging his gloved fist at the bounty hunter's head. Kal ducked under the blow and slashed at Armand with his sabre. It skidded off the armour plates. He dove into a forward roll as Armand's follow-up punch came down at him. Jerico popped back up to his feet, and the two men began to circle each other.

'They're good, hard-working people,' said Kal. He searched Armand's Spyrer rig for the hole Valtin had mentioned as they talked.

'Ha. They're hardly people at all,' said Armand. His red eyes flared beneath the dome. 'You forget. I've tasted them. The Hivers are fouled by pollution and waste.'

'But they are proud of their heritage,' said Kal. He found the hole. It was right over Armand's heart. In his vampire rig, Armand was at least a head taller than Kal and it would be a tough shot. Kal would only get one chance. He needed to keep his brother talking while he looked for the right opportunity to strike.

'They work hard to make the Hive what it is,' he said. 'Hivers live and die in the filth, always striving for a better life for themselves and their families. They are the true nobles. They have nobility of heart, and mind, and spirit. Not some worthless birthright and fancy armour.'

'And there it is,' said Armand. He chuckled. 'The birthright. That's what we're fighting for, isn't it?' Armand stopped circling the lift and leaned back against the rail. 'Father offered to give you back your birthright if you brought me in.'

Kal could feel the red eyes of the rig staring at him. 'Hah! I'm right. I knew it,' shouted Armand. He clapped his hands and then rested them on the rail behind him. 'All that talk about nobility and purpose? What a load of sump waste. You're doing this for the money and the power. You're no better than Father.' Armand howled with laughter, bending his head back as it escaped his helmet.

LYSANNE GRITTED HER teeth as she pressed the tip of the dagger against Themis's skin. She knew what she had to do, and Themis had little time left. She pushed the dagger into the skin next to the protruding tailfin and cut through to the ribs. Dropping the knife, she pushed her hand through the enlarged hole and felt around inside the elder Escher's chest cavity for the tip of the missile.

Before starting, she had ripped off the hem of her black robes. She took a piece of the cloth and packed it in around the wound to hold back the bleeding. Her probing fingers found the missile cone, which was lodged between two ribs. She pushed her thumb and forefinger in between the ribs and tried to pry them apart. The missile moved slightly as she applied the pressure, so she grabbed the tailfin with her free hand and pulled.

The missile slipped right out of the wound, which immediately began to fill up with blood again. Lysanne threw the missile over the edge of the lift and turned back to Themis. As she stuffed her ersatz bandages into the wound, an explosion from below rocked the platform.

YOLANDA HUNG UPSIDE down beneath the lift, her feet clasped around the bottom rail of the platform. With her hands encased in webbing she could do nothing but hang on at this point. She could feel the web ropes moving, as if someone was climbing up the webbing. After a few minutes, she finally saw Scabbs emerge into the dim light surrounding the lift. He climbed, hand over hand, toward her.

'Good to see you again,' she said.

'Just hanging around… waiting for me… were you?' He asked in between breaths.

'Very funny. Just climb onto the lift and pull me up.'

'At least your pants didn't fall down,' said Scabbs. They both chuckled, remembering the similar predicament Scabbs and Kal found themselves in no more than three days ago. Scabbs grabbed hold of Yolanda's shoulders and began to pull himself up toward the platform.

Before he could reach the bottom rail, an explosion on the far side of the shaft rocked the lift. Yolanda lost her foothold and they both plummeted back into the darkness. Yolanda didn't know if she could activate the web shooters with her hands encased, but it was their only hope.

She clenched her fingers inside the webbing and pointed her hands at the walls rushing by. Nothing happened. She pressed harder and a line of web sprayed out and fastened to the wall. She stuck her other hand into the stream and let it harden around the bulb of webbing already there. The webbing hardened, and Yolanda and Scabbs swung toward the wall of the shaft

They slammed into the wall hard, but the web line held and Scabbs, who had been hugging Yolanda during the fall, held on around her neck. They ended up face to face, Yolanda's amazon body pressing the much smaller Scabbs against the wall. He smiled.

'If you try to kiss me, I'll let you fall,' she said.

'I'm smiling because we landed next to the ladder,' said Scabbs. 'Roll off of me, and I'll get us out of here.'

Yolanda rocked back and forth until she finally turned them around. Scabbs reached out and grabbed a rung of the ladder and dragged them toward it.


As Armand laughed, Kal rushed. Now was his chance. He leapt through the air, his sabre held high, ready to be driven home through the hole in Armand's armour. Kal swung his arm forward just as the missile exploded beneath the lift. Staggered by the explosion, Armand fell to his knees.

Kal sailed over the domed head of Armand, toward the edge of the lift. He waved his arms wildly, but knew he would never be able to stop before flying head first off the lift and plummeting down the shaft.

At the last moment, Armand's hand whipped out and grabbed Kal by the wrist. Jerico's legs and torso spun around and slammed into the rail. Armand stood and lifted his little brother off the ground by the arm. Kal could swear he saw a smile beneath the mirrored helmet.

Jerico reached for the sabre with his free hand. Armand shook his head. 'No. No. No,' he roared. He squeezed Jerico's wrist hard, forcing the bounty hunter to drop the sword. 'Now what should I do with you?' he asked. 'Should I throw you back down into your beloved Hive or keep you here and make sure your noble blood doesn't go to waste?'

DERINDI PULLED HIMSELF over the edge of the lift and dropped onto the mesh floor, wheezing. His arms and legs ached. His chest felt like someone was standing on it and he could feel his heart pounding all the way up to his ears. 'I made it!' he said. 'I can't believe I made it.'

'Excellent. Tell me what you see.' The voice was in his ear. Nemo had obviously been monitoring his channel the entire time.

Derindi raised his head and looked around. 'Jerico is fighting some black-armoured monster…'

'That would be Armand, the vampire.'

'…It looks like Jerico is losing. The vampire is holding him off the ground by the arm.'

'Excellent. What else? Do you see the item?'

Derindi had no idea what the item looked like or even what it was. He decided to describe everything. 'There's two Escher women. Looks like one is killing the other. I don't see Scabbs or Yolanda, but I heard a lot of people fall in the darkness as I was climbing. There's two dead Spyrers. No, one of them just moved, but he looks pretty bad. And some guy is sitting in a tunnel next to the lift.'

'Nothing else? What about that tunnel?'

'I can't see into the tunnel from here. There's a lot of junk on the lift. Some of it looks like guts. Wait a minute, I do see a small object near the tunnel.'

'Describe it.'

Derindi crawled closer to the tunnel. He was breathing a little better, but he could barely move his arms or legs. 'It looks like a metal rat, kind of like a toy I used to have.'

'Idiot, tell me what it looks like, not about your childhood toys.'

'It's kind of roundish, maybe ten centimetres long, with a metal tail. You know, like little round segments all linked together so it can wiggle around. Oh, and I can see little metal wires coming off the body, all over, like hair.'

'That's it!' said Nemo. 'It must be. Has anyone seen you?'

Derindi shook his head, and then remembered that Nemo couldn't see him. 'No,' he said.

'Get it and go before anyone else does. Bring it to me right away!'

Derindi grabbed the Chamberlain's brain, stashed it in his pouch, and crawled back to the steps. He sighed. 'Going down should be easier, right?' he said to himself.

This time there was no answer in his ear.


'You KNOW,' SAID Armand, 'All of this exercise has left me feeling a little drained.' He lifted Jerico's arm higher into the air, bringing them face to face. The strain on Kal's shoulder was almost unbearable. It felt like his arm would rip out of its socket at any moment and spikes of pain shot through his arm, chest, and back.

'Aren't you afraid I've been tainted by the Underhive atmosphere?' he asked 'I'm sure I'm carrying any number of diseases. I touched Scabbs's face the other day.'

Armand brought his other arm up toward Kal's neck. Long needles extended from the tips of his first two fingers. The ends glistened as beads of clear liquid grew on the needles. 'These inject an anti-coagulating agent and a sedative into your blood stream before drawing out your blood.'

'So, you're more of a mosquito than a vampire,' said Kal. 'Father must be so proud.' Jerico tried to pull away from the needles, but he couldn't get free from Armand's grasp, and he was now too far away to even kick him effectively.

As he squirmed, Kal got a good look at the hole in Armand's armour. He could almost reach it with his free hand. He needed a weapon, but his sabre was on the floor, and lasguns were useless against Armand. The energy would get sucked into his mirrored helmet.

'Proud enough to make me heir apparent,' said Armand. The needles moved back and forth in the air as Kal squirmed. 'What did he ever give you?'

The spear. How could he have forgotten about the spear? It had been on his back so long now that he'd finally gotten used to the constant scraping and banging every time he moved. 'As a matter of fact, Dad gave me a birthday present not too long ago,' he said. 'Want to see it?'

Kal reached over his head, grabbed the spear and pulled it out. Armand reached for the weapon. Jerico whipped the spear down toward Armand's chest. Armand's arm stopped and his body went rigid. The spear slammed into the armour. It was a perfect shot, sliding through the hole in the armour. Gems scraped off of the shaft as Kal drove the spear deep into his brother's chest, impaling his heart and lungs.

'How do you think it's going up there?' asked Bobo. They stood at the door to the shaft, peering into the darkness. Wotan had wandered off a while earlier and hadn't yet come back. Bobo was a little worried that the steam had fried the robot dog's brain, but then again, Kal Jerico would never know how it happened.

Dutt hadn't answered yet, so Bobo glanced at his companion. The tilt of Dutt's head told him that the other spy was getting instructions or new information via his inner ear receiver. While that was obviously a very useful piece of equipment, Bobo preferred the old-fashioned, non-body-intrusive methods of communicating.

'I understand,' said Dutt. 'I'll be ready.'

So, it was instructions. 'Care to share?' asked Bobo. 'Don't forget you owe me.'

Dutt considered. He pulled the tooth out of his mouth and looked for a spot to hide it.

'Here, I'll hold it,' said Bobo, extending his hand. 'It hasn't picked up my voice from inside your mouth, so it should be safe in my hand.'

Dutt dropped the tooth in Bobo's hand. 'Well, it turns out your last bit of gossip was dead on accurate, so sure. It won't matter soon anyway.'

'Go on,' said Bobo. 'I'm dying to find out what happened up there.'

'Well, things did not go well for Kal Jerico and crew,' he gloated, a huge smile plastered on his face. 'It looks like Armand killed most of them, and Jerico's next. And would you believe it, that little snitch actually found the item and lifted it from underneath their noses in the middle of the battle. He's on his way down right now. In fact, you might want to leave. Nemo's muscle will be here soon to help me escort the weasel back to Nemo.

'I can take care of myself,' said Bobo. 'Besides, I'm still holding out hope that Jerico will come through and save the day, like he always does.'

'I'm serious,' said Dutt. 'These guys are a couple of wild thugs, from what I hear.'

'You don't even know them?' asked Bobo. 'How do you know they're so bad?'

'I know them by reputation,' said Dutt. 'They're a pair of twins named Seek and Destroy. Plus Nemo's sending some hired help from out of town. If these guys see you, they'll kill you.'

'Not if they think I'm you,' said Bobo. The dagger flashed across Dutt's throat in an instant, severing his vocal cords and slicing open his jugular. Dutt's eyes went wide in pain and surprise as a torrent of blood poured down his neck and onto his shirt. A moment later he slumped to the ground. Bobo gave the body a little shove with the heel of his soft leather boot, pushing Dutt over the lip of the shaft.

He looked down at the tooth and thought about dropping it down the shaft as well, but decided to keep it and stuffed it into a deep pocket in his trousers. 'You never know when that might be useful,' he said.

The only thing left to do was wait. His next move would depend on who arrived first, the twins or Derindi.

# 10: END GAME

'A LITTLE HELP here!' Kal called out. Armand was dead, but the Spyrer rig had powered down just as he delivered the death blow, and now Kal was stuck. The joints of Armand's power armour seemed to have locked into place, leaving him suspended off the floor of the lift, and he couldn't get his arm free of the dead man's grip.

'Help me!' cried Lysanne. 'She's dying. I can't stop the blood. Someone help me.'

Kal tried to turn around to see who was alive and who was dead. He heard two pairs of feet run across the mesh flooring. 'I've got Kal,' said Yolanda from behind him. 'Get the Spyrer medi-pack and help the girl.'

'I hope you're not talking to me,' said Kal.

'No,' said Yolanda. She was right behind him. 'Scabbs, hurry!'

'Good,' replied Kal. 'Because I'm just going to hang around here for now, if that's okay with you.'

'Shut up and let me get you down.'

Then it dawned on him, what she had just said. 'Scabbs? Scabbs is alive?'

'Of course he is,' she said. She climbed onto the railing beside Armand. 'Who do you think powered this guy down?'

Kal regained his composure. 'Well if he was alive all

this time…' he twisted around to find the scabby little
sidekick. '…then what took him so long? I was fighting
a vampire for you while you were, what, having a
smoke?'

'We were a little busy,' said Yolanda. She grabbed
Armand's fingers with one hand and his thumb with the
other. As she pulled, Kal could see the pistons in her rig
pumping.

'Wait!' he said, just as Armand's hand opened up and
he fell to the floor of the lift in a heap.

'Kal!' called a weak voice from behind him.

'What now?' asked Kal. He stood up and looked
across the lift. Valtin was leaning against the side of the
service tunnel. He took a step forward and fell to his
knees.

'Kal,' he called. 'He took the brain. You have to hurry.
He took the brain.'

'What in the Hive?' said Kal as he rushed to his
nephew's side. Scabbs kneeled next to the young
Wildcat, using the medi-pack on Themis. Kal smiled
at his friend and gave him a thumbs-up as he ran
past.

He slid to his knees as he reached Valtin and grabbed
the young Helmawr around the shoulders. Valtin kept
saying, 'He took the brain. Hurry. He took the brain… '

Valtin's face was as white as the sheets in the comfy
bed Kal had shared with Candi, Sandi and Brandi not so
many hours ago. He laid his nephew back down on the
floor of the lift. 'Hold on, Valtin, we'll take care of you.'
He glanced back at Scabbs. 'When you're done there,
Scabbs, Valtin needs help.'

'It can't wait,' said Valtin. 'The item we were sent to
find. It was the brain of the Royal Chamberlain. We
have to get it back. He took it.'

'Who?' asked Kal. 'Who took it?'

'A weaselly-looking man with a bandage over one ear took it while you were fighting Armand. I tried to stop him. I'm just so weak. We can't let it fall into… the information inside is too–'

'Don't worry,' said Kal, 'I won't let anyone hurt the family. Not anymore. Not even Father.' He laid Valtin's head down on the mesh floor and stood.

'Kal! Somebody! Help!'

'What now?' asked Kal. He looked around. Jonas was lying on the floor. His rig had lost power as well and he couldn't move. 'Scabbs, Yolanda. Help Jonas with his rig. I've got to go see a man about a thing.'

'Sure thing, boss,' she said with only the slightest hint of sarcasm. 'Here, you might want these.' She tossed his sabre and the spear toward him. He caught them both and slipped them into their respective sheaths with a little flourish and then ran toward the ladder.

BOBO HEARD SOMEONE climbing down the ladder. He slipped back down the tunnel and watched to make sure it was Derindi. When the snitch emerged from the shaft, Bobo trotted down the corridor toward him.

The little weasel turned at the sound and started backing away. 'What?' he asked. 'What do you want? Who are you?'

'Don't worry,' said Bobo. 'Nemo sent me. My name is Dutt. I'm supposed to take you back to the… master.' He almost choked on the last word, but Derindi didn't seem to notice.

'Nemo didn't say anything about an escort,' whined Derindi. He continued backing away down the tunnel.

'It's okay,' said Bobo. He moved forward slowly. He didn't want to spook the snitch. Running wasn't Bobo's forte. 'Nemo had me watching your back all day. I saw you on the roof outside the Fresh Air. I ruptured the steam pipe to get Jerico's dog off your rump, for Hel-mawr's sake.'

'That was you?'

'Yeah, now come on. There's not much time.' Bobo was telling the truth about that. Nemo's real men could show up at any moment, and he was a little worried that Armand might fly down the shaft once he was fin-ished with Jerico's crew. He led Derindi down the tunnel away from Hive City.

'Where are we going?' asked Derindi. 'I came from that direction.' He pointed back past the shaft entrance.

'Yeah, this is a shortcut,' said Bobo. 'Follow me. It's not far.' If he could just get Derindi out of sight of the shaft entrance to make sure they couldn't be seen and weren't being followed, Bobo would gut the little snitch and take the item. Then it would be off to Noritake's to send a secure message to Kauderer and spend a little quality time with Jenn.

But nothing about this mission could ever be easy. He heard a low growl ahead of him that sounded frighten-ingly like the buzzing of a chainsword. Up ahead, sitting in one of the pools of light, was Wotan. He growled again as he got off his haunches and stalked his way down the tunnel toward them.

'Maybe we should turn around and go the long way,' said Derindi, backing away from the metallic hound.

'That wouldn't be my first choice,' said Bobo. He backed away as well, though. It really was the only choice. He just hoped they could get out of the tunnels before the twins showed up.

'Then what?'

Bobo turned and dashed off. 'Run!' he yelled. Wotan barked, and Bobo could hear the dog's steel paws scrap-ing the concrete floor behind him. Bobo pumped his legs as fast as he could, but the spy was quite a bit shy of two metres tall, and Derindi, as short as he was, soon passed him.

Bobo kept running. The barks and scrapes got closer and closer. They had almost made it back to the shaft. They could possibly climb down and look for another access point, but Bobo knew he would never make it there in time, and he couldn't afford to let Derindi get away. Time to let the dog do his work for him.

Bobo dove to the ground as Wotan nipped at his heels. He curled his shoulder under him as he fell, and rolled to the side underneath the banks of pipes lining the tunnel. He kept rolling until he hit the wall before looking back. Wotan sniffed at the pipes and then turned and ran after Derindi.

Bobo crawled beneath the pipes down the tunnel as fast as he could, which was nearly as fast as he could run. Being short had some advantages, especially for a spy. Any second, he expected to hear Wotan tear into Derindi. He had to find some way to lure the dog away or get the item from the snitch before the metallic hound destroyed everything.

But instead of snarls and screams, he heard laser blasts and cheers from down the tunnel. Wotan ran off back down the tunnel again as blasts hit the floor and pipes around him.

'Yes! I hit him!' yelled one voice.

'No, you did not. I hit him!' yelled a second voice.

'Why you!'

'I'll kill you!'

Then there was the sound of fighting. Bobo had no idea what in the Hive was going on, so he crawled out to the edge of the pipes and looked. Two Orlock gangers wearing leather vests over coloured shirts, one red and the other blue, rolled around on the concrete floor, clawing and hitting at each other. Three other people stood back and watched. The shortest of those three, a stocky man with huge arms, a plump, red face, and combat boots, held Derindi by the collar.

Bobo recognised the short one. It was Hern, the bounty hunter, which meant the other two were Lebow and Gorgh. The three bounty hunters from Dead End Pass always worked together. Lebow wore a shiny, black, collared shirt open down to his chest. He had a large cigar tucked into the corner of his mouth. Gorgh wore what looked like a thick, red sweater. The material looked odd until Bobo realized the sweater was woven from thin leather strips. He'd just taken the stopper off a flask and was watching the fight with a smile on his face.

Bobo realised that the two matched gangers fighting on the ground like only brothers can, had to be the twins, Seek and Destroy. He was too late. Nemo's men had gotten to Derindi. But Bobo wasn't ready to give up just yet. He pulled himself out from under the pipes, brushed off his pants, and walked up to the group. Lebow and Gorgh both whipped pistols out of their holsters as he approached. Hern carried no visible weapons, but smiled in a way that said, 'Move another inch and you die!'

Bobo put his hands in the air and smiled. 'Relax, men. Name's Dutt. K W Dutt. I work for Nemo. Hold onto that one, Hern. He's worth more than what Nemo's paying all three of you for this job.' The mercenaries didn't waver at all. Bobo looked at the twins. The red one had the blue one in a chokehold, while his brother tried to claw his eyes out. 'Seek! Destroy! Stop that nonsense.' Bobo had brothers as well, and that's how his mother always spoke to them when they got like this. 'We have a mission here.'

The twins paused and looked up at Dutt. 'Who are you?' they asked at the same time. Lebow and Gorgh clicked the safeties off their weapons and took a step forward.

Great, thought Bobo. I'm going to die because these two idiots were too busy killing each other to listen to me. 'Whoa, whoa!' he said. 'I'm Dutt. Nemo's agent. Didn't he tell you I would be here to help you escort Derindi?'

'Dutt?' asked one.

'Oh yeah,' said the other. 'The spy.' The boys got up and straightened their shirts and vests. The one who'd been in the chokehold poked his brother in the ribs with an elbow as he dusted off. The one in red slapped his brother in the head, knocking off his blue bandana as he resettled his dark glasses over his eyes.

'Right,' said Bobo. 'The spy. And you're Seek and Destroy. The twins.'

'I'm Seek,' said the one in blue. 'He's Destroy.'

'And don't call us "the twins" – ever!' said Destroy.

'Fine,' said Bobo. What did it matter? They were identical, right down to the colour-coded clothes and the bandana-covered, bald heads. If they wanted to be treated as individuals, they should at least dress differently, aside from the colour.

Bobo turned to Derindi. He'd gained everyone's trust for the moment. It was time to make his move, before everything fell apart again. 'Let's get going,' he said, 'but maybe you'd better give the item to me, Derindi. After that dog attack, I'm worried about its safety.'

Derindi had cocked his head to the side, as if listening to something that nobody else could hear. 'Dutt,' he said. 'Short, kind of wiry. A little squirrely looking, to tell you the truth.'

'What in the Hive is he babbling about?' asked Seek.

Bobo took a step back, knowing all too well what was coming next. Damn Nemo and his implants.

'That's not Dutt,' said Derindi.

Lebow and Gorgh whipped their weapons up again.

'Then who in the Hive are you?' asked Seek.

'That's what I'd like to know,' said a voice from behind them.

Bobo turned to see Kal Jerico standing by the entrance to the shaft. 'Who in the Hive are you people, and what are you doing with my snitch?'

SCABBS CARRIED THE medi-pack over to Valtin and set it down. 'How are you doing?' he asked.

'I've had better days,' said Valtin. A weak smile flitted across his pale face. He could barely keep his eyes open.

'I need to get your coat off,' said Scabbs.

Valtin tried to rise, but couldn't. Scabbs reached down and pulled Valtin's leather coat off one arm. The skin was clammy and cold. He attached the leads from the medi-pack near his patient's shoulder. After flipping a few switches to account for the different mass and sex of his new patient, Scabbs sat back and scratched at some dry skin on his neck while the medi-pack analysed Valtin's condition.

He looked around while he waited. Lysanne sat with Themis over to the side. He'd been able to stabilise the elder Wildcat, but she'd still need a real medicae to repair that nasty wound once they got out of this scav-forsaken shaft. Lysanne had hugged him again when he'd told her Themis would live.

As he looked at Lysanne, who sat holding Themis's head in her lap, Scabbs wondered if they could ever... Nah, he thought. They lived in different worlds. More likely she'd go rogue one day and they'd have to hunt her down for the bounty.

Near the Wildcats, Yolanda worked on getting Jonas out of his dead rig. She was having some trouble with his mangled monomolecular sword, from the looks of it. Jonas sat and glared at her, waiting to get free.

Leoni's remains lay opposite the Wildcats. Scabbs tried to avoid looking at it or at Armand's body. He was always a little squeamish around corpses. Perhaps because he'd seen too many of them rising back up. He glanced back at Valtin. 'What should we do with Armand and Leoni?' he asked.

'Jonas and I will take them back to the Spire for a royal cremation.'

'Huh,' said Scabbs. 'Down here we normally just chuck bodies into a waste pool. Usually does a pretty good job of cremating the remains.'

He peered into the nearby tunnel. The work lights on the lift illuminated some of it. He could see racks of tools and spools of copper wire hanging on the walls. 'What is that; some sort of maintenance tunnel?'

Valtin turned his head to look. 'I don't know,' he said. 'But Armand spent a lot of time in there. You should take a look to see if there are any more bodies back there.'

'Yeah,' said Scabbs as he picked at an old sore on his arm. 'I'll get right on that.' He stared at the copper and tools. 'Still, that stuff sure would bring a lot of credits.'

'I'm sure those items are for official use only.'

'Right, well I'll only sell them to official people, then.' Scabbs was about to get up and go take a look when the medi-pack beeped. He read the display. 'Anaemic,' he said. 'Well, I could have told you that.' There were other instructions on the screen. He pulled out a syringe with a tube that extended from the side of the pack and jabbed it into Valtin's arm. A clear solution snaked its way through the tube.

'Looks like that's going to take a while,' he said, and then stood to go into the tunnel. A hand on his shoulder made Scabbs jump. He swivelled, half-expecting to see the vampire, risen from grave. But it was just Jonas, free from his rig at last.

'How's my cousin doing?' asked Jonas. He draped his good arm around Scabbs's shoulder as if they were old friends. It was just a little creepy.

Scabbs looked at Jonas and then down at Valtin. 'It's too early to tell, but this medi-pack of yours is pretty good, so I think he'll be fine.'

Jonas just nodded. He tightened his grip, giving Scabbs a slight twinge in his shoulder, and then pulled Scabbs hard against him. 'So, Scabbs,' he said. 'Can I call you Scabbs?'

Scabbs nodded. He was starting to get worried now.

'What was that device you used to ruin my rig?'

'I, uh, I mean I was aiming for Armand. I'm sorr–'

'It was a power cell disruptor,' said Valtin. His voice was sounding stronger already. 'Father gave it to me. He thought it might come in handy against Armand.'

Jonas smiled and eased his grip on Scabbs's shoulder a little. 'Pretty nifty device,' he said. 'I've never heard of anything like that.'

'It's actually a prototype,' said Valtin. 'Father "acquired" it from a Van Saar tech with dubious morals.'

'Interesting. Can I see it?'

'Well I don't… '

Scabbs pulled the device out of his pocket, desperate to do anything to get out of Jonas's grasp. 'Here it is,' he said.

Jonas released his hold on Scabbs and plucked the device from his hand. 'Thank you very much,' he said. 'Honestly, I don't know how Jerico stays alive with you by his side.' He punched Scabbs in the nose, knocking him to the floor with the blow. He then pointed the device at Yolanda and pushed the button.

'Now to complete my orders,' said the Spyrer leader. He dropped the device and pulled out his plasma pistol, aiming it at Scabbs first. 'Rule one: leave no witnesses.'

Scabbs closed his eyes. He heard the plasma pistol fire, and then heard something hit the floor. What happened? Did he kill Valtin first? He snuck one eye open and screamed. Jonas's body lay on the floor, blood and guts oozing out of a hole in his chest and running through the metal mesh.

Scabbs sat up and looked around. Lysanne smiled at him as she slipped her own plasma pistol back into the folds of her black robe. 'I never liked him,' she said.

Scabbs smiled back at her. Maybe they weren't that different after all, he thought.

'THESE ARE NEMO'S men, Jerico,' said Derindi, 'and they're on my side. You can't intimidate me this time. I'm more than just a snitch.' He quivered as he spoke, and Kal couldn't help but notice that he was being held by a bounty hunter already.

Kal rested his hands on his holsters. 'Yeah, you're a thief, now,' he said. 'And I want my property back.'

'You're playing some mighty long odds, Jerico,' said Derindi. 'Those two are called Seek and Destroy. They're Nemo's personal guards.'

'And we got our own bounty hunters,' said Seek. 'The best Nemo's money could buy.'

'Hey, Hern,' said Jerico. 'How's it going? Gorgh, Lebow?'

'Hey,' said Hern.

'Good.'

'Fine.'

'That's my property you got there, Hern,' said Kal. 'Not the snitch, just an item he's carrying. Call it a family heirloom.'

Gorgh and Lebow lowered their weapons. 'Wait a scavving minute,' said Destroy. 'You work for us. Kill him and let's go.'

'Sorry kid,' said Lebow. 'A bounty is one thing, but property is property. We can't take what belongs to another bounty hunter.'

'It's not right,' said Hern. He released Derindi and stepped back.

'Against the code,' said Gorgh, holstering his weapon. 'You're on your own.'

The three bounty hunters melted into the darkness down the tunnel.

'Come back here!' yelled Seek at the retreating mercenaries. 'You three are dead, do you hear me? Dead!'

He turned to face Kal, who now had his weapons drawn.

'Now give me back my snitch,' he said, pointing one lasgun at Seek and the other at Destroy. 'And you two boys won't get hurt.'

'Wrong word,' said Bobo, who was standing beside Kal.

'We're not boys!' roared Seek. He threw open his leather vest, pulled out twin blue-plated autopistols from his shoulder holsters, and began firing as he ran toward Derindi. Bullets ricocheted off the pipes and floor.

Destroy lifted a flamer hanging at his side and pulled the trigger, sending a sheet of fire toward Kal and Bobo. Kal fired his lasguns as he leapt to the ground and rolled out from under the line of fire. When he came back up, he couldn't see Bobo any longer, or much of anything except the gout of flame coming from Destroy's weapon, which he sprayed back and forth across the tunnel.

As the flame came at him again, Kal retreated down the tunnel toward the shaft. He thought, briefly, about taking his chances on the ladder, but didn't relish the thought of fighting while suspended above a three-kilo-metre drop. Several more bullets zipped over his head and Kal fired several laser blasts back.

Where had Bobo gone? He could use some help about now. He fired a few more shots, trying to blast the flamer, but hitting nothing as far as he could tell. Then, from behind him, Kal heard a sharp, metallic bark. His prayers had been answered, assuming he had been pray-ing to a robotic canine god. Kal looked over his shoulder as he continued to shoot and back away from the flame. He finally saw Wotan bounding toward him.

The dog looked ready to leap on his master again, which would have been deadly considering the current circumstances, so Kal called out to his metallic friend. 'Wotan,' he yelled. 'Fetch the gun!'

Wotan ran past Kal, right into the gout of flame. Kal hoped his dog was fireproof. He delayed his shot, wait-ing to see if Wotan would come through for him. He heard a growl and a bark, and then more growling. Then he heard Destroy. 'Let go, you rusty mutt!' he yelled.

The flames died away as Wotan wrenched the flamer from the ganger's hands. The dog shook his head back and forth as if he were trying to rip meat from a carcass, and then let go of the flamer. It flew straight through the doorway and down the shaft.

'My flamer!' called Destroy. 'I'll kill that dog.' He lunged for Wotan and grabbed the metallic hound around the collar, trying to wrestle him to the ground. Kal couldn't believe his eyes. He looked up at Seek, who was also staring in disbelief at his brother. Seek looked up and he and Kal locked eyes.

They both raised their weapons at the same time, but Kal was just a bit faster and a much better shot than

Seek had proven to be. He fired a lasblast from each of his weapons, hitting Seek in both hands simultaneously. The Orlock ganger dropped his pistols and stuck his laser-burned fingers in his mouth.

Kal kept his weapons trained on Seek, but glanced back at Destroy. He had somehow managed to get himself underneath Wotan. The dog was just standing there, seemingly paying no attention to the enraged ganger, even as Destroy pulled on his neck and kicked at his back legs. 'Wotan,' said Kal. 'Sit!' The dog sat down on top of Destroy, pinning him to the floor and winning the wrestling match in a single move.

'I've got him, Kal,' said Bobo. He walked back down the tunnel, dragging Derindi behind him by his one good ear. Bobo held up the snitch's satchel. 'And I've got what you came for right in here.'

'I'll take that, if you don't mind.' The voice had come from behind Kal.

Kal knew that voice. Kal hated that voice. Every time he heard it, bad things happened to him. Bad things that usually included getting hit. A lot. Or getting shot at. A lot. 'Hello, Nemo,' he said, without turning around.

'If you would be so kind as to drop your weapons, Jerico,' said Nemo. Kal felt the barrel of a large calibre gun press into his back. 'Then I won't be forced to shoot you.'

Kal dropped his lasguns at his feet.

'Now kick them into the shaft.'

'But…' The barrel pushed a little harder into his back. He kicked both guns over the edge, and winced as he heard them bang their way down the shaft.

'Now, Mr Bobo, I believe it is?'

'Yeah?' Bobo still held Derindi by the ear in one hand and the satchel in the other.

'Whatever did you do with my spy?'

'Kal's guns should be hitting him in the head any minute now,' said Bobo.

'Pity,' said Nemo. 'Ah well, I knew this operation would be expensive. If you would be so kind as to give that satchel to Mr Derindi, then we'll leave you to your fun.'

'What about us, boss?' asked Seek. His voice was somewhat muffled from the fingers stuck in his mouth.

There was a pause. 'You get the most important job, boys – covering my escape.'

'Thanks boss. You can count on us.'

'I'm sure I can,' said Nemo. 'Now, Mr Bobo!'

Bobo pulled Derindi to his feet by the ear and hit him in the chest with the satchel. He stepped aside to let Derindi pass, and then looked right at Kal and winked. Jerico didn't know what Bobo had planned, but was ready for anything. Plan W always worked, right?

As Derindi walked past Bobo, he dropped to the ground and spun around, sweeping Derindi's legs out from under him with a swift kick to the shins. Kal stomped on Nemo's foot and slammed his elbow into the master spy's midsection. Derindi pitched forward and lost his grasp on the satchel, which went flying into the air toward Kal and Nemo.

Kal only had a second, not nearly enough time to catch the satchel and escape from Nemo's blast, so he grabbed the spear off his back, chucked it at the incoming satchel, and dived to the ground. The spear ripped through the satchel and hit something metallic inside. The force of the gem-encrusted missile drove the satchel off course. It and the spear sailed through the opening and down the shaft.

Kal rolled forward and came up running, zigzagging down the tunnel. An explosive slug from Nemo's bolt pistol whizzed past his ear. He kicked Destroy in the head as he went by and called Wotan. 'Bobo, come on!' he yelled as he and the dog ran past the spy.

Bobo pulled something out of his pocket, leaned down, and jammed it into Derindi's ear. The next moment, Kal heard Nemo and Derindi screaming in pain. The bolts from Nemo's gun stopped flying and the three of them ran off into the darkness.

'What in the Hive did you do?' asked Kal as they ran.

'Feedback loop,' said Bobo. 'I jammed one of Nemo's transmitters into Derindi's ear, up against his receiver implant. The sound cycles through the system over and over until it creates an awful screeching noise.'

'I'm glad you're on my side.'

Bobo smiled.

SEVERAL HOURS LATER, Kal and Valtin sat on the couch in Madam Noritake's sitting room. Kal had a cigar in one hand and a bottle of Squatz's House Special he'd liberated from the Fresh Air in the other. Valtin looked much better, but had opted to pass on the libations due to his recent blood loss.

Scabbs and Lysanne sat in a loveseat across the room. Kal avoided looking at them and hoped they were simply swapping war stories, for the thought of anyone swapping anything else with Scabbs just turned his stomach. Bobo sat in a comfy chair next to a fake fireplace, with the pretty young girl Kal had met earlier sitting on his lap.

Yolanda had taken Themis to the medicae and hadn't come back yet. Kal wasn't worried. Yolanda was a big girl, in every sense of the word.

'I want to give you something, nephew,' Kal said in between puffs.

'You gave me my life,' said Valtin. 'That's more than enough.'

'Call it an early birthday present, then' said Kal. He handed Valtin a data cartridge. 'Or an insurance policy.'

'For who, you or me?'

'Both of us, really,' said Kal. 'Something to make sure that keeping you alive doesn't become a full time job.'

Valtin turned the cartridge over and over, but Kal knew there were no markings. 'What's on it?'

Kal took a long puff from his cigar, held the smoke inside for a moment, and then blew a large smoke ring that floated off toward Scabbs and Lysanne. 'I'm not sure. Scabbs found it in that maintenance tunnel next to the lift. Said it came out of a terminal that had a web-like network of wire leads plugged into it. I think Armand had been duplicating the contents of the Chamberlain's brain. If so, whatever he found is probably stored on that cartridge.'

Valtin stared at the cartridge in silence and then handed it back to Kal. 'I can't take this,' he said. 'You take it. Give it to Grandfather, so you can get paid.'

'I don't want the money,' Kal replied before whispering, 'I can't believe I just said that,' under his breath. He pushed Valtin's hand away. 'And I don't want my father or anyone else to have that cartridge either. It's too dangerous. You have to take it.'

Valtin sighed and nodded his head. He tucked the cartridge away inside his coat. 'Why me?' he asked.

'It's family business,' said Kal. 'It should stay in the family, and you're the only family member I trust – besides myself.' He smiled and took another puff from his cigar.

'But what about the money?' asked Valtin. 'I can probably get Grandfather to at least give you some of it.'

Kal exhaled, blowing an arrow of smoke through the expanding ring. 'Nah,' said Kal. 'I'd just blow it on women and booze, and I've got more than enough credits for that already. You could get me another spear, though. I lost the last one.'

# EPILOGUE: BUSINESS AS USUAL

VALTIN SAT AT the desk in his new office. He wore a neatly-pressed white suit with a royal blue silk tie. The torn leather jacket he'd worn on his recent adventure hung on a brass coat rack by the door. Sunlight streamed in from a bank of windows behind his chair, shining right in the face of his visitor, Hermod Kauderer. Kauderer had to squint to keep the sun out of his eyes. Valtin knew of the man's preference for standing at meetings, and had chosen the time carefully to make sure the sun was at the right height for maximum discomfort.

'It's been quite an eventful week,' said Valtin. 'Stiv's death, Armand's rampage through the Underhive, rogue Spyrers unit destroying several sections of Hive City, and you, Hermod, uncovering not one but two spies within the palace.'

'Just doing my duty to our Lord Helmawr,' said Kauderer. He tried to look down his hawkish nose at Valtin, but, with his eyes nearly shut, he looked more like a mole than a bird of prey.

'And yet I can't help but think that had you done your job a little more efficiently, we wouldn't have had spies in the palace in the first place,' said Valtin. 'Senior advisors at that. Right under your nose, as it were.'

'Excuse me?' asked Kauderer.

'And a bad job, letting Colouri and Clein kill each other like that,' he added. 'Bit of a bungled operation there, wouldn't you say?'

'I don't know that I would go that far…'

Valtin opened a folder on his desk and spread out several sheets of paper that were all densely covered with notes. 'And now I have quite a lot of political fallout to deal with on account of the horrible way you handled this entire mess.'

'Now see here,' said Kauderer. 'You may be the new senior political officer…'

'*And* Lord Chamberlain,' added Valtin.

'… but you can simply cannot talk to me in this manner.'

'Oh, but I can,' said Valtin. He stood and stared the master of intrigue in the eye. 'I know who it was that sent that Spyrer team down into the Hive. I also know they had special orders to be completed once their primary mission had been achieved.'

Kauderer was getting flustered. He sat in the chair and looked up at Valtin. 'How could you know…?'

Valtin smiled. 'I have friends in low places.'

'That means nothing,' said Kauderer. 'You may be Helmawr's grandson, but you're not the heir apparent. As advisors, we are still equals.'

'You never seem to tire of being wrong, do you, Hermod?' Valtin's smile grew as he looked down at Kauderer. 'Lord Helmawr and I had a long talk after I got back. I am the heir apparent, and I will be taking an active role in the running of this family from now on. So, your future within House Helmawr depends completely on keeping me happy.'

'How? What do you have on the old man?'

Valtin sat down and pressed his fingertips together in a steeple. 'Let's jut say I have access to the information needed for the job,' he said. 'And don't get any funny ideas. I keep my data stored in a much safer location than poor Stiv ever did, and if anything should ever happen to me, that information will find its way into the hands of one of my relatives, an uncle with whom I recently spent some "quality" time.'

KAL SAT AT his usual table in the Sump Hole, with his big boots propped up on the table, a busty, if not terribly clean, barmaid on his lap, a bottle of Wildsnake in his hand and his two partners arguing across the table. After one of the craziest weeks since the last time he'd been hauled up into the Spire, it felt good to be home.

A dull roar permeated the bar, making every conversation at every table as private as if the people were talking in their own homes. More private, probably, since a bug planted in the Sump Hole wouldn't get much more than snippets of conversation.

'I say we should have kept it,' said Scabbs.

'They needed it more than we did,' replied Yolanda.

'But I could have worn it,' said Scabbs. 'You know, for protection and power.'

'Aw, you never would have figured it out,' said Yolanda. She grabbed her bottle of Wildsnake and downed it in one go. She bit the snake in two and spat half of it at Scabbs. It wasn't Yolanda's normal method of dealing with the 'Snake, but spitting seemed suddenly more appealing with Scabbs involved. 'It's a complex machine, and you're, well, you.'

Scabbs wiped the snake off his forehead, causing a cascade of dead skin to fall on his shoulders.

'What in the Hive are you two arguing about?' asked Kal.

'Yolanda gave the last working Spyrer rig to those two Wildcats!' whined Scabbs. 'I wanted to keep it.'

'They needed it,' Yolanda said to Kal. 'The vampire and that unit wiped out all but the two of them. The creds they can getting from breaking that thing down and selling it for tech will more than rebuild the gang.'

'Okay,' said Scabbs. 'I guess it's the least we can do for Lysanne, after she saved our lives. At least we've got that cartridge. It's got to be worth something.'

'I gave it to Valtin.'

'You what?' asked Yolanda and Scabbs at the same time.

'He needed it more,' said Kal. He stroked the barmaid's arm aimlessly as he spoke. 'Besides, if we had kept it, Nemo would still be after us.'

Scabbs scratched his chin. Amazingly, nothing fell off his face afterward. 'Well, that's true,' he said. 'At least we got the bounty on the vampire.'

'I had to spend most of that on new lasguns,' said Kal. Yolanda stared at him. 'They're scavving sweet guns,' he added. 'Pearl-handled, wood grip, laser sights. Just gorgeous.'

'You mean we're broke?'

'Not quite, but we're going to need work soon enough,' said Kal. He took a drink of his Wildsnake and shifted a little in his seat to make himself and the barmaid a little more comfortable. 'Maybe you should go check the Wanted posters, Scabbs.'

'I sure wish you hadn't thrown away that spear,' said Scabbs. 'That thing must have been worth a fortune.'

Kal remembered something. 'Say, some of the gems on that spear scraped off when I killed Arma… the vampire. Did either of you pick those up?'

Scabbs's face sported its normal blank stare, but Yolanda looked sheepish. 'Yolanda?'

She reached into her special hiding place and pulled out a few small gems, and reluctantly scooted them across the table. Suddenly she looked a lot less cold.

'I could have sworn more fell on the floor than that,' said Kal.

Yolanda brushed her blonde spikes out of her eyes. 'I might have given a few to the Wildcats, you know, to help them rebuild.'

The table fell silent. Kal stared at his drink, stewing about the lost gems.

'Do you regret losing out on all that Spire money?' asked Yolanda, finally.

'What?' said Kal. He put his arms around the barmaid. 'And give up all of this?'

Just then, a huge Van Saar ganger pushed his way through the crowd up to their table. 'What are you doing with my sister?' he bellowed. He broke a bottle of Wildsnake over Kal's head.

Kal jumped up, dumping the barmaid on the floor in the process. 'Your sister?' he said. 'I thought she was my sister.' He threw a punch that knocked the ganger onto the next table, and then jumped on top of him.

The table broke, and all of the drinks went flying. The owner of one of the drinks grabbed Kal and punched him in the gut. 'Now, this is the life for me!' Kal yelled as he kicked his new assailant in the groin.

## ABOUT THE AUTHORS

Will McDermott has written two Magic: The Gathering novels – *Judgment* and *The Moons of Mirrodin* – as well as eight gaming-related short stories for Wizards of the Coast and Malhavoc Press. The former editor-in-chief of *Duelist* and *TopDeck* magazines has also written strategy books for the Magic and Pokémon trading card games, an interactive electronic book for Fisher-Price, a chapter on writing in a shared world for *The Fantasy Writer's Companion*, and recently co-wrote a Dungeons & Dragons source book. Will lives in Hamburg, New York, with his wife, three kids, and one large dog.

Gordon Rennie lives in a state of befuddled cynicism in Edinburgh, Scotland, where he writes comics, novels, computer game scripts and anything else anyone's willing to pay him money for. In between waiting patiently to become the main writer on the 2000 AD Judge Dredd strip, he spends his time getting into internet flame wars and pretending to be a lifelong supporter of Hibernian FC. He's recently started smoking again, and so hopes his wife isn't going to be reading this.